# WINDS OF ALLEGIANCE

## HEART OF INDIA SERIES

*Silk*
*Under Eastern Stars*
*Kingscote*


## THE GREAT NORTHWEST SERIES

*Empire Builders*
*Winds of Allegiance*

# LINDA CHAIKIN

# WINDS OF ALLEGIANCE

## BETHANY HOUSE PUBLISHERS
MINNEAPOLIS, MINNESOTA 55438

Winds of Allegiance
Copyright © 1996
Linda Chaikin

Cover illustration by Joe Nordstrom

Cartography by Philip Schwartzberg, Meridian Mapping,
Minneapolis, Minn.

Published by Bethany House Publishers
A Ministry of Bethany Fellowship, Inc.
11300 Hampshire Avenue South
Minneapolis, Minnesota 55438

Printed in the United States of America.

**Library of Congress Cataloging-in-Publication Data**

Chaikin, L. L.
   Winds of allegiance / Linda Chaikin.
     p.  cm. — (The Great northwest ; 2)

   I. Title.  II. Series: Chaikin, L. L., Great northwest ; 2.
PS3553.H2427W56  1996
813'.54—dc20                        95–45788
ISBN 1–55661–442–X               CIP

Dedicated with love to

Jeanne Chaikin Marr

and her Alaska cruise
to New Archangel [Sitka]

PROVERBS 31:27, 31

# CONTENTS

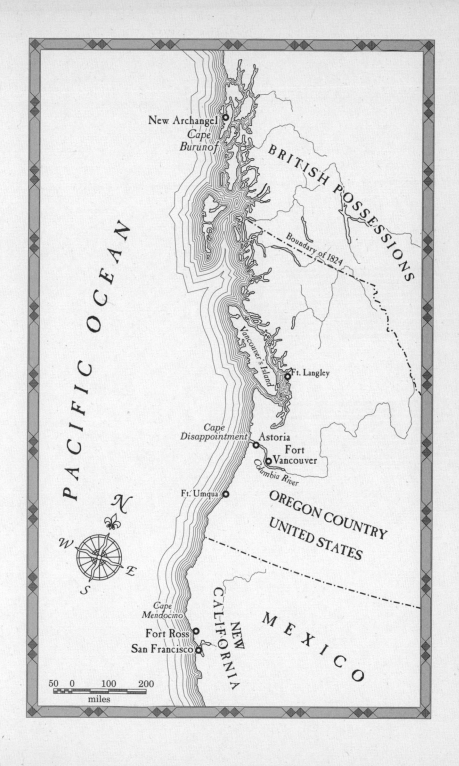

# 1

# NEWS FROM A FAR COUNTRY

*San Francisco, 1834*

Savana shivered and drew the white ermine cape about her slim body for warmth while the wintry dawn made a feeble effort to penetrate the drizzly fog. It failed, and the fog continued to silently creep toward the deserted wharf like some sinister living thing wishing to smother the light of the sun.

She stepped down from the carved barrel seat at the back of the mule-drawn hackney and handed the driver a peso. "Wait for me."

He lifted his wide sombrero and pulled ahead into the empty lot near the wharf. Savana stood watching warily until the gray mist swallowed him.

Alone, she turned to look down the sloping terrain toward the bay just as the daylight insisted on its right to rule, and the mist parted to reveal what looked to her like a gigantic graveyard of ghostly ships buried at anchor, their ratlines cluttered with perching gulls.

She lifted the hood of her fur cape to conceal her flaxen hair, remembering Zoya's comment that it stood out like a beam of light in a storm.

Zoya, the elderly Russian nurse who had attended Savana at birth, was the one person who had known Savana's mother, Nadyia Rezanov, at Baranof Castle at the Russian-American colony in the Pacific Northwest. Only Zoya, with her tender tongue, had been able to explain about the young Russian girl who had died in the lonely process of giving Savana birth while the thick swirling flakes of white slowly buried her with heaven's soft blanket.

Faithful Zoya had managed to escape the blizzard and bring the newborn to her father, an outcast Hudson's Bay Company chief factor by the name of James Mackenzie, who was being sought by the czarist officials and who faced imprisonment in the frozen Siberian wasteland.

And now Savana's father may also be dead, though the young woman harbored hope that she may yet find him among the forgotten prisoners in the Russian territory. In the five years since his unexpected disappearance, she had prayed continuously for a chance to search for him.

Savana's soft pearl gray eyes misted, and though they were considered her most feminine feature, her jawline, a little too square, indicated a tenacity of heart not easily vanquished. With a door now appearing to open in the search for her father, nothing would deter her from moving ahead, cautiously but with resolve.

Savana blinked against the dew and stroked back the delicate ermine brushing the sides of her face. With her raw emotions mollified, she switched her chain of thoughts to last night's mysterious message.

Her traveling companions from the Sandwich Islands, Mrs. Warrender and her young daughter Roslyn, had not long retired to their room at the Hudson's Bay Company fort on Montgomery Street in San Francisco when a message had discreetly arrived for Savana by the hands of a young errand boy from the local Spanish mission.

Further questioning of the lad had proven to be unproductive. "No sé nada, señorita, I not know," he had insisted, his luminous brown eyes wide in the amber light spilling down from the lantern above her bedroom door. "I get peso to bring letter to Señorita Savana Rezanov Mackenzie," he gushed breathlessly, and then was gone, slipping soundlessly down the wooden steps on quick bare feet.

The message, written on a torn piece of faded yellow paper, had sent her heart pounding. And so . . . she had come. She would hazard a covert meeting in a warehouse.

Savana left the dirt lot and walked gingerly along the wharf, trying to avoid the mud oozing through the wooden planks. The damp daybreak was drenched with the reek of brine and filled her lungs with messages from the open sea.

What did the writer of Proverbs say? *"As the cold of snow in the time of harvest, so is a faithful messenger to them that send him; for he refresheth the soul of his masters."*

But, *"Confidence in an unfaithful man in time of trouble is like a broken tooth, and a foot out of joint."*

"What message will the stranger waiting in the warehouse bring me?" she murmured. *Please, Lord, turn the quest of finding my father into good, and bless the path of my feet.*

Gripping her small black velvet handbag containing the written message, she hastened onward, hearing little except the hollow sound of her footsteps on the warped boardwalk as each step brought her closer to the warehouse. She wavered in the fog, her tension rising, peering ahead.

Through the fingers of gray mist that reached to twirl about the tall masts of sleeping merchant ships, a small lighter emerged, heaped high with bales of fur—no doubt from the internationally disputed Pacific Northwest. The lighter's flag, now visible, identified the loading vessel as American, or, as referred to by the British and Russians, a "Boston" trader. A scant glower pulled Savana's brows together as sight of the flag provoked her resentment.

Years earlier the Boston men had won their second victory with England in the war that had claimed the life of her cousin Boyd Bellomont at the Battle of New Orleans. Boyd, the only son of her powerful uncle, Sir Douglas Bellomont of the Hudson's Bay Company, had died from a musket shot while fighting. The Boston men had served under Andrew Jackson, who was now, she thought unpleasantly, President Jackson in Washington City.

"Rebels and traitors to His Majesty, that's what they are," she murmured, and yet her curiosity about the lighter grew, for it was the only vessel she could see out doing business in the fog-shrouded bay.

Savana stood watching until the lighter drew closer and bumped alongside the dock. Then, quite by accident, her studious gaze collided with a Boston man—a compelling young rogue wearing a black woolen coat and a wide-brimmed hat from Madrid decorated with silver pesos.

He sprang ashore, as agile as the California cougar she had noticed the day before, and stood on the wharf, hands on hips, as though he didn't see her.

*Which is quite impossible,* thought Savana, *since we're the only ones about.*

Her eyes skimmed over his bold good looks. Unfairly or not, she judged him an ill-mannered American full of himself and the Boston cause of "Manifest Destiny." He also looked to be a man born to wild places and difficult circumstances, and comfortable to be so.

As she walked past she cast a glance in his direction, careful to be discreet, and a faint stirring from the distant past tapped her memory.

*I've seen him somewhere before.*

As the thought blew across her mind it vanished in confusion when he turned his back and stared out toward the sea where an even thicker fog crept steadily toward the wharf.

Someone else in the lighter called to him, and as a heaving line was tossed, he snatched the monkey's fist with a one-handed catch and swung his muscular frame onto the boat.

Removing his coat as though he wished to be free of encumbrance, he began tumbling the bales within reach of the crane.

Savana dismissed him as a dock worker and walked on.

Minutes later she became sensitive to the fact that she might not be alone and glanced behind her, but no one followed.

Her heeled slippers clicked on the sodden planks. Water lapped against the creaking pilings. Above, a lone gull sounded a cry and winged its way into the mist.

Stopping briefly, she stared down the wharf toward a pile of stacked crates and a large rustic building, and was just able to make out a painted sign: Diego Brothers Warehouse.

This was it, her meeting place. The words on the sign blurred and she quickened her steps. From behind her she heard the town's mission bells tolling a Sunday morning welcome.

Despite the friendly chimes, she couldn't rid herself of the odd sensation that she was being watched by unfriendly eyes. The boards beneath her feet creaked and groaned like underground prisoners seeking release. When a shiver tightened her back, she turned about suddenly.

Nothing but mist trailed her footsteps.

She peered back toward the lighter that was yet visible, but the man in the black coat and Spanish hat was nowhere in sight. More curious than that, she thought, neither was anyone else. Where was the captain of the loading vessel? Where were the other dock workers? The fur pelts appeared to be abandoned and the crane hung frozen.

The wall of fog that had begun to creep in was now all about her, its veil descending in silence as Savana neared the warehouse where the door stood ajar. A warm lantern glow welcomed her inside.

With a white-gloved hand she gently pushed open the warehouse door.

"Mr. Yuri?" came her steady voice, surprising her with its calm. "I'm Miss Savana Mackenzie."

In the lantern light were more stacked crates and a desk cluttered with soiled papers, but the chair in which she expected to see the man named Yuri was vacant.

She glanced about her uneasily, then looked toward the rafters. From a low overhead pole, red chili peppers and white cloves of garlic hung like festive decorations, adding their strong odor to the smell of damp wood.

A soft, furtive sound moved from behind the shadowed boxes. Savana whirled about. "Mr. Yuri?" she repeated.

He walked toward her now, a tall, angular man wearing a calf-length coat. "Step into the lantern light so I may see you."

His Russian accent brought relief, yet her instincts prompted her to hesitate, and she lingered in the shadows of the doorway.

He must have sensed her wariness because he added softly in an apologetic tone, "So I may see if you resemble your father, James Mackenzie. I have come as an ally."

She walked with a soft rustle of skirts closer to the desk. She reached for the lantern base, her cold fingers wrapping about its warmth, lifting it in front of her as she turned to him.

The glow shone upon her pale face, highlighting the mist-dampened flaxen strands, her serious gray eyes, and resolute chin.

His breath released, and she wondered who else he might have expected in her place that made him as careful as she.

He came toward her, but because of the glare from the lantern she could not distinguish his features. With shaking fingers she stepped to the side and set it on the desk as he neared.

As she saw his face, her relief was audible. Yuri must have been in his late fifties, a slim, military-straight figure with a stoic but benign expression. His coat bore a wide lapel, and beneath it, he wore a blue Russian fitted surtout with a white vest, giving her the impression that he was a czarist official.

"I am most sorry for secrecy, Miss Mackenzie. Unfortunately it is necessary."

She mused again why it was necessary and asked the question that had bolstered her courage to come here alone. "What news about my father do you bring?"

His stoic face, waxen in the yellow light, changed perceptibly, and she sensed his tension, noting that his eyes scanned the other side of the dark warehouse.

"We must speak hurriedly," he said in a low voice. "There is not much time."

Savana's head turned toward the shadows. Had she heard a faint footstep? That sound—was it a rat?

"It was necessary to mislead you, Miss Mackenzie. It is not your father I must speak with you about."

As if struck, she took a step backward. "Mislead me?" she repeated accusingly.

The single lantern exaggerated the lines of strain etched down his cheeks and above his brows. "Do not misunderstand. I remained a friend of your father until the end."

Disappointment thudded like a heavy rock in her stomach. *Until the end.* The sound of her breathing mingled with his and she said dully, "Then he's dead?"

He spread his hands helplessly. "Few survive the weeklong blizzards in the frozen wastelands of Siberia."

Her desire pleaded for a faint whisper of hope. "But my father knew the North. He was strong, an outdoor trapper before he became an officer in the Company. And he was traveling in a *tarantass* with Russian-bred horses," she protested. "He couldn't have just disappeared."

"The blizzards, Miss Mackenzie, bury everything. They could not even find his vehicle. And if he wandered away in search of shelter as officials in the Russian-American Fur Company suspect he did—"

"Suspect?" she interrupted with a desperate scoff. "The Russian-American Company was no friend to my father, nor to the priest who journeyed with him. They were going to report to St. Petersburg, to the czar himself, and bring proof of the Russian fur hunters' cruelties to the Aleut Indians. That report might have cost Russia its charter in the Pacific Northwest. Profits were at stake, Mr. Yuri. And my father stood in the way. It's human nature to lie and cheat and even kill for the age-old lust for wealth."

If she thought to shock him with her knowledge, he remained unmoved. "Are you suggesting officials in Russian America deliberately had your father killed?"

Was she? Even she didn't know. Her energy had crested with the emotional outburst fed by her disappointment, and in its place came a wave of weariness. "I confess to instances when I've thought his disappearance was deliberately arranged, yet even I can't bring myself to fully believe it." Her restive glance settled upon his face. "Why did you ask me to meet you like this? The report of his death in the blizzard has circulated for nearly five years." Still daring to hope, her eyes searched his. "Last night when your message came, I thought the report may have been in error."

His thin mouth twitched. "We had no intention of bringing you false expectations."

Alert, she understood that he'd not come on his own. "Who sent you?"

"I am not at liberty to tell. I can say, however, that I did know your father and considered him a friend, a champion against the violence done to the native peoples of the North, of which I was never in agreement. The *promyshlenki* can be brutal," he said of the free-roving fur hunters who worked for the Russian-American Company.

Her eyes questioned him, but he held up a thin hand. "It is Baron Peter Sarakof I came to speak to you about."

The mention of the nephew of the countess was unanticipated. "What about the baron? Did he send you to speak with me?"

"Then he wrote you in England?"

She hesitated again. "Yes . . . several times. Was it the baron who sent you to me?" she asked again, this time curiously, for she could see no cause for secrecy.

The flicker of a disparaging smile mocked the suggestion. "Send me to warn you? The baron would do most anything in his authority to stop the information I bring from reaching you. It is because of the baron that I insisted our meeting be in secrecy. There is danger."

His words riddled her nerves. Savana assumed he somehow knew of her recent decision to aid her uncle in England's cause of gaining supremacy in the Pacific Northwest. Sir Douglas was in line to become the next governor-general of the British Northwest, and his request that she serve His Majesty King George had been intriguing, providing her the opportunity to journey to New Archangel, where her father had disappeared.

Her uncle had arrived in London unexpectedly, bringing important news of the Hudson's Bay Company's various forts throughout Oregon, and at York and the Red River Colony near Manitoba. America and England had signed a joint occupation treaty in Oregon after the War of 1812—"*But Russia has not yet fully dismissed imperial claims to territory all the way to the Columbia River,*" her uncle had told her. Three nations vied for the same land, and while war seemed far away, intrigue, sabotage, and the murder of national agents was an expanding fire that threatened to control the entire Pacific Coast from Alaska to San Diego.

Sir Douglas had gravely informed her that her Russian ancestry could become extremely valuable to England. Her role in serving His Majesty would actually be quite small. She was simply to journey with her uncle to Baranof Castle, accepting the long-overdue invitation by some in the Rezanov family. She was to be "nice and jolly" to the handsome Russian baron who favored a treaty with England and opposed the Boston traders in the region. If the baron entertained thoughts of a possible future betrothal—which, of course, was quite unlikely—she was not to offend him by refusing to at least "consider" the possibility.

Besides aiding her uncle in gaining the treaty to route the Boston traders from the rich fur region of the Northwest and the islands, Savana had a personal mission: to satisfy a desire to know more about the Christian work her father had done with the Aleut, and to see for herself the home of her Russian mother, Nadyia—a dream she had nourished since a young girl when she discovered that her grandmother was the powerful Countess Catherine Rezanov.

Savana looked at Yuri and offered a brave smile to throw him off. "You must be mistaken, Mr. Yuri. Why would my casual introduction to Baron Sarakof be dangerous?"

He did not return her smile; on the contrary, tiny beads of sweat glistened on his upper lip. "Because the information I bring you comes from St. Petersburg."

St. Petersburg! The word exploded with visions of imperial Russia.

"I don't understand," she repeated in a rush. "Information from whom?"

"From one," he whispered, "who warns you against any involvement with the baron, however seemingly trivial."

"Why do I need to be warned? I wish no ill to my mother's family, even if they were callous to my feelings while I was growing up," she said, masking the pain that had festered since childhood. "The baron invited me to journey to Baranof Castle with my uncle on trade matters with the Hudson's Bay Company."

"You must stay far from Baranof Castle," he said forcefully.

Savana's suspicions were strengthened by his taut face. What if an enemy had sent him to keep her from learning the truth about her father?

"Why is it dangerous to visit Baranof Castle?" she persisted. "And dangerous to whom? To me, or to my uncle?"

His mouth formed a tight line. "Perhaps to both of you. I am only the bearer of news, Miss Mackenzie, a messenger, but a most faithful one, I assure you."

Savana proceeded with caution. "Is it dangerous because of who my mother was—the daughter of a countess—or has it to do with my father's unexplained death?"

"I am afraid your questions are too involved for me to answer."

*Or dare to answer, perhaps?* She was not convinced as she looked into his remote gaze. "Then who sent you to warn me? At least tell me that much."

He stood as straight and proud as the bodyguard of the czar himself. "A friend sent me. One who must remain anonymous."

She pondered. An anonymous friend. Did she believe him? He made it difficult. A friend of her father? Certainly not of her mother. From what Zoya had told her, the Rezanov family had been avidly against Nadyia's marriage to the British official in the Hudson's Bay Company who had turned private missionary to the Aleut Indians. They had disowned Nadyia, and after her death they had also rejected Savana. Her father had received a terse letter informing him that the infant was better off in London with his sister Hillary, the wife of Sir Douglas Bellomont.

The prickle of her misgivings now convinced her she'd been too bold in meeting him alone. What if this man who called himself Yuri, of whom she knew nothing except the little he had disclosed, was not a friend of her father but an enemy? Might not he have some motive of his own? Perhaps he was against the treaty his Russian government might sign with England.

"Am I being warned against the baron?" she whispered. "If so, why?"

He did not look intimidated by her doubts. "Because Baron Sarakof is cold, efficient, and deadly."

She stared at him. How could she reply to such surprising charges?

Savana knew little about Peter Sarakof through any personal relationship of her own. She had heard stories about him, and some bore credence to his rigidly ambitious appetite. She had a small portrait and several letters of correspondence, nothing more. Lady Hillary had approved of the introduction, and Sir Douglas had said that the baron was crucial to getting the treaty signed by the czarist officials at Baranof Castle.

"Peter Sarakof is the nephew of the countess," she protested. "Surely he is a trustworthy man. He's also important to Sir Douglas."

A twitch of disdain tensed his lower lip. "What you mean, I think, is that an arranged marriage between you and the baron will greatly benefit England's interests in the Northwest. Lest you are offended at my bluntness, I hasten to say it is also of importance to Baron Sarakof's ambitions."

The unpleasant note in his voice could not be mistaken.

"I take it, Mr. Yuri, that you do not approve of this treaty with England?"

"It is not for me to approve or disapprove. My loyalties are to another, and to certain friends in St. Petersburg. As for the baron," he warned, "his objectives will be favorably enhanced by working closely with Sir Bellomont. He is a military man, recently placed in command of the patrol boats at New Archangel to thwart the Boston traders.

"You must return to London, Miss Mackenzie. Leave the matter of politics to ambassadors and soldiers. As for your deceased parents, there is nothing you can do to change the past, but if you insist on coming to New Archangel to uncover an injustice, you will endanger others besides yourself. And I'm sure you do not wish to do so."

"You will not tell me who sent you? And whom I might endanger?"

"I cannot. No one must know—it would mean my death."

Savana's breath caught. She watched as he reached within his coat and removed a sealed document.

"I am authorized to see you have this information from St. Petersburg. There is proof here of the kind of man Sarakof is." His lean face hardened. "You would do well to think again before allowing England to turn you into a British agent."

Savana accepted the envelope and placed it carefully inside her small bag. "I shall give careful consideration to your warning, but I can't promise my immediate return to London. As for marriage to the baron, I assure you, I've little anticipation either of us will wish to make anything serious of our families' introduction. I have plans of my own and I will not surrender them easily."

He studied her soberly. "I hope you will reconsider—" He stopped.

His head turned sharply to look into the shadows, with fear carved across his face. Swiftly he took hold of her arm. "Go!" he whispered. "Tell no one of our meeting, not even Sir Bellomont."

A faint sound came from behind them. Her eyes left his to swerve to the thin curtain that was drawn over a doorway, which appeared to lead into another office or clerk's room. Or was someone hiding in the darkness behind the crates where she had first heard that furtive sound like a scampering rat?

A floorboard squeaked, and Savana's nerves snapped. She broke and ran toward the warehouse door where a crack of daylight seeped in.

She rushed through the door into the wet stillness of the early morning, clutching her bag with the document, her mind and emotions in a tumult. What could it all mean? And whom could she trust? Was there anyone?

The fog had thickened while she met with Yuri, and Savana rushed ahead down the wharf losing herself within its swirling wisps, her pounding heart in her ears.

As she ran, an overpowering fear of being alone and rejected stalked her trail like a hunter forcing her toward a trap. She had felt the fear many times since being torn as a child from her father's embrace, knowing there was no one left to whom she truly belonged. Lady Hillary Bellomont had never been a caring woman. There was only Zoya.

Out of the whirlwind of her thoughts, words formed in her spirit—like silver in a furnace, shimmering with confidence and everlasting love: *When my father and my mother forsake me, then the Lord will take me up.* No, never abandoned, no matter how dark the shadows, how dangerous the path beneath her running feet.

She slowed, her panic easing, and drew in several deep breaths. She had the greatest and wisest Father to turn to in her need, her confusion, her feelings of isolation.

For a moment she closed her eyes and felt the fog softly touch her skin.

"I need someone, Father, someone to trust, someone who will prove a friend . . . yes, even more than a friend. Is it Peter Sarakof? Send me someone I can depend on."

Wet with drizzle and shivering from more than the cold, Savana hurried ahead, anxious to reach the wagon to bring her back to the Hudson's Bay Company fort.

Out of the fog arose a man with a dark pea coat and a wide-brimmed hat. The lighter loomed up like a sea monster rising from the hissing deep, and it seemed the dock worker was standing on its back. He appeared to be tumbling some bales of fur within reach of a crane—

Unexpectedly he lunged toward her! She tried to scream, but the sound died in her throat as the impact knocked the breath from her.

Together they landed, rolling hard on the wooden wharf.

# 2

# KEEP ME FROM THE SNARES

Dazed, Savana imagined herself having collided with a statue, but it proved to be warm, solid muscle gripping her. After the incident in the warehouse, her fear turned to fury. She tried to wrench away, but the arms around her might have been a prison bolt. She opened her mouth but found she was so overwhelmed she could make no sound.

Her captor peered at her from the swirling fog, and Savana had an impression of height and a handsome profile carved in an outline of granite strength. A pair of flinty blue eyes held hers.

With dismay she recognized the same American dock worker whom she had noticed earlier on the lighter. His hat had been knocked off in the fall and a swatch of rich brown hair fell across his forehead.

Into her subconscious rushed the same sense of recognition she had felt earlier that morning, perhaps diminished by a rush of confusion beneath his level stare.

25

With affected calm he released her. "Lovely morning, isn't it?"

Savana sat up and, under his gaze, whipped the hood back over her hair. Uncertain as to what had prompted the rough-and-tumble escapade, she saw it as a brash American display of supposed gallantry. His confident smile remained, convincing her she was right. She remembered what Aunt Hillary in London had said in her frosty British tone: "Beware of knaves, my dear. Untrustworthy scamps are everywhere about like nettlesome fleas."

She averted her eyes and drew in a breath. "It will do you no good," she stated coolly. "I've been warned in advance."

His suave mood vanished as quickly as though he had discarded a mask. "Who would be foolish enough to risk warning you?"

The sudden change in his tone of voice surprised her, and she thought his question quite odd. "If you knew Lady Hillary as well as I do, you'd not be so arrogant as to ever call her foolish." Her fair brow arched with British superiority, and she felt satisfied with her successful ability to so easily sober his hopes.

A mere flicker within his vivid gaze responded. Then— "Lady Hillary?" he repeated smoothly.

Savana managed a dignified expression, despite her discomfiture. "My aunt. She warned me about you before I ever left London."

"She couldn't have. No one knew—"

"She knows your type of rogue all right! She's an intelligent woman and knows a great deal about men of the knavish sort."

As if trying to decipher a garbled message, he was silent, contemplative, weighing her words.

Slowly he relaxed. "I've been called a good many things recently but never this. Still, I can understand your misfortune in meeting many of these knaves running about England in white periwigs and red coats. I always thought them rather odious myself."

He was deliberately choosing to misunderstand her. "I speak of Boston men turned traitor to His Majesty."

He lifted a brow. "Perhaps your aunt Hillary is a wise woman after all. So I will humbly accept your scathing denunciation, apologize for my knavish ways, and vow to hold them in abeyance from henceforth."

She had first interpreted his accent as a mixture of American sounds, but now she wasn't as certain. There was a tinge of something British about him that vaguely suggested an ancestry gone awry.

Savana's irritation was unwilling to allow for any charity. She began to think he was not the least troubled by what he had called her "scathing denunciation," but rather he was relieved by it. She wondered why. He had been more abrupt when she simply told him she had been warned about him.

"Not that it appears to matter to you," came his satiny drawl, "but I gallantly rescued you from a glancing blow from that pile of pelts."

She trusted no worker on the dock, especially the unscrupulous Boston sea traders who secretly prowled the northern waters of British and Russian territory in the Pacific Northwest. American spies were everywhere, and after the frightening incident in the warehouse she wasn't inclined to believe his excuse.

"I doubt it."

"Thanks. Your crumbs of grace, princess, are appreciated."

She drew in a breath. "If it's my gratitude you wish, you have it," she said in a chilly tone, for she wished to keep him at bay. "Would you mind—" and she pulled at her skirt. "You're sitting on it."

He glanced toward her yards of skirt and crinolines. "A thousand pardons," and he stood to his feet, a bounty of muscular and energetic good looks. He reached to snatch up his Spanish hat, pausing a moment longer to place something else inside his pea coat. Flecking off the dust while his gaze held hers, he settled his hat firmly on his head, giving it an arrogant twist as he extended his other hand.

She accepted only because she felt rather weak in the legs after the morning's diverse experiences. She managed to stand to her feet, drawing her now smudged ermine cape closely about her.

He scanned her with disinterest, yet challenge. "Take a suggestion from an ill-mannered colonial knave. Avoid the wharf at dawn, or at any time for that matter. Even at daybreak on Sunday mornings there are more than boorish Americans prowling about." A smile formed. "You may run into a few mad Englishmen with ice in their veins, out for a sprightly morning jaunt; not to mention Russkies with spy telescopes hiding behind crates. All in all, you'd better take the advice of Aunt Hillary. Go home to London."

Her eyes met his coolly. *Russkies*, she knew, was the name the Boston traders called the Russians. It was almost as if he knew she had Russian ancestry.

"Thank you. Perhaps I'll take your advice." She scanned his rugged garb and the handmade Spanish leather boots, wondering who he was but not willing to show enough interest to inquire.

He stood there, the mist encircling him. As if to play upon her charge that his American manners were lacking English refinement, he swept off his wide-brimmed hat and bowed deeply at the waist as elegantly as an English cavalier in the court of King Charles, his flint blue eyes amused. "Your servant, madame!"

She couldn't help but smile and turned her face away before brushing past him.

"Good day, señorita," he said with affected sobriety.

When she had walked farther down the wharf she was prompted by a whim to look back, but refused.

*Strange,* she thought as she walked ahead, musing. For all his spoken concern for her safety, he didn't inquire about what she was doing on the wharf alone at dawn, or whether she was even with someone else. She had a hunch that he might know who she was. And yet, how could that be true, and why?

"It's as if I've seen him somewhere," she told herself again, "but I've never before been in California."

Leaving the wharf, Savana hurried toward the lot where the wagon waited, thinking of Yuri and the document on Baron Peter Sarakof she had placed inside her handbag. She was anxious to read it and—

"Handbag!" She stopped with alarm and whirled, looking toward the wharf. "No—"

Had she dropped it?

With a stifled groan over her negligence, she snatched up her skirts and began running back in the direction of the dock. *Surely the American would have discovered it lying on the planks,* she thought, wincing as she realized she might need to apologize for her behavior.

Precious minutes had elapsed before she once again was rushing across the ominous wharf to where the lighter was anchored.

She ran up, peering toward the boat but seeing no one. She decided he must be inside the pilothouse. She made a quick search for her bag in the area where they had collided, but it was not there. She thought back, glancing in the direction of the warehouse now concealed with fog. Yes, she had it with her when she fled.

"Then my bag must be here, unless—"

She turned, her breath pausing, peering through the wisps toward the lighter. "Unless," she repeated, and her heart raced with a newly emerging suspicion.

Not a soul was in sight, not even a guard for the fur pelts.

Her mind retraced its steps over the encounter . . . the falling pelts . . . the embarrassment . . . the bewildering conversation they had engaged in. The moment had so arrested her attention that she had not even thought of her bag.

Why—the distraction he had caused must have been deliberate. The American had taken it! Of course he had, and it all was making sense now—even the change in his behavior when she told him that she'd been warned beforehand.

She walked to the edge of the dock where the lighter was anchored, hearing the water lapping. It was now reasonable to believe the lighter had only been a clever ruse.

Dare she risk going aboard to confront him? There was no telling a man's character by his looks, and if he'd been after the document he wouldn't have waited for her to return.

The ropes creaked. She whirled around and looked again in the direction of the warehouse, barely visible through its gray shroud. Suddenly she backed away and, turning, fled from the wharf.

Minutes later, she neared the wagon where the driver waited, dozing. Wet and exhausted from her own folly, she recalled the faint mockery in the flinty eyes of the tall American.

*He must think himself quite clever,* she thought. How had he known that Yuri was waiting for her in the warehouse? What motives did he have for wanting the information on Peter Sarakof?

"Then I was right in my suspicion of having seen him elsewhere," she murmured to herself.

Try as she might to recall where, she could not. Whenever the meeting had occurred, it certainly had not been as dramatic as the one on the wharf. And of course, he had wanted this one to be dramatic! He had used whatever props were available to accomplish his purpose. And he'd been successful!

As the wagon brought her back to the Hudson's Bay Company fort on Montgomery Street she drew her cape tightly about her and tried to sort through the reasons for his actions. Surely he'd not taken her bag for hopes of monetary gain!

No, not that, she concluded. It was the document he had wanted. The next question was equally disturbing: Why would he be interested in her affairs?

He could be an agent.

She thought of Yuri. What would the Russian do if he knew she had foolishly lost the document to a Boston agent?

As the wagon neared the double-storied wooden frame house, she debated whether or not she should inform Sir Douglas about her meeting at the warehouse. Yet Yuri had warned her to silence.

Wet and shivering, she slipped silently through the back door, smelling bread baking in the hearth.

Yuri's warning rang in her ears. *Do not go to Baranof Castle.* If she were right in her conclusions about the rogue she had met on the wharf, he would soon know the reason for Yuri's warning.

Would the American contact her again?

# 3

# THE RUSSIAN BEAR

Captain Trace Wilder climbed the wooden stairs to his hotel room and entered to find his brother Yancey waiting patiently, lying on the bed with his hands behind his head.

Yancey was a year younger than he, his eyes a deep blue, his hair as dark as coal. Their father, Zachary Wilder, had been a friend of Andrew Jackson and had served him and the country well until Zachary's death in the war.

Committed to America's "manifest destiny"—determined to see his country rule the continent from shore to shore—Trace had thrown himself into the unfinished work of his father in the Northwest and was serving the President as an agent. Recently Trace had been contacted by Senator Baxter of Missouri, a political ally of Jackson, who'd given Trace more information on his assignment.

It would be a difficult one, but a job that best suited him, since he was related to Sir Douglas Bellomont of the Hudson's Bay Company, and was committed to seeing Oregon become a territory of America, as was Senator Baxter. Trace was expected to marry Miss Callie Baxter, the senator's daughter—unless Yancey had his way.

Trace couldn't think about Callie now. He was commissioned to sabotage England's plans to sign a trade treaty with the Russian-American Fur Company at its headquarters in New Archangel.

In that treaty, the Hudson's Bay Company hoped to open a new trading fort on the Stikine River, thereby undermining the Boston traders' ability to profit from fur trades with the trappers and Indians, and terminating their viable presence in the Pacific Northwest. Although there was the Joint Occupation Treaty of Oregon signed between Boston and England, President Jackson knew, as did Trace, that possession of the Northwest depended upon settlers and merchant ships. The Hudson's Bay Company at Fort Vancouver knew it as well.

As boys, Trace and Yancey had cared for their wounded father in a cabin for the month of his intense suffering until their father's friend and serving man, known as the "Colonel," had found the three of them in hiding from the British.

Trace had become more fervently committed to his country after seeing his father suffer and die for a cause, but Yancey had become withdrawn and somewhat cynical. In a certain sense Trace didn't blame him. Yancey had also witnessed the death of their mother in the fire that had destroyed the family plantation in Virginia.

They had lost everything in the war—everything except each other and their Christian faith. Trace held tenaciously to his upbringing, but Yancey refused to discuss the matter.

While Trace was wholeheartedly involved in a race to claim Oregon ahead of England and Russia, Yancey drifted across the Northwest with the American pathfinder Joe Meeks and his trapping brigade. Meeks had forged some of the first cross-country land routes through Oregon Country, and Yancey had risked the journey with him through Indian territory.

Yancey now had a new interest, one that Trace did not approve of, not that Yancey appeared to care. He raised himself onto an elbow and scanned Trace.

"You look like a cat whose mistress left the canary cage open," came his smooth Virginian drawl. "I assume you got what you wanted?"

Trace reached within his pea coat and pulled out a sealed document, tapping it against his palm. "Delivered by the Russkie Yuri."

"You think she's cooperating with St. Petersburg?"

"Don't know, maybe England." Trace threw off his pea coat and sailed his sombrero to the bed against the wall where it landed at Yancey's polished black boots. Trace walked to his desk.

He lighted a second lantern. "What better secret agent could Bellomont employ in his service to good King George than a woman with a Russian mother and an English pappy? Particularly when he hopes to arrange a marriage between her and the baron."

Yancey lounged on the bed, saying nothing, and Trace glanced at him. Because of Yancey's relationship with Joe Meeks, President Jackson wanted him as a scout for the first wagon train of immigrants soon to be heading into Oregon Country, perhaps to the Willamette Valley near British Fort Vancouver. Missionary Jason Lee and his party had arrived to set up their compound, and word had reached an American agent that British Chief Factor McLoughlin had received Jason cordially.

Trace frowned. He rather liked McLoughlin. So far, as director of Fort Vancouver, he'd treated the arriving Americans fairly.

A seasoned guide was needed to lead a route from Independence to the Columbia River, one who knew the mind of the Indians and had traveled the route that few others had ever seen except the Sioux and Blackfeet. Trace intended to talk Yancey into the job, but he would say nothing now, for he knew his brother would refuse. Yancey was on his way back to St. Louis to buy a riverboat.

Trace worried about Yancey. . . . His brother's once-strong faith in God that he had as a boy had taken a whipping over the years. Trace hoped to get him involved with some missionaries who planned to join that wagon train to Oregon.

Neither the wagon train nor the missionary work was likely to succeed if he failed to thwart the Hudson's Bay and Russian-American Companies from their purposes.

"Leaving already?" he asked as Yancey stood and caught up his new black broadcloth coat. Yancey slipped it on over a satin vest and a white shirt with stylish ruffles. He looked every inch an untrustworthy gambler.

"I only stopped by to let you know where you could find me after this mission of yours in the North."

"St. Louis. Why don't you come with me to Fort Vancouver? Rebecca's there," he said of Callie's sister. Trace mentioned Rebecca even though he knew Yancey was interested in Callie.

Yancey picked up his hat and settled it on his head, then took his gunbelt from the peg, strapping it on. He looked at Trace and smiled. It was a smile that Trace knew, and didn't like.

"Nope," said Yancey. "I've a hankering for St. Louis. The daughter of Senator Baxter has some notion of joining the missionary party heading into Oregon. She's making a mistake. More than likely she'll get herself scalped if I don't convince her to stay in the senator's brick mansion."

Senator Baxter's daughter, of course, was Callie. Trace's eyes narrowed a little. He didn't like the notion of leaving Callie to his brother's devices while he was away serving the Boston cause.

"You don't need to concern yourself about Callie," said Trace smoothly. "The senator will never allow her to head west in that wagon train."

Yancey's dark blue eyes flicked over Trace. "Maybe you don't know her as well as you think. Callie always manages to get what she wants."

There was more to his words than first appeared. "Does she?" asked Trace tonelessly.

"You ought to know," said Yancey, meeting his gaze evenly.

He might have told Yancey that it was his arrogance and interest in a riverboat that had turned Callie toward Trace. Even to this day he believed that she still had a secret infatuation with Yancey, though she'd never admit it.

"You could lead that wagon train north as a scout," said Trace, leaning against his desk. "The President has asked for you in particular. He's heard you've traveled that way before with Joe Meeks."

"No thanks. I'm no scout. I don't want to be responsible for a wagon train in Indian territory. I'll see you in St. Louis when you get back, Trace." He walked to the door and opened it, looking back, his blue eyes amused. "Be careful Miss Mackenzie doesn't win you over to the wrong side. I'd be disappointed to hear my patriotic brother had settled down at Baranof Castle." Yancey went out, closing the door behind him.

Trace heard his steps disappear down the stairs. He sighed and stood looking at the closed door between them, folding his arms.

A moment later he was forced to dismiss his brother from his mind. He had his own work now and nothing must interfere, not the dreams he'd left in St. Louis in the quiet, sheltered drawing room of the senator's mansion, nor Yancey's ambition to have Callie for himself. Trace had his duty. Nothing else mattered much, or so he told himself.

He picked up the sealed document, but in his mind he saw instead the woman he'd taken it from, a woman with gray eyes, flaxen hair, and an almost regal expression. Did she know she was the granddaughter of a Russian countess?

His flinty eyes narrowed slightly and his handsome features grew sober. She made a troubling spy, he thought. Without a moment's more hesitation he broke the St. Petersburg seal and brought it closer to the lantern light to read:

*Baron Peter Sarakof is an able officer in the Imperial Russian Navy, but he has been reckless in his personal life and has been sent to New Archangel as a mild reprimand for his significant gambling debts. He is hardly the manner of man who is fitting to become the husband of a young woman of your religious cause. A woman who hopes to follow her father's work with the Aleut.*

*Baron Sarakof is deeply entrenched in the inner circle of men who hold the charter for the Russian-American Fur Company at New Archangel, by which he hopes to regain his lost wealth and position. You should know that he is misusing the native people for his gain and at the same time misappropriating dividends to the stockholders and the government.*

*The baron has secret plans of which I dare not write, except to inform you of your grave mistake in considering marriage to a man of such cold and calculating schemes. This I can tell you: When a friend of mine, a czarist official, threatened to ask for an investigation by the czar, he was "accidentally" killed in a hunting expedition of which the baron and several of his men were also attending. If you wisely ask why I do not make this information known publicly, it is because there is more at risk than even my life.*

*The baron hopes to return to St. Petersburg and become elevated to the inner circle of the czar. How and why you would play into his plans I cannot say, but it is not to your good.*

*A Friend*

Trace stood frowning to himself, staring at the letter. The information was not what he had hoped for. The entire fiasco on the wharf had proven to be of little value. He sniffed the fine linen paper, but there was no feminine fragrance. He tossed the letter on his desk, his eyes narrowing. This was not the secret document on the plans of England in Oregon! Nor personal information on the whereabouts of his American friend Fletcher, imprisoned in Russian America.

As he looked down at the letter his thoughts were troubled by what he had read. Evidently Bellomont's niece didn't know what she was getting into—unless she was actually working not for England but St. Petersburg.

His American contact had been right about one thing: There were members of the Rezanov family at Baranof Castle as well as in St. Petersburg who didn't want Bellomont's niece to visit the Russian-American Fur Company's headquarters.

There was good cause to worry about the baron, thought Trace. Sarakof was a ruthless and ambitious scoundrel who evidently hoped to use Miss Mackenzie to further his influence with the czar.

Trace paused reflectively, stroking his chin, considering the St. Petersburg postmark. Who had found it necessary to send Yuri to warn Bellomont's niece not to come to Baranof Castle? A true friend? An enemy?

Perhaps Yuri was the man to ask. . . .

Trace studied the handwriting, holding it close to the lantern. It told him little about the individual who had written it, since it was likely to have been dictated. Who would be injured most by Savana's marriage to Baron Sarakof? Who did not wish her to come? Her parents were dead . . . perhaps someone in her mother's family?

Trace had been told about Countess Catherine Rezanov, Savana's maternal grandmother. Obviously she wished nothing to do with her granddaughter, or else she would have contacted her during the years she'd grown up in London. A grandfather? Trace had heard nothing about him from his sources in Washington, so he assumed him to be dead.

He scowled and set the letter aside again. He had expected a map, secret plans, times, dates, Russian and British contacts at Fort Vancouver and New Archangel. Instead he had a warning about the safety of a young woman with whom he hoped no further contact.

Was she misguided enough to be considering a marriage to Sarakof, or was she working with her uncle for England? He tapped his chin and looked at the letter impatiently, realizing it added more problems to a situation that was already troublesome. If he warned her, she would have more opportunity to learn what he was about, and she'd accuse him of staging the incident on the wharf to get the document.

Trace leaned by the desk, debating his own logic. He was likely to get involved against better judgment if he tried to warn her. But if he simply decided to forget what he had read and proceed with his mission, she might be walking into a trap she didn't know was there.

He muttered his impatience, lifted the letter to burn it in the oil lamp, then paused, unable to destroy it. His gaze narrowed. In the reflection of the lantern's glow he envisioned the girl with a modest flush of indignation on her cheeks when he had held her on the wharf. . . . He smiled wryly, remembering, then rebuked himself for wavering in his rigid intentions. Toying with her problems would complicate matters, perhaps in more ways than one.

He slowly folded the letter and placed it on the desk, then took his time removing his shirt and the inner holster he carried next to his chest.

There was a creak on the stairs outside his door. Yancey had changed his mind, after all, and returned. Trace waited until he heard a low tap. He opened the door, and a wide-eyed Mexican boy of perhaps twelve stood looking up at him, nervous and frightened.

"Señor Wilder, there—there is a girl waiting downstairs to see you."

"What does she want?"

"She say—she say please come quick."

His gaze searched the boy, who watched him, licking his lip. . . .

*A bruised lip,* thought Trace. *Someone has roughed him up, but why?*

Just as Trace stepped back from the door, five men with seamen's knives and bare knuckles rushed him. One vicious blow after another struck him, and as he fell, a boot rammed his side.

In a moment of fading consciousness he heard their Russian accents: "The document from Yuri is here. Set his desk and trunk on fire."

The smell of smoke and a child's weeping stirred Trace. "Señor Wilder, wake up, wake up!"

With his last vestige of strength, he struggled awake to see hot flames licking their way through his trunk. The boy was beating the fire with a blanket, and other voices clamored up the stairs as the boy's father and brothers came rushing in to stop the flames from spreading.

Trace heard the hiss and sizzle as water splashed, and heat and smoke drifted to him from the floor. The women were bringing buckets of water and yelling in Spanish. Trace managed to get to one knee, but it was too late for his belongings. Everything was in smoldering rubble.

His head was splitting with searing pain, and he realized he must have put up more of a fight than he had thought. He felt the sticky blood on his arm where a knife wound gaped open. He pushed himself up onto his feet only to collapse.

# 4

# THE BOSTON KINSMAN

Savana and her maid, Zoya, had arrived two days ago at the Hudson's Bay Company's new trading fort in San Francisco with Reverend Angus Withycombe and Mrs. Warrender and her daughter. Their first stop after a tedious voyage from London had been a refreshing two-week rest at the Company's trading fort in a warm-water port called the Kingdom of Hawaii. From there they had sailed on to Spanish California at San Francisco's port.

Her uncle had briefly informed her that she would also be aiding the fastidious Withycombe in an important cause for beloved England at Fort Vancouver in its race with Boston to claim sole authority to the Oregon Country. Since Savana was more concerned with obtaining information on her father's disappearance at New Archangel, she had not given Reverend Withycombe and Fort Vancouver much thought until today.

The Reverend was being sent out from London as a representative of the Anglican Church at Fort Vancouver to maintain the chapel service for the Hudson's Bay Company workers and Brigade trappers. While Angus was to conduct the services, Mrs. Warrender was to aid in the school that Chief Factor John McLoughlin had already established at the fort.

Oddly enough, Sir Douglas Bellomont had been instrumental in having the Hudson's Bay Company urge the unlikely Withycombe to serve as a representative of the "Christian cause," as he had put it, at the British fort. He had also prearranged for his niece Savana to voyage with them, and at Honolulu they had boarded a Company trading vessel named the *Beaver* for San Francisco. They would only be on the California coast for a week before reboarding the Company vessel and, along with her uncle, voyage up the coast into what was known as Oregon Country. Along with the Pacific Coast, Oregon was a vast, mostly unexplored territory, deemed to be valuable for its rich fur trade and desired by three international powers.

At the noon meal on the day following the incident on the wharf, Savana sat at the dining table in the Hudson's Bay Company headquarters in San Francisco silently engrossed in her own dilemma while Sir Douglas and Withycombe argued the fate of Oregon Country.

She shivered, remembering yesterday's scene as though the fog that had clung to the wharf continued to wrap its tentacles about her. But in the sunshine that filtered pleasantly through the lace curtains the next day, there was nothing mysterious or threatening hovering about the dining table where she and the others took their noon meal with Sir Douglas.

Her uncle had arrived late the night before, and as she sat beside him at the table, an inland breeze had risen to chase away the mist that had covered the bay for several days.

Sir Douglas's square hand firmly gripped the silver urn of strongly brewed tea as he refilled his cup. His heavy British accent reinforced his monologue on the absolute necessity that England, and England alone, rule the Pacific Northwest and perhaps all of the Great Rockies.

Sir Douglas was a relatively short and energetic man in his fifties, wholly dedicated to England's colonial dreams and to keeping every inch of the expanding empire—whatever the cost.

His thick neck, with its layer of leathery skin overlapping a high-winged white starched collar, gave an unflattering impression of a turtle's small head above the hard, humped shell of his shoulders. His straight-clipped iron gray hair was jaw length, and the quick, assertive dark eyes teemed with little flashes of brittle humor. He was a man of insight and sagacity, though somewhat portly in size, his barrel chest often popping buttons. His "fat," as he claimed, "is solid, my dear ladies, not flab," he would inform his wife Lady Hillary in London, and he would wink at Savana when Hillary's coldly smiling blandness refused the good humor of a husband too long away from home.

Yet regardless of his misleading appearance, he was far from a soft, tea-sipping Britisher, content in satin finery beneath chandeliers while expounding upon the destiny of England. He was, Savana knew with amusement, an expert wrestler who heartily enjoyed besting the rowdy French-Canadian Brigade trappers who served the Company on the Columbia River and in New Caledonia.

It was no secret to Savana that her uncle, to whom she was greatly attached, often displayed more of the temperament of a trapper than a man knighted by King George, though he wouldn't admit it. He thrived in the rigorous outdoors like the beaver the Company hunted. And she'd heard him comment to Aunt Hillary, when she complained that he was away from Bellomont House too much, that he'd much rather own a canoe and sing lustily with the brawling nor'westers—surging downstream with their season's pelts to rendezvous with trappers and Indians for their yearly fair—than hobnob in London with her humorless aristocratic friends.

"Far kinder to parley with the Indians and exchange rope tobacco with the Brigade than wear lace at my cuff and take a snort of snuff with the lords and merchant investors," he said in his clipped British brogue.

His tough mind could be callous at times, and he was known for taking risks that involved others to fulfill his loyalties to King George, but he was not a malicious man. Savana believed him reasonable, and she shared his dedication to England and his interest in Russia.

Savana's "arranged" meeting with the Russian baron was due to Lady Hillary's wishes as well as her uncle's. When her introduction to Baron Peter Sarakof was explained to the family as lucrative for England, the family all agreed that the best possible plan for the orphaned daughter of James Mackenzie was to make the voyage to New Archangel.

Not all in England agreed with the political determination to make Oregon Country a territory of the empire. On the voyage, Savana had already experienced Mrs. Warrender's impatience with international politics, and she could see now by her expression as Reverend Withycombe continued his speech—not for God but King George—that the widow was in no mood to be silent and genteel.

"My dear Reverend," she stated at last with a bored voice, "as far as I care, Boston can have the forest wasteland, and His Majesty can retire to his herb garden of posies." She had declared this while inspecting a forkful of Mexican-style omelette dotted with bits of red chili pepper. She laid her fork down without tasting the spicy dish.

Mrs. Warrender's indifference was all the dry brush Reverend Withycombe needed to fuel his scorn. "A wasteland did you say, my dear woman? Oregon Country? By the king! 'Tis a land coveted by three nations," he corrected her apparent ignorance. "That should tell you of Oregon's importance, now and in the future. Isn't that correct, Sir Douglas?"

Savana's uncle was busily enjoying his meal, heaping spoonfuls of omelette into warm flour tortillas and adding a splash of hot pepper sauce.

Mrs. Warrender shrugged her thin shoulders in the worn black dress. The newly furbished lace added to the high collar must have scratched her throat, for she kept thrusting her chin forward as she gazed birdlike across the table at Withycombe.

"Important or not, I dare say we've wasted too many lives in war with Boston already. Will His Majesty welcome a third? What do we have to show for it? What has the king?"

"Rubbish indeed," scoffed Withycombe, and lifted a hand impatiently as though shooing away a bothersome fly from his orange marmalade toast. "I'm disappointed in you, madam, thoroughly so. I must admit before Sir Douglas that you talk appeasement."

"Call it appeasement if you wish," said Mrs. Warrender. "I'll tell you what I've already told Sir Bellomont. I wouldn't be sorry if I saw the Joint Occupation Treaty flung to the north winds for good."

"Treason!" declared Withycombe, two splotches of color forming in his hollow cheeks.

Savana thought he would make the perfect dour judge in white wig and black robe peering down the bench at the condemned prisoner about to be hanged and quartered. A minister in name only, his passion was not roused by the truth of Scriptures but by politics.

Savana had learned on the voyage from the Sandwich Islands, where Reverend Withycombe had served previously, that he had requested of her uncle to be transferred to Fort Vancouver to serve in the new Company chapel built for the Company workers.

"Angus is right," came the gravelly voice of Sir Douglas. "Joint occupation with America is out of the question."

Roslyn, Mrs. Warrender's young daughter, winced. "Are we going to argue politics all through luncheon?"

Savana silently agreed with her uncle and took another bite of her omelette made with black olives from the mission and red chili peppers. . . . In her mind's eye she could see the peppers hanging from the rafters in the warehouse. It reminded her of those furtive footsteps she had heard when meeting secretly with Yuri, and she lost her appetite.

Mrs. Warrender swished her spoon energetically in her teacup, looking in no mood to squelch an argument.

Sir Douglas wore a thin smile. "Perhaps," he said, "you feel strongly against British interest in Oregon because of friendships at Fort Vancouver?"

Both Mrs. Warrender and her daughter looked at him. Savana moved uneasily in her chair. She thought she knew the path her uncle was heading with his honey-coated accusation. Mrs. Warrender's blue eyes sparked with a temper unsubdued by the Christian graces she espoused so eloquently, and Roslyn looked down at her plate.

"Indeed? And is it now deemed treason to be friendly with American missionaries come to Oregon to intervene for the savages, Sir Bellomont?"

"That, my dear Mrs. Warrender, depends on whether or not those said missionaries have truly come for such a worthy purpose."

"Mother . . ." began Roslyn, "I'm feeling ill again. Let's go to our room."

"I can think of no other purpose why Jason Lee and his friends would sacrifice to journey there and build a missionary compound," she retorted. "Living in the wilderness with a troop of savages darting about naked in the trees is cross enough to bear, without being accused of aiding Boston expansionism."

Savana knew that Mrs. Warrender's main reason for going with her daughter to Fort Vancouver was to join a certain American missionary with whom she'd been corresponding since she'd met him in Honolulu two years before. Her own husband, who had worked for the Hudson's Bay Company on the island, had contracted a tropical disease and died four years earlier. And young Roslyn was on her way to Fort Vancouver to marry the Company teacher at the school.

Savana laid aside her napkin and attempted to smile cheerfully to head off further debate. "We're not likely to solve international disputes between three nations over the luncheon table now. It's a pleasant afternoon, Mrs. Warrender. Why don't we take Roslyn for a walk in the garden? The Company has planted some Spanish roses and the smell is intoxicating."

Mrs. Warrender sat stiffly. "I'd rather not. I didn't sleep well on that hard mattress last night. I vow it must be stuffed with rocks instead of feathers."

Reverend Withycombe emptied his cup and set it down quietly. He pushed back his chair and stood, sweeping back the tail of his long black coat. He was a big-boned man with a shock of graying red hair and a long chin, from which grew an anemic, pointed beard.

"Then if you will all be so good as to excuse me, I'm anxious for a bit of a stroll now that the fog has retreated." He added with ironic humor, "I should like to see why England hopes the Mexican government will exchange California to pay us for some old debts in dried salted salmon. So far the Mexican government impressed me as having more common sense than that."

Sir Douglas chuckled silently, his chest shaking, and poured more tea. "You can't blame the Company for hoping. If we don't get California, imperial Russia will, or far worse, Boston. They already have their eyes on Texas. That Sam Houston is a dangerous renegade, and Daniel Boone is no better. Let's hope they stay in the Southwest."

"The sunshine does look wonderful," sighed Roslyn. "Sure you won't come, Mother? I'd like a clear look at the bay for a change."

Mrs. Warrender shook her head as though preoccupied with her own thoughts and smoothed a wisp of her auburn hair, pushing it back into the large knot weighing heavily on the back of her neck.

As fifteen-year-old Roslyn stood and Savana prepared to scoot back her chair, Uncle Douglas laid a restraining hand on Savana's wrist. "Wait a minute, my girl, I need to speak with you in private after luncheon."

She hadn't spoken to him alone since before leaving London, and she supposed that he had much to tell her about their visit to New Archangel to meet the baron.

But Reverend Withycombe decided he was not yet done with his speech, and he crossed his long legs at the knee, taking out his long, skinny pipe to jab toward her uncle to emphasize his words. "There's no doubt in my opinion, Sir Douglas, but that the Russians are the true threat to our aims in Oregon, not Boston."

"I think not, Angus. And here, I differ with McLoughlin and the governor-general in London. I think the Hudson's Bay and Russian-American Companies have much in common. We should operate jointly to oppose the Americans."

Withycombe raised both brows. "A risky bit of trick if you ask me. Count Aleksandr would be as well pleased to see us booted from the coast as the high-flying Boston traders."

"Not if matters go as I and some others in the Hudson's Bay Company expect they will."

Mrs. Warrender had evidently taken all the political talk she could endure, and stood from her chair. "Come, Roslyn," she ordered, and with cold dignity walked across the bare floor of the Company dining room, where she stopped at the door and looked back. "Are you coming, Reverend Withycombe? I do believe you told Roslyn and me that you had some interesting tales about the Methodist Jason Lee."

Savana caught an exchanged glance between Withycombe and her uncle; then the minister stood. "Indeed, Mrs. Warrender, most interesting. I shall join you at once."

Savana watched him stroll from the dining commons, her curiosity pricked, a small frown forming. "He makes a poor minister. Somehow I think if a man is going to serve the Lord he ought to do so by teaching the Scriptures instead of arguing earthly kingdoms." She glanced at Sir Douglas. "You're certain you did the wise thing transferring him to Fort Vancouver?"

"The best move I could make, seeing as how he'll make an unsuspected agent to sabotage Jason Lee's work."

"Sabotage?" Savana turned to him with a frown. "But Jason Lee is a minister, even if he is an American."

He shot her a bright look, his hefty brows pointing upward. "So now I've two lecturing females to nag me about the man's pristine motives each morn at the table."

"I've no habit to nag," said Savana.

He gave a brisk pat to her arm, and Savana added smoothly with a smile, "Because it wouldn't do any good if I did."

He gave a short laugh, then took the last swallow from his teacup and refilled it, scowling at his own musings. "Mrs. Warrender would be a sprightly woman if she had more sense."

"Uncle!"

"Unfortunately for the cause of England, her emotions get in the way of what needs to be done. She's not dependable. Yet every Britisher at Fort Vancouver who buzzes about Lee and his colleagues can be useful to our cause. If I didn't need you at Baranof Castle . . ." He looked at her thoughtfully.

His hesitancy intensified her curiosity, though she wasn't certain she truly wished to know enough to become involved.

Sir Douglas studied her keenly, then seemed to decide to change the subject. "I've news from Baranof Castle that you'll find interesting."

Yuri's warning about the baron flashed across her mind. If the American had the document in his possession and it proved important, she might be doing an injustice to England by keeping silent.

"You've news from the baron?" she asked, expecting him to produce a letter, but he reached for another dessert cake and added more butter. Pleasure kindled a flame in his eyes as he stared thoughtfully at the cake, and Savana wondered if the pleasure were directed toward the sweet or in contemplation of what he was about to say.

"The baron is here at Fort Ross. We'll meet with him tomorrow night at an official dinner held in our honor."

Strain held her in silence. While the baron remained far away at New Archangel, he seemed less of a threat. Learning that he was nearby at the Russian colony toppled her walls of security. She picked up her cup and finished the now-cold tea.

"So soon? What's he doing in California? How did he know we'd be here?"

"I sent him news months ago."

"You were quite certain I'd come," she accused mildly.

"For England? I never doubted you a moment, my dear. Peter's here with a delegation sent by the count. They're looking to buy a shipload of wheat for the colony before their winter sets in." He peered into his cup thoughtfully. "A bit of an oddity . . . the wheat they usually get from the Mexican government isn't available. There isn't a bagful to be had from here to Los Angeles. Getting wheat is a matter of urgency for the count, but a stroke of luck for us."

She wondered how that could be as he looked at her with glinting eyes. "If Hudson's Bay can guarantee a wheat delivery, the Russian colony will see the importance of signing that treaty. England can deliver when Fort Ross cannot. And when the Boston traders have their schooners sabotaged dead in the water, Hudson's Bay will come through." He drummed his fingers. "But where can I get wheat? Odd," he repeated again to himself, "that there isn't any to be bought, when the season elsewhere in California has been good."

Savana was still contemplating going to Fort Ross to meet the baron and wasn't listening wholeheartedly.

"By the way," he said, changing the subject, "Zoya left for Fort Ross this morning. The baron requested her early arrival to prepare your stay."

Savana was bewildered that her uncle had sent Zoya without first informing her, or that her maid would leave without explaining. Zoya had been her mother's maid before she died, and was now as dear to Savana as a grandmother. "Was there any need to send her ahead? It's not as if I'm royalty needing large preparations for an overnight stay," she said with a laugh.

He shrugged. "Peter thought it best. He's a meticulous man who is concerned for your comfort."

She stirred. "Is he?"

He looked at her across the table and changed the subject. "Peter's also brought interesting news from Baranof Castle."

Savana recognized the satisfied gleam in his eyes.

"Someone else wishes to meet with you when you arrive at the castle." He smiled. "Countess Catherine Rezanov."

Savana's breath caught. "The countess?" she said, overwhelmed.

"Your grandmother, no less. She's pleased you have come to meet Peter. He's her nephew by marriage, but keep in mind she looks upon him as a grandson. You've done well for yourself, my dear Savana."

Savana felt the blow of his words as something physical. *My grandmother,* she thought, unbelieving. Was it possible after all these years that her mother's family had a change of heart toward Nadyia's "peasant" child? Savana hungered for acceptance, and her heart pounded.

"You're certain? When Father was alive he told me Nadyia had no living relatives that could be accounted for, or if there were family in St. Petersburg, they held no interest in me."

"Bah! My guess is that James wanted it that way. He didn't want you in New Archangel when he worked with the Aleut. He insisted the political environment was dangerous for you. Matters change with time. You have the baron to thank for this meeting with the countess. A clever man, Peter." He smiled, musing, "He's convinced her that her granddaughter is worth meeting."

Savana's emotions floundered in bewilderment. The countess wished to meet her granddaughter!

"Savana," he said gravely, "however this situation of meeting Peter turns out, it's crucial you go out of your way to please him."

Savana's Christian convictions would allow her to co-operate only on certain conditions. She had already told him so in London.

"The baron holds great sway over the countess," he was saying to her. "She's the one who can privately exert pressure on Count Aleksandr to sign the treaty, and I will ultimately need to deal with him."

Sir Douglas studied her. "We can't do it without Peter. And he's the one man who can arrange the meeting with your grandmother."

Her eyes swerved to his. "Arrange? Did you not say the countess wished to meet me?"

"There are those who prefer the meeting to not take place. Political enemies of the Rezanov family are against friendly ties with England in Oregon. They're rethinking Czar Nicholas's withdrawal from the Columbia River. He was young, they say, and made a grievous error. The countess prefers to keep territorial lines closer to Alaska. As such, she fits well into our plans, as does the baron."

Had Yuri been sent by those who hoped for a strained relationship between St. Petersburg and London? She was not now in a position to discover who was telling the truth.

"Who in St. Petersburg does not wish me to meet my grandmother?"

"Unfortunately, that's a question to which I have no answer and must wait for the countess and Peter to explain."

"You don't think I'm suspected of wanting the Rezanov inheritance?"

"You are her granddaughter. From what Peter has written of the countess, she was deeply attached to Nadyia. You can imagine how she will feel when she sees you for the first time. You look so very much like your mother."

Savana didn't know why, but his words made her ill at ease. "You've seen my mother's portrait?" she asked wistfully. "I should like to have it. I've never seen her, though Zoya says I'm not as attractive as my mother."

"Zoya! That croaking old frog! She's filled your mind

with stagnant tales for too many years. I specifically wrote Lady Hillary that she was to remain in England."

Savana was mildly surprised by his outburst. She held affection for Zoya, who for years at Bellomont House had been her nearest and dearest companion, giving her the one important link to her Russian past and to a mother she had never seen.

"I wouldn't have come without her," she stated calmly. "And I intend to bring her with me to Baranof Castle. She also has a brother there she wishes to see again after so many years. He's a priest at the Russian Orthodox church."

He waved an impatient hand. "I expected that. I suppose he may even prove useful as an interpreter. Peter Sarakof speaks English well, so do the countess and Count Aleksandr, but many do not. A pity, as I would expect that anyone with any sense would learn English," he stated as he bit off the end of his cigar.

"There's some risk to us going there, Savana. I wouldn't want you to think otherwise, but I've a mission to accomplish for His Majesty, and I intend to see it done."

"I'm not afraid," she said. "I'd be disappointed if I were left behind."

His humorous but shrewd eyes twinkled. "It isn't often a future governor-general is fortunate enough to have someone in his immediate family with crucial ties to an opposing nation."

He chomped the end of his fat cigar thoughtfully. "I also have some assistance from one of our kinsmen."

She was alert. "From St. Petersburg?"

"He's been there once on a matter of trade . . . not a happy visit, I suspect. The Russians are harsh on any trader buying furs in their territory and selling to China. He's also explored the region of the Stikine, going upriver forty or fifty miles, so he says." Again he mused, his eyes half closing. "So I've contacted him through Don Diego. He refused my offer." He struck a match and held the fire to the tip of the cigar. "I've recontacted him. I think he expected it—that he was waiting. I'm suspicious of him, but I need him."

"Mild deceit, Uncle, seems to be the norm in the world of national intrigue," she said warily, and a new sobriety settled over her concerning New Archangel. "Whoever he is, please don't trust him."

He reached over and patted her hand. "Give your uncle more credit than that," he said, and with a smile leaned back in the velvet chair and rested his hand across his rounded belly, tapping his fingers while he smoked his cigar. "We shall have a jolly time at Baranof Castle. They serve marvelous meals I'm told—but are a bit too much on the vodka. Fortunately for us, the Russian colony can no longer depend on Fort Ross to produce their growing need for food supplies."

Savana had done some research on her own. The colony was officially called Ross, taken from the root word for Russia, although the English as well as the Spanish called it Fort Ross, recognizing the strength of the colony with its mounted cannon.

The stalwart immigrants at the colony, however, had failed to turn the fort into an agricultural production base in California for the czar's interests in Alaska, and if England and America had their way, the objective would never be realized.

When the fort was built in 1812, the colonists had come for furs, even as they had in Alaska. It infuriated Savana to learn of the reports about the ruthless treatment of the natives in Alaska, and the methods that were used by the Russian-American Fur Company for gathering pelts for trade with China. Even in California many of the same tactics had been used.

The Russians at Fort Ross and the Aleut who had come with them from Alaska had hunted thousands of California sea otters, sea lions, and seals into near extinction all the way from San Francisco Bay and the Farallon Islands to their oceanfront at Fort Ross. As fur became sparse, the Russians had turned their attention to farming in order to supply the New Archangel settlement farther north.

Now the early and optimistic years at Fort Ross were fast running to an end, and the cool foggy coast of Bodega Bay, just north of San Francisco, was producing less viable crops each year.

Sir Douglas had lapsed off into meditative silence, and like a contented lizard on a warm rock, he stared ahead with a drowsy gaze. Savana smiled and stood to go up to her room when she heard a tap on the door. It opened, and she recognized one of the Hudson's Bay Company serving men.

"Sorry to interrupt, Sir Bellomont. The captain of the *Okanagan* has arrived."

Her uncle chomped on the end of his stubby cigar and pushed himself up from the chair. He looked, thought Savana, like a man enjoying mental chess. "Ah! Send him in."

Savana prepared to leave, but he waved a hand. "No, no, stay. You're included in this discussion."

She was included? She curiously turned as a man entered the sitting room. Sir Douglas was saying, "Savana, this is Captain Trace Wilder from Virginia. He's an American cousin of ours."

# 5

# RENEGADE OR PATRIOT?

Savana stared at the dock worker she had met on the wharf. As she recovered from her shock, Trace Wilder, from what she could tell by his outward expression, was not at all surprised by her uncle's announcement. She came to the uneasy conclusion that Captain Wilder had already known who she was the morning they met on the wharf when he claimed to have rescued her from falling pelts.

If that were true, why hadn't he introduced himself? The wharf—*her handbag*.

The information on Baron Peter Sarakof that Yuri had so painstakingly wished her to have rushed to mind. While she remained uninformed, Trace Wilder had the information at his disposal, and for what ulterior motive?

Her eyes met his with restrained accusation, for as yet she couldn't explain the meeting with Yuri to her uncle. She suspected that Trace Wilder knew as much and was also willing to remain silent for some reason of his own.

Savana looked at him, scanning the leather jerkins and jacket . . . and then saw that he carried his left arm in a sling. Her eyes rushed to his face and his equally hard jawline—but there was discoloration above his brow near his temple and a cut on his mouth. There was no mistaking the results of a dreadful brawl. *Probably acquired in a saloon on the wharf.*

Savana's emotions withdrew behind cool isolation as she looked away. *He's a worse scoundrel than I thought.*

She turned her shoulder toward him with a rustle of satin skirts and busied herself rearranging the cluster of pink geraniums in a cut-crystal vase on a table near the window.

It was all she could do to remain serene while Sir Douglas greeted him graciously enough, regretting his inability to see him sooner.

"Looks as though you've bucked heads with a bit of trouble. On the wharf, I suppose? Well yes, it's understandable. Lawson tells me they've been having some trouble with a gang of roughs down there. Broke into a Hudson's Bay Company warehouse last week." His eyes shot over him as he reached for a match from the brass holder on the mantel. "You're no meager lad yourself from the looks of you. Whoever he was, he must have been a gorilla."

"Five gorillas," came his Virginian drawl. "With Russian accents."

Sir Douglas's bushy brows lifted. "Russian, you say? Interesting."

Savana's head turned sharply in his direction.

"They all rushed me at once. Left me for dead and set fire to my trunk. Rather unsporting of them, don't you think?"

"Beastly. You notified the Mexican authorities?"

"No need to. I'll find them myself eventually."

"A good deal of trouble to handle alone."

"I'm used to it. Anyway, Diego's a friend. He's asking around. These men weren't common wharf rats out for trouble. I know the men who swarm the docks, and I've had no trouble with them before. We've a silent agreement to leave each other alone. These were strangers. . . . I thought you might know them, Sir Bellomont."

The suave insinuation in his tone caused Savana to look at him, totally taken with the brief discourse.

"Me?" Sir Douglas clamped down on his cigar as though bewildered but captivated by the thought. Striking the match he relit his dead cigar. "I find that insulting, my boy. I'm a politician. I've no need for hoodlums."

Savana's hand tightened on the vase of flowers. In the brief silence the wooden ceiling creaked above them.

"Just thought you might have heard of strangers in town," said Trace.

Savana bit her lip, weighing the tension in the gaze between her uncle and Trace Wilder.

"I'm sorry I can't help you," Sir Douglas said flatly.

"Guess I was wrong," stated Trace in a completely expressionless voice.

"Man has a right to be wrong once in a while. Been so myself on a number of occasions. Don't tell Governor Simpson," he said in a vain attempt at light humor. "I'm after his position, you know."

"I've no doubt you'll get it, sir."

Savana moved uneasily away from the window into the shadows of the log room, and Trace's gaze followed her. She looked at her uncle and watched as he flipped open the brass cigar box and offered it to Trace, along with a carved decanter of Peruvian wine.

Trace shook his head.

"There's a fine physician here at the post," said Sir Douglas. "He's straight out from Honolulu, as tanned and relaxed as a native. If that arm's broken, my boy, he'd best have a good look at it or it'll be worth nothing. Saw a man's broken arm heal on its own once. Bone was so crooked he couldn't lift a cup."

Savana winced.

"Thanks," said Trace. "It's only a knife wound. It will heal."

While her uncle appeared to go out of his way to make the son of his deceased American cousin welcome at the British Hudson's Bay Company headquarters, Savana tried to make sense of the unexpected situation playing out before her, but the reason for the attack was as much of a mystery as the man who called himself Trace Wilder. Why had he questioned her uncle? Had he been right when he said the thugs spoke with a Russian accent?

Yuri and the document from St. Petersburg—what might that have to do with the attack?

Savana came wide awake hearing the name of Baron Peter Sarakof, and found her uncle speaking of the arrangement he had made with the rest of the Bellomont family in London to introduce his young niece to the Rezanov family. He ended casually—

"And you say you'll be taking the risk of trading fur in northern waters again? Imperial Russia will not be pleased, but the Hudson's Bay Company is. We hope to make good use of your newfound allegiance to King George."

Savana's mind raced to keep up. Newfound allegiance to England? She might have laughed aloud! Just wait until she informed Uncle Douglas who this scoundrel was, and how he had deliberately stolen important information on the baron!

"I've heard of your exploits, Trace, make no mistake about that, and despite our differences in the past over the destiny of America, we share the same blood. There've been times when I've been as proud of you as my own son."

At the mention of his son, Trace appeared curious. "Boyd was killed in the war, wasn't he?"

Savana was surprised that he even knew Boyd's name, and she looked at her uncle. There was a moment when sentiment broke through his blustery expression, but he appeared to shove the feeling away as he sank into the leather chair behind a desk. "Battle of New Orleans," he stated. "Boyd was a soldier. There were none better."

Trace moved the subject away from the war. "My father is dead. You knew that?"

Sir Douglas shot Trace a hard look. "Yes. Must have hurt to care for Zachary all those months before he died." His face softened and he rubbed his chin, scanning Trace. "Did he suffer long?" he asked quietly.

"Long enough. The leg amputation didn't heal. He died of infection."

Sir Douglas studied him. "About eighteen then, you and Yancey?"

Trace remained indifferent. "Twelve. But we have an excellent memory." Something in his voice caused Savana to look across the room at him, but he was not watching her. He had hardly looked at her twice, but she knew he recognized her.

"You must have had a hard time of it," said Sir Douglas. "Two boys alone."

"We made it."

"A bedeviled situation. Always did think we should have brought you boys to London and into the good graces of His Majesty."

Savana expected to see displeasure. Somehow she was quite certain he was not only proud of his father's death, but willing and anxious to have joined him had he been old enough. She scanned him casually, trying not to notice his obvious good looks.

"Suppose you buried Zachary on Heritage . . . always did like that plantation," he mused in a puff of cigar smoke. "Zachary and Anne gave it a class all its own—had a touch of Essex—"

"My father's buried on public ground in Washington City. There wasn't any plantation left to bury him on. They burned it."

Savana knew who "they" were. While she felt an odd degree of sympathy that she tried to hold down, she was also irritated with Trace for bringing to mind the results of the war. She found herself saying in a clipped voice, "At least you know where your father is buried. Boyd was so destroyed by fire that they never could identify him. We've all suffered in the war and—"

"Captain Wilder didn't come about the past, but the future," interrupted Sir Douglas calmly, and Savana felt her cheeks turning warm as Trace looked at her long and meditatively.

Sir Douglas stood, pushing himself up from the desk. "I understand you've friends in the Russian-American Fur Company, even sailed with them to sell furs in China. A remarkable achievement for a planter's son from Virginia."

"I always liked the sea . . . my brother prefers to wander."

"Ah yes, Yancey—a friend of the pathfinder Joe Meeks?"

"Was. The Indians along the Snake River killed Joe."

"Too bad." He chomped his cigar. "Best wilderness man around. Crossed the Rockies on horseback into Oregon Country. Yancey go with him?"

She believed she understood the reason for her uncle's question, but Trace seemed almost indifferent to the obvious. Nor was her uncle being very tactful. Surely they could see through each other's motives!

"Yancey prefers St. Louis," said Trace.

At the mention of St. Louis her uncle bit his cigar.

"He's bought himself a riverboat," said Trace.

"Ah, St. Louis. A growing spot—so is Independence, I hear."

"Never been there."

"I see. . . . I hear you are also somewhat of a gambler, at least when it comes to tempting the Russian patrol boats in the North to buy and sell furs."

"I take risks only when needed. Russia seems to think they own the Pacific Northwest, and that Boston traders are intruders."

Sir Douglas smiled. "So does England."

Trace returned the smile. "As long as I get paid well for my furs I don't care who owns it."

"Far different than your father's allegiance," came his unconcerned voice.

Trace tapped his fingers against his slinged arm and appeared distant. "He's dead. Yancey and I had to scrape up enough money to give him a decent burial. A lot of good his sacrifice did."

Whether her uncle accepted this was uncertain, for he turned toward Savana.

"Forgive my rudeness. I have not yet introduced you. Trace, this is my niece, who has just arrived from London. Savana Rezanov Mackenzie."

From Trace's response to the introduction they might have never seen each other before. There was a lack of expression in his tanned face and little except official gravity to the light bow in her direction. As their stoic gaze held for a moment longer she saw a flicker of smile. His all-too-brief acknowledgement was precise: "Miss Mackenzie."

"Captain Wilder," she echoed flatly.

"My mother, I believe, was a cousin of James Mackenzie," said Trace easily.

"Indeed?" she responded stiffly. "How pleasant, Captain Wilder." Under his intense gaze she turned her back and looked out the window.

"I've decided to accept your offer, Sir Bellomont," he was saying.

"You'll work for the Hudson's Bay Company?"

Startled, Savana restrained her reaction and casually turned her head toward him. *Work for England? He can't! He won't do that. Not when he's obviously an American agent. What about the incident on the wharf? What of my handbag?*

She could hardly wait until they were alone so she might openly confront him. Yet, why she did not do so now was curious even to her. *Naturally,* she thought, *because Yuri made me vow I'd not say anything to anyone.* She noted Trace's rugged clothing and wondered what manner of work her uncle was offering him. He had said something about an expedition.

Uneasily, she eyed Trace. Would he be transporting them to Fort Vancouver? Evidently he had a ship. Hadn't her uncle said something about wheat? The notion brought mixed feelings. She wondered about the Wilder land in Virginia. Lady Hillary had once said that her father's cousin Zachary had done well for himself, even marrying an English-born wife from one of the better families in London. She had voyaged with just her maid all the way to America to become his bride, and had been the mother of several children. Was Trace the firstborn?

She drew in a quiet breath. *So . . . that is where I saw him. In the family hall of portraits at Bellomont House.*

Not long after Savana's arrival from school on her fifteenth birthday, Lady Hillary had decided to introduce her to the only side of the family that was worth mentioning: the British blood. Russians, of course, were untrustworthy, she had said; nearly as notorious as Napoleon's Frenchmen. And then Lady Hillary had gone on to mention some British traitors in the family who were now infamous "blackguards" who had betrayed England to fight for America both in 1776 and 1812.

The traitors' portraits had been taken down in disgrace, but one day Savana had noticed a cedar chest in the corner and suspected there was too much pride in the family to destroy the portraits, even if they were mistakenly "Boston" sympathizers.

Lady Hillary admitted that she was supposed to have destroyed them but didn't have the heart. "Cousin Zachary's sons were such fine-blooded kin," she had said. "We had hopes at one time to unite you and your cousin Julia to Virginians, but alas."

Having piqued Savana's interest even more, she had wheedled until she'd gotten her aunt to relent. The cedar chest was unlocked and Savana was introduced, portrait by portrait, to the scandalous American side of the family. Sir Zachary Bellomont Wilder and Lady Anne Mackenzie Wilder had a lovely plantation in Virginia, although it was their two sons Savana remembered. Both had been painted in fine Virginian wardrobe, with majestic horses and hounds. Even then she had thought Trace and his brother forbidden fruits of treason—young men to reject at all costs. After all, their father had been disowned and disinherited. "He betrayed the king," she heard Lady Hillary whisper in her scandalous voice. "In England they'd be beheaded and quartered!"

*Beheaded and quartered*—the horrid words echoed loudly in her mind. They mingled with the present as she heard Trace saying pleasantly enough but with a certain aloofness to his voice—"I'll serve the Hudson's Bay Company on the condition the pay is worth the risk to my ship and my crew. I'm not exactly on friendly terms with the officials at New Archangel."

"It is just as well you are not," her uncle was saying. "Wooing Count Aleksandr will be left to me and my niece."

Savana didn't like the way Sir Douglas had arranged his words, and she noted that Trace looked across the room at her, briefly taking her in. She turned her head away. Did he think she had agreed to deliberately deceive the baron about her romantic intentions?

"I'll need more information on what the Hudson's Bay Company expects of me," said Trace.

"There's no reason why we shouldn't trust you," said Sir Douglas. "I have a map."

Savana turned her head as her uncle walked into the next room. A quick look at Trace and she saw nothing in his expression until his gaze met hers. A faint smile played on his mouth and Savana's eyes turned frosty. She raked him bluntly to let him know that she at least didn't trust him and started to walk across the room to stop her uncle from getting the map.

Trace moved lithely but swiftly to intercept her, his hand catching her arm. His boldness took her by surprise and she paused, noting the gravity in his flinty eyes.

"I can try to explain if you'll give me opportunity," he said in a low voice.

"I'm certain you have quite a tale," she whispered.

"I must talk to you alone. When can we meet?"

"Meet *you* alone? You jest. What information from St. Petersburg do you wish this time? I know you're an American agent and—"

"Ah, here we have it," interrupted Sir Douglas as he returned. "After the wheat delivery to New Archangel I need you to explore this region. Come have a look, Trace."

Something in his eyes silenced her from unmasking him. Her gaze swerved, and his hand casually drew away as he turned to Sir Douglas bent over a drawing, the stubby cigar still in his mouth.

Savana brushed past and walked over to the desk to stand next to her uncle. Trace came up.

"I admit the map is not as detailed as it could be," said Sir Douglas.

"I've a better one," said Trace indifferently.

She was quick to note her uncle's pleasure, but it wasn't clear if Trace noticed or not as he retrieved the satchel he'd been carrying on his arrival.

Savana watched as he opened it and removed a roll and, coming to the wide desk, spread it out with his one good hand as her uncle secured the corners.

"Ah," was all her uncle grumbled under his cigar, and Savana too wondered at the size and intricacy of the map of the Pacific Northwest, including San Francisco and the rugged coastline to New Archangel and beyond.

Sir Douglas's robust gaze ran over him in a comprehensive glance that Savana knew all too well and read as easily. Her uncle's summing-up glance said that his erring American cousin Zachary had a son that could not be taken lightly, even if he apparently had lost everything of value in the war.

"A splendid map. Where did you come across it?"

"I've assembled it over the past several years," came the toneless reply, and he leaned over the desk with Sir Douglas, explaining the differences. Somehow Savana believed that showing the map had not been part of his first plan, but he had felt the need to do so to convince them he was indeed on the side of King George's quest for Oregon Country.

Her mouth turned a little. Her uncle would put the information his wayward American kin had gathered to good use, she was sure of that much.

Her eyes left the map to glance at Trace. Unwillingly she noticed that his dark brown hair pleasantly brushed the back of his coat collar.

She walked over to the window and glanced below to see if he had arrived in a carriage. A fine-looking horse was tied near the gate. The entire Virginian family appeared to think highly of horses, she thought, remembering the portrait.

Once again the fog was floating in from the bay, and she became aware that the room was chill and damp. She glanced at the hearth and saw that the coals were dying out. There were logs in the bin, and she stooped to choose one to lay on the coals, brushing her hands afterward on a towel. Minutes later the flames crackled and jumped, and she warmed herself while carefully listening to their low conversation.

It seemed the map contained information that Trace had acquired from various shipmasters, common seamen, trappers, Boston traders, and several Indians. Her uncle was especially interested in the Indians and how he knew them, and Trace seemed at liberty to explain everything.

They were both testing the other's qualifications and sincerity, and she could not surmise whether or not they trusted each other. She did know that she did not believe Captain Trace Wilder had the slightest allegiance to King George. There could easily be truth to what her uncle said about the indifference of Sir Zachary Wilder's son, or both sons perhaps, to the cause of Boston. Why this should be she hadn't as yet found out. If they had lost everything in the war, wouldn't Trace and his brother be more inclined to hate London? Then why did her uncle seem to trust him?

Suddenly she was alert, listening, and turned her head in his direction while she warmed her hands toward the fire.

"In selling wheat and buying pelts I've had occasion to

listen and ask questions. Most of the traders and mariners are eager to share their successes or discoveries, whether British, Russian, or American."

"I agree the Company's charts on the New Archangel area are miserably inadequate," said Sir Douglas. "Nevertheless, you should have them at your disposal. If not, I have several here."

"I've secured copies and studied them already," was the smooth reply.

"I see. . . . You are just the man we need, Trace. And the fact your bloodline mingles with the Bellomonts' only adds to my good pleasure. I can't tell you how pleased the family in London will also be when they hear from me how you've come back to your true heritage and to His Majesty. And hear about it they will—this very night I shall write a letter to Lord Charles, your grandfather. You do have some title somewhere, you know, and the king will surely bestow it again when this venture of ours for the Company is completed successfully."

"I'm honored, Sir Bellomont. And yet, I wouldn't expect either you or the family to believe I've utterly repudiated my birth, or the honor in which my father fought and died under the American flag."

Sir Douglas bit his cigar and made no comment.

"This is strictly financial," said Trace.

"And you represent no cause other than your own dreams to regain your Virginian heritage?"

"None. The war is over. The scars remain and will for years to come. For myself, I intend to rebuild my father's plantation and settle there."

"You've a fine girl in mind, of course?" asked Sir Douglas amiably.

"Yes."

Savana glanced at him and heard her uncle say, "British, no doubt. They don't come any better, or prettier."

Trace smiled. "American. She lives in St. Louis."

"Ah . . . Senator Baxter's younger daughter by any chance?"

Trace hesitated, and it was the first time Savana saw his casual mood falter. Had her uncle unearthed a secret?

"Yes, Callie hopes to work with some missionaries near Fort Vancouver."

"And you expect to bring her back to Virginia?"

"If I can rebuild from the rubble."

"A wise decision. Oregon is best left to the Hudson's Bay Company."

"My exact conclusion, Sir Bellomont."

Savana stood, hands behind her, warming herself by the fire as though totally composed. When Trace looked over at her, she wondered that his intense gaze seemed to see through her indifference. She impatiently brushed a wisp of flaxen hair from her cheek and turned her back, only to hear him saying casually, "May I suggest, Sir Bellomont, that Miss Mackenzie remain in San Francisco during the delivery of the wheat and your expedition north?"

Savana started to protest, then looked at her uncle and saw a confident smile on his face. Trace remained calm and expressionless.

"That is quite impossible. You see, she is necessary to England's negotiations with the Russian-American Company at New Archangel. Without her presence and assistance, the success of my mission—our mission—will most likely fail."

As Trace listened to her uncle's words Savana almost suspected he had asked that she be left behind in order to learn her position in the negotiations.

"She must come for the good of England," her uncle concluded.

Trace turned and briefly scanned her, his gaze casual. "Anything for His Majesty," he said with the barest hint of humor.

Savana couldn't keep still. "Coming from a devoted Boston trader, Captain Wilder, I'm sure my uncle and I are deeply appreciative of your return to the fold of his loyal subjects. We can, of course, trust you wholeheartedly?"

Unconcealed amusement flickered in his eyes. "You'd best ask Sir Bellomont. He's destined to become the next governor-general of British America. He's the one who wishes my services for the king. You don't mean to question your uncle's judgment?"

Sir Douglas chuckled and clamped down on his cigar. Savana retained her cool composure.

There was a faint scowl on his brow, and his penetrating gaze convinced her that there was much more to his motives than what he wished to pretend. He had said he must speak to her alone. Well . . . she had more than enough reasons to accept, but arranging it would be difficult.

Her uncle appeared pleased with the interview and stood up, ending what was for Savana an uncertain meeting that left far too many questions unanswered. How could her uncle so readily put their fate into the hands of a man they knew so little about?

And the letter from Yuri? What explanation could he give for his incriminating actions?

Savana waited until the two men had left the sitting room and were in the outer hall, then rushed to the window and looked below into the yard where Trace's horse was tied. Except for a worker here or there, the afternoon fog had sent the Company men indoors for their meal.

She couldn't risk anyone seeing her run after Trace, but if she took a back door she might manage it.

Minutes later, skirting the edge of the yard to avoid detection, she emerged on the far side of the Hudson's Bay Company residency. Breathless from her exertion, she concealed herself among the trees directly across from his horse and waited.

The fog lay thicker under the overarching boughs that lined the outer wooden wall, and they appeared grayish white and dripped with moisture.

Savana felt a cold drop down the back of her neck. She'd

been in too much of a rush to bring a cape, and now shivered as her clothes turned damp and her hair was misted with dew. Overhead she heard the coo of a gray dove.

Savana made a grimace mingled with relief as her ear caught what at first seemed an echo. Someone was walking across the yard and she guessed from the certain stride of bootsteps that it was a man, sure of himself and in a hurry.

She stepped out from her concealment. A moment later he emerged from the mist, quickly untied the reins, and was about to mount when his gaze confronted her.

# 6

# THREE FLAGS
# IN THE NORTH WIND

Trace stopped at seeing Savana. He hadn't expected the good fortune of speaking with her yet, and concealed a sense of admiration that she had managed to slip away.

As yet, he hadn't made up his mind about her motives in coming from England to meet her uncle, and he wondered if her apparent guilelessness was genuine. Perhaps to safeguard his emotions, he wanted to doubt that the girl with dove eyes and a noble expression existed, except as a misleading influence for the English cause—or was it Russian?

If he doubted her, he told himself, he could feel less responsible for her safety. The image of a fawn trapped in a thicket with the hunter moving in made him restless.

He noted her guarded expression and reminded himself that he too must be cautious, and he stood for a moment, one hand resting on the saddle horn, considering her.

Savana's wealth of smooth flaxen hair was drawn straight back and confined in a net of white silk with seed pearls so that its weight lifted her dignified chin with a look that he reluctantly found charming.

If Baron Peter Sarakof was any kind of man he would find her fairness of face and form worthy of his fullest attention. The paraded lamb before the hungry wolf was likely to evoke the response that Bellomont hoped for, but did she know what the baron was like?

The thought that she might not added to his irritation over the entire matter that he had stumbled upon. After the incident on the wharf she was not likely to believe him if he unmasked Sarakof for what he was. The more he villainized the Russian, the more she was apt to align herself with him.

He searched her face for guile, for some of the clever machinations that compelled the decisions of Sir Bellomont. She might very well be an agent out to collect information, not for her uncle but Sarakof. What plans and dreams motivated this woman so that she would confront a deserted wharf to meet with Yuri? Or if she served the Hudson's Bay Company and England, was she also willing to hazard the trap certain to be waiting for her at Baranof Castle?

What of himself? What better way was there to detour him than with a lovely young woman? She could prove as dangerous as Sarakof's patrol boats.

She moved from the trees like the graceful breath of an April breeze on the Virginia plantation, and he found himself remembering the past: a summer's day, beauty, and the laughter of hope—

The fog rushed in, damp and cold as she whispered, "You have much to explain, Captain Wilder. Suppose you do so—quickly, lest I decide to call a guard in service to Sir Douglas."

His warm, flinty gaze turned ironic. "Unfortunately, Miss Mackenzie, you are right. And equally bothersome is the fact that you're not likely to believe the truth even if I explain in detail."

"If you do not, I could advise Sir Douglas that you are a Boston agent."

His smile was tinged with mockery. "And be hanged for good measure? Is that any way to treat a long-lost kin?"

She had a way of turning her shoulder to him while she regarded him with thoughtfulness. He noticed her upswept lashes. He decided that he disliked Sarakof even more.

"If I sound harsh, Captain Wilder, it's because the times demand it. You don't deceive me with your heartrending tales of being attacked by 'Russian' gorillas."

"No?" He deliberately winced as he touched his arm.

She winced too. "You must see the doctor and have it examined."

He smiled, for she'd given herself away. She didn't reject him outright as she wished to pretend. He took a step toward her in order to keep out of view, but she quickly stepped back, holding on to a branch. "Stay where you are, Captain Wilder. It's not so far to the residency that I can't cry out for help."

His brow lifted. "I imagine you can scream well enough." And seeing her chin lift, he added ruefully, "If you're so convinced I'm dangerous, why did you come here?"

"Not to feel sorry for your bruises, I can assure you. I'm not at all certain you didn't get them in a saloon. And I don't believe in gorillas with Russian accents. You can tell me what you know about Yuri."

He leaned against the tree and frowned, feeling the drizzle.

She folded her arms. "Oh come, Captain. You were spying on me on the wharf. You knew who I was before I arrived. And I'm guessing you also trailed Yuri to Diego's warehouse before that."

"You do a good deal of guessing. In a court of law it is the facts that matter. Will you judge and sentence me on mere suspicions?"

"I suppose it was a mere 'suspicion' I heard in the warehouse puttering about in stocking feet."

He tried to keep his interest casual. She was talkative if

he asked the right questions, but wiser than he had first given her credit.

"Did Yuri also hear 'the mouse in stocking feet'?"

He saw her hesitate. She knew more than she was willing to trust him with.

"Yes," came her quiet voice.

"Did he suggest who might be scampering about?"

"No, but maybe it was you," she said, her voice wary.

"It wasn't," he stated flatly. "Not that I expect you to believe it. It's my guess it was one of Bellomont's informers," he said in order to illicit a response.

"My uncle? It couldn't have been," she protested. "He didn't know about Yuri's message asking me to meet him." Her tone changed. "But you did."

"You think so?" he said smoothly. "I suggest it was one of the baron's agents, since both he and Bellomont have the most to lose if you should wisely decide against going to New Archangel."

"Then you've no notion of explaining yourself to me?"

Trace watched her, then smiled. "I'll explain all about Trace Wilder anytime you have a sympathetic ear."

"That's not what I meant." She shivered in the fog and folded her arms, glancing back toward the residency. In the afternoon shadows the lamps inside had been lit, offering the tug of warmth and security.

"Your glib tongue won't get you off the hook, Captain. Suppose you begin by returning the document from St. Petersburg."

He was irritated with himself. "I can hardly do that, Miss Mackenzie."

"No? Dare I ask why?" came her cynical voice. "Have you sent it on to Boston?"

"I assure you, it wasn't worth the postage."

Her gaze narrowed. "So then. You finally admit you have it, that it was planned."

He mocked innocence. "Saving you from the pelts? Are you still ungrateful for my daring rescue?"

"Where is the document?"

His smile faded. "What wasn't worth the price of postage to me, my dear, was of great value to someone else who wishes to keep his reputation from you. It was stolen," he admitted flatly.

"Stolen—" She stopped, surprised.

Trace saw her expression turn to doubt, then she gave a disbelieving laugh that rankled his pride.

"After your clever little escapade on the wharf, do you now expect me to believe you permitted someone else to steal it from you?"

A wry expression formed on his mouth. "Unfortunately, yes. It was stolen after they left me for dead and set my trunk on fire. I underestimated Sarakof—or Bellomont," he stated with deliberate underemphasis. "Next time, I won't."

"Why shouldn't I go immediately to my uncle and inform him that he's just hired an American agent?"

He smiled easily. "Because, madame! You have no proof except your suspicions. Bellomont needs me for the expedition and I need the five hundred dollars, especially after the fire."

"And because you need the money you're willing to play true and faithful to England?" she asked with a scoff.

"Bellomont is willing to take a chance. He has little choice, and neither will Sarakof if wheat for New Archangel is to be delivered."

"And when a man is needed—especially a long-lost Yankee cousin who now swears oath to King George—it allows him the freedom to move into the very circles he's come to spy on."

"What of you, Miss Mackenzie? Are you willing to hear what I have to say about the baron?"

She remained cautious. "I suspect you'll tell me the same thing Yuri did."

"Then he did warn you about him?"

He saw her uncertainty; then she let out a breath.

"All right, Captain Wilder, you might as well know. He

warned me about the baron's ruthlessness and asked me to return to England."

He saw her expression reflect concern that she appeared to try to conceal. "Yes?" he persisted. "That's a good beginning. What else?"

Her gaze turned remote. "What was in the document? Surely you read it before it was 'stolen.'"

"It was a letter from an anonymous individual in St. Petersburg warning you against coming to Baranof Castle. I can see, however, you're not willing to take that advice."

"If you have anything more to tell me, then do so."

"The baron killed an opponent under questionable circumstances while serving the czar in St. Petersburg. He has gambling debts which he cannot pay. And as a disciplinary action, he was sent to New Archangel to command the patrol boats under the authority of Count Aleksandr. Sarakof is out to regain his losses, to return to the czar with trumpets blaring." He stopped and regarded her. "And it's my guess he needs you in some way to accomplish it." He looked at her steadily. "I thought you could tell me how you benefit his career with the czar—or perhaps someone else close to the czar."

She was able to restrain her alarm, and his eyes narrowed as he scanned her, grudgingly admiring her cool nerves. Her poise, in spite of the character of the man she was about to marry, was nevertheless odd.

"Even if I knew how I might benefit these odious plans you say the baron has, you surely don't think I'd share the information with you?"

"The reason is simple enough. You're in danger. And a gallant Virginian always risks his neck to come to the aid of a lady, especially an attractive one."

"I'm flattered, Captain Wilder, but that's no cause for me to trust you, is it?"

"I beg to differ. Unlike Sarakof I don't need you, so you needn't worry about what I'm after. Even if I were a Boston agent," he said flatly, "I could have accomplished what I wanted without contacting you again. I knew you were here with Bellomont, and I wanted to see you."

He saw a slight change in her demeanor, and a thoughtful glance drifted over him.

"You wished to see me to warn me about the baron?"

"That was the idea, yes. My willingness to risk involvement should tell you I'm on your side, at least where Sarakof is concerned. I've had a run-in with him before in the northern waters. Boston ships have disappeared around New Archangel and Sarakof is behind it. He is ruthless and without pity. Men have been beaten and hanged on false charges, some sent to Siberia, their ships confiscated. And if he has any aims toward you, you can bet they benefit him at your expense."

He saw her flinch then steady herself. "You've indeed spoken plainly, but your accusations against him are not enough. As for the letter containing information from St. Petersburg against the baron, it could be the work of enemies. Except for the baron, no one in the Rezanov family has bothered until now to show interest in me," she said. "I am in his debt."

"Just where he wants you to be. And maybe the family had no cause, until now, to pretend interest. Have you heard from them before? In London perhaps?"

The suggestion of suspicion behind Sarakof's sudden interest seemed to give her pause.

"No," she admitted tonelessly. "Only the political unrest in the Northwest has afforded opportunity for Sir Douglas to contact the family in Russian America."

"Maybe. A curious coincidence." Trace noted the uncertainty reflected in her face. "Who first made the contact asking you to come to Baranof Castle, Bellomont or Peter Sarakof?"

He watched her pause and reflect, but whatever decision she came to she wasn't about to share it with him. "You admit that the baron has his enemies. So why should I believe what is contained in the letter just because it bears a seal on the letterhead? Lies are not turned into truth by imperial seals."

"A wise deduction where truth is concerned. Unfortunately men and nations seek to mastermind their own deceptions and call them truth. Then nothing I can say will cause you to reconsider going with Bellomont to New Archangel?"

She drew in a breath. "No. I shall go through with my plans, Captain. I'll meet the baron as my family has arranged, and in so doing, I shall make up my own mind."

His brow lifted. "The baron will wish to make up your mind for you. He'll want to arrange a marriage. You'd best be prepared."

She moved uneasily. "I'm not convinced he will, but I'm quite prepared to say no."

"Are you?" He watched her, wondering. He could still be wrong about her. What were her ties to the Rezanov family and how deep were her Russian loyalties?

She turned away, glancing toward the residency. "I must get back before I'm missed. Goodbye."

Trace said nothing. He watched her slip away into the mist-shrouded trees until she was gone.

A minute later he was still standing there.

So much for the false conception that his gallant interjection into the situation would prove helpful to the girl in the end.

He touched his arm and gritted with frustration. Until the knife wound healed he was forced to move more slowly than he had intended. He felt a sudden notion to throw the entire mission overboard and join Yancey in St. Louis.

He frowned. He knew he wouldn't.

He was a fool to think about her.

He walked to his horse and with some difficulty swung himself into the saddle. Whoever was responsible would answer for the beating he'd taken. It might not be Sarakof at all. He looked back at the Hudson's Bay Company, where his father's cousin had received him on gracious terms. He still hadn't ruled out Bellomont.

Anxious for action rather than intrigue, he turned swiftly to ride, giving the fine-blooded animal its freedom to run.

Savana was still thinking of Trace Wilder after dinner that night as she walked to her room. She wondered if she would judge him so harshly if she had not met him on the wharf. Was he worthy of her trust, and had he actually come today knowing she would be here with her uncle? The idea that he might be concerned for her safety was flattering, but she warned her emotions that she must avoid involvement. His assertiveness would have set her on guard anyway, she decided. She would remain vigilant where Trace Wilder was concerned.

# 7

# A RUSSIAN FORT
# NEAR SAN FRANCISCO

The brisk, chilly morning did little to brighten Savana's mood as she tried to reconcile her emotions after yesterday's meeting with Sir Douglas and Trace Wilder. She managed a bland expression so that Mrs. Warrender, Roslyn, and Reverend Withycombe would not guess her tension.

She walked across the yard toward a sleek black carriage belonging to Sir Douglas where the others were already gathered and waiting to leave for the Russian colony of Fort Ross. There would be a dinner reception that evening, where Sir Douglas planned to meet with the Russian delegation that had come to buy wheat for New Archangel. She thought it likely that Yuri would be among that Russian entourage. If so, she could try to see him when they arrived at Fort Ross for the official dinner in their honor.

Savana would also meet Baron Peter Sarakof for the first time since they had begun their correspondence. The thought made her stomach flutter nervously. Unlike many young women who worried about not being appreciated by the man they were to be introduced to, Savana was concerned that the baron might actually decide that she was suitable.

Surely that was not likely, even if her family wished it so, she consoled herself. *My destiny has already been committed to the Lord. All my tomorrows are His,* she thought, allowing the knowledge to snuff the small flame of doubt within her heart.

Such a man as the baron would not seriously be interested in pursuing a relationship with the rejected offspring of a British fur trapper! The baron was much more likely to find her family's hopes to kindle a romantic flame an amusing comedy of the British. How had Sir Douglas arranged for her visit to Baranof Castle? His story differed. In one version he had arranged the meeting; in the next, it was Peter Sarakof. Now there was the added excitement of actually meeting her grandmother and learning firsthand of her mother as well.

What of the plans she had privately cultivated and prayed about in England before the family had ever arranged that she should meet the baron? They seemed like an unfinished statue in her mind, more like a glob of wet clay in the potter's hand. In London she had thought long about the idea of carrying on her father's work in New Archangel, but it would be dangerous.

"You look a trifle ashen this morning, Savana," said Mrs. Warrender as they walked to the carriage where Sir Douglas waited to meet them, looking in good humor.

"Ashen is she? It must be her introduction to Mexican cuisine," he jested, taking her arm to hand her inside. "It's not exactly British, is it?"

Savana smiled. "On the contrary, I found the food wonderful," she said sincerely. "The tortillas and—what was inside?—was quite good."

"Frijoles," explained Reverend Withycombe. "Beans, I think, is the American way of saying it."

"It's Russian *borscht* you must cultivate an appreciative

taste for," Sir Douglas continued in good humor. He climbed in after her and heaved a weighty sigh as he sank his heavy frame into the leather seat. "Yet if you become a baroness living in St. Petersburg you're likely to have better fare than beet soup."

*St. Petersburg* . . . Savana felt a chill blow across her heart like the blizzard winds sweeping across Alaska. Her mind shot back to something Yuri had told her at the warehouse. *"He wishes to return to St. Petersburg to serve the czar."*

Sir Douglas had already informed her that the baron was a soldier of reputation as was his father and grandfather before him. Peter's father was killed in the war with Napoleon, and his grandfather in Poland. She had no doubt that if the czar had sent him to command the gunboats in Russian waters, he would perform his duty explicitly. How was she to explain the contrary information in the letter from St. Petersburg that Trace had told her about?

"There's always the likely possibility that the baron will see that he and I are quite ill-matched," said Savana, keeping hope from spilling over in her voice. "There must be many lovely Russian girls who are first on the Sarakof family list. Girls with Russian nobility far more suitable than I."

"That is what we hope to discourage," said Sir Douglas briefly. "For the sake of the British flag and the beaver trade."

As the carriage raced along the oceanfront trail leading north from San Francisco toward the Russian colony of Fort Ross, Savana felt the wind buffeting the carriage door where she sat. She stared out the small window, watching the choppy gray Pacific with its wind-waves frothy white. Mist sparkled upward in the early sunlight, causing a jewel-like mirage.

Beside her, and across from Sir Douglas, Reverend Withycombe sat fully engaged in reading a small newspaper the Mexican serving girl had given him before they left the Hudson's Bay Company.

The carriage was drawn by two black horses, and Savana commented on their strength and beauty.

"Magnificent creatures," agreed Sir Douglas. "I bought them from the Spanish don Marcos Diego. He's a partner in the rancho with wheat to sell to the Russian delegation."

Savana remembered the warehouse owned by the Diego brothers on the wharf. The same man? She dare not give away that she had been there. Was her uncle involved with the Spanish dons? Could the intruder she heard have been one of the Diego brothers? Why had Yuri chosen to meet at that particular warehouse?

"Why does New Archangel need Diego's wheat?" asked Mrs. Warrender, eyeing Sir Douglas suspiciously, for it was no secret she distrusted him. "Was it not the purpose of the Russians at Fort Ross to grow food commodities for New Archangel?"

He looked impatient. "Foggy weather, my dear woman. The fort is quite a miserable location for farming. I would have thought them to move on to the Sacramento River area."

"It's a pity about the fort closing down," said Mrs. Warrender. "People will suffer. What will they do?"

"Sell out to an American colonist named John Sutter. He's out to bring in immigrants to settle on the Sacramento River, diverting them from Oregon. In that," he said dryly, "the American has my appreciation."

Mrs. Warrender was watching Sir Douglas accusingly, as though the Russian colony's misfortune were due to his personal conniving. "And what will Mr. Sutter do with Fort Ross if the Russians can't farm it?"

"Buy it up lock, stock, and barrel. He'll purchase all outbuildings, animals, even the harvested crops. The Orthodox chapel will be moved as well."

Mrs. Warrender looked indignant. "I've never heard of such a thing! How can he haul an entire fort to the Sacramento River!"

"By ship, my dear Mrs. Warrender. Sutter's bought the Russian vessel the *Constantin* as well, and renamed it the *Sacramento*. Fitting, don't you think?" he mocked. "They'll make trips from Fort Ross about a hundred miles up the Sacramento River until they haul all movable sections of the fort. Grudgingly, I can't help but admire the American's frontier spirit."

Reverend Withycombe looked up from the paper, his eyes speculative. "The padre at the mission informed me of an old Indian who carries a gold nugget looped to his belt. Swears he found it around Sutter's area."

"Gold?" Mrs. Warrender breathed, and even Savana and Roslyn looked at him.

"Perhaps the Russians should have moved to Sutter's place," quipped Withycombe.

Sir Douglas smiled tolerantly. "Sutter won't find any gold. He'll lose out in the end. So will the Americans trailing after him. As for the colony at Ross, Russian America faces a dilemma. If they are to remain in viable competition with America in the Pacific Northwest, they must rely on the Hudson's Bay Company. If we form a trade alliance, England will become the mighty wedge to hold back the troublesome Boston traders and keep Russia in check at the same time." He settled comfortably into the leather seat with his hands clasped lightly across his rounded belly. "America will need to withdraw south of the Columbia River—where they belong."

Mrs. Warrender stirred uncomfortably and Rosyln glanced at her. Savana thought she understood their unease, since both women were romantically involved with American missionaries serving with Jason Lee. The discussion died and even Reverend Withycombe returned to reading the small San Francisco paper.

Sir Douglas removed a cigar from his water-silk doublet and lifted it to his prominent nose to whiff appreciatively. "Ah, Don Diego buys the best tobacco in Cuba."

Reverend Withycombe rustled the paper. "It seems Cuban tobacco and race horses are not the only commodity Señor Diego deals in."

Sir Douglas looked at him evenly above a puff of smoke,

waiting curiously for his explanation—as did they all—for it was obvious even to Savana that the minister meant to imply something unpleasant.

He looked up from the page he was reading and gazed at Sir Douglas for an uneasy moment, then swerved to look at the others.

Savana unconsciously played with the white silk ribbon that fell softly from her hat. She did not like the look in his face, and for some reason her heart began to beat rapidly as she waited with the others for the explanation.

"Good mercy, the paper says Don Diego found a dead body in his warehouse yesterday. Imagine."

Savana was momentarily frozen by the news. A second later she released a quiet breath, and afraid that her eyes would give her away, she did not look at either of them. *No, it couldn't be Yuri.*

"A murder is not an unlikely incident to take place on the wharf," said Sir Douglas tonelessly. "Knifings and robberies take place frequently by a growing gang of thieves. Captain Wilder himself was attacked."

Savana looked at him.

"The Russian must have been a sailor," continued Sir Douglas. "They're known to jump ship to settle in a warmer climate and take up farming at Fort Ross."

Savana turned her head slightly and looked at her uncle from beneath her large hat with its cluster of white silk flowers. *How does he know the dead man was Russian? Or that he's been murdered?*

Restraining her growing anxiety, Savana watched the churning gray sea. As the carriage picked up speed down the road leading to the Russian colony, she could hardly restrain herself from snatching the paper to read the details. Had anyone else noticed Sir Douglas's explanation?

Reverend Withycombe appeared to lose interest in the subject. He set the paper aside on the seat and now busily wrote in his leather journal.

Mrs. Warrender grew drowsy and shut her eyes as she

swaycd with the carriage. Her ailing daughter, as always, remained morose and untalkative.

Savana hid a shudder. *Is it possible that the dead man is the one who followed Yuri to the warehouse? What if Yuri has killed the intruder instead?* She remembered how she had been alone with him in that dank and dark warehouse with rats and the smell of old wood. Her eyes fell to the paper beside her, but she kept her hand in her lap. She mustn't alert anyone to her interest.

*If Yuri is dead, I was the last one to see him alive in the warehouse. What if the authorities find out and come to question me? Although, who could possibly know of our secret meeting except—*

The handsome image of Trace Wilder flashed across her mind. She tensed, remembering his injuries. *Might not he have gotten them as Yuri fought to defend himself?*

Near Bodega Bay, the tawny plateau lay bare above the ocean, a dull gold in the afternoon light with gray-blue ocean waves rolling toward the horizon. They were perhaps eleven miles from the Russian River, nearing Fort Ross.

Savana peered intently through the window, sizing up the wooden fortress constructed from the first cutting of the coastal redwood trees. Seventeen small-caliber cannon smiled down through wispy fog onto the carriage as the horses trotted through the gate of the Russian colony. The cannon, she decided, were quiet proof of the czar's military interests in California.

"Shakespeare was wrong," she murmured to herself. "It is not events that ride the saddle of history, but God who raises empires, and it is He who blows upon them, scattering their feeble military and global ambitions into dust." She looked about at the Russian colony's faltering attempts at expansionism.

"What are you whispering to yourself about?" asked Roslyn Warrender with a small laugh.

"The sovereign purposes of God," said Savana brightly. "If a sparrow can't fall without His notice, then no country can rise without His providential care."

"Rubbish, my dear Savana," said Sir Douglas. "I fear your Scottish Calvinistic doctrine is coming to the forefront. It's the free will of man that governs nations and charts the course on the sea of life. And if we fail, *we* fail. To win the race we must fight and sweat. The runner must be swift; the soldier must be strong."

"Maybe it's a bit of both," said Savana. "Napoleon must have shared your belief. He said that God was on the side of the strongest battalion. If that were true, France would have won at Waterloo—and Spain would have defeated England in the reign of Queen Elizabeth. Both France and Spain had the largest armies. God's snow and wind decided the outcome of both battles. What if Spain had won? What if Napoleon?"

Sir Douglas gave a short laugh and chomped his cigar stub. "Rubbish," he repeated. "If I didn't know better I'd fear you could fall prey to Boston's naive claim to manifest destiny in the West."

Savana smiled. "You know I'd never agree with a Boston Yankee. It would mean denying His Majesty's own claim to destiny. The sun never sets on the British Empire! It is interesting, though, that America has maintained its independence through two wars," she mused. "Maybe God does have plans for nations as well as individuals. Who knows what the future holds, or what His purpose may be for the Northwest?"

"Just as long as their westward drive doesn't bring them north of the Columbia."

"He's quite right," interjected Reverend Withycombe. "If any nation is destined to colonial rule, it is glorious England."

Fort Ross had a Russian commander's house built of planks, a windmill, a forge, a tannery, cattle sheds—and a cemetery. Savana's spirits lifted when she saw the chapel called St. Nicholas. Her gray eyes fixed upon the plain bell

tower and the familiar design of the onion-shaped dome roof
that was Russian Orthodox.

Had her mother known Christ's salvation? Had her faith
gone beyond the external and beautiful ritual to a living faith
in the One crucified and resurrected from the dead?

The sunlight broke through the fog and glinted a rain-
bowlike prism on the windows of St. Nicholas. At the same
moment, the light pricked her heart and it seemed that He
asked her whether or not *she* had fully trusted Him with her
future. *"You have not even trusted me with your past."* Her past
remained as an open wound that could easily bring fresh pain
again and again. It sprang up in a sunset, a ripple of wind
through leaves, a lone cry of a bird, in the shadows of a dying
sunset. That feeling of being abandoned. Alone. What was
it the soul ached for? Father God? The true home where His
family gathered safely around the table?

*Through life's mundane steps He walks beside me. He is the
joy erupting from the fountain of Living Water. . . .*

"Wake up, Savana," whispered Roslyn. "We've arrived.
Look—here comes a group of Russian officials. You poor
thing—I'll wager that awful-looking man in the lead is Baron
Peter Sarakof."

Sir Douglas was the first to step down from the carriage
onto the fort grounds to greet the party of three men who
approached. Savana's eyes were on the newspaper.

"After you, Roslyn," she told her, and when the girl was
alighting from the carriage, Savana gathered her cape from
the seat and slipped the paper beneath.

A moment later she turned toward the Russian soldier
who offered a hand to help her down the carriage step.

"My niece, Miss Savana Rezanov Mackenzie," said Sir
Douglas.

A thin-faced official with pale eyes and a rigid uniform
buttoned tightly at his neck bowed his head briefly.

"Welcome to Fort Ross, Miss Mackenzie. We regret
Baron Sarakof was called away on urgent business. He will
return in time for the official dinner tonight."

"Not anything to be alarmed about, I hope?" asked Sir Douglas, and Savana couldn't tell if her uncle was sincere in his concern or not as he watched the Russian thoughtfully. She rather thought that the news came as no surprise.

"The wheat we were to buy is no longer available, Sir Bellomont."

"A regrettable circumstance," he said. "How fortunate that Hudson's Bay has a seller. He will arrive tonight to meet the baron."

# 8

## THE REZANOV INHERITANCE

Sir Douglas's party had been given accommodations at the commander's two-story house where the Russian delegation from New Archangel was also staying. As soon as she arrived and greeted Zoya, Savana gratefully accepted hot tea and lighted another lantern on the desk in the dim room made of logs. She brought out the newspaper and smoothed it across the desk beneath the light.

Savana's eyes skimmed the words until she found the line she was searching for but had hoped wasn't there. *"The body of Yuri Bering, secretary in the delegation of Count Aleksandr visiting Russian Fort Ross, was found on the San Francisco wharf in the Diego Brothers warehouse. He was the victim of an apparent stabbing. . . ."*

Savana stood without moving. What did Baron Peter Sarakof and the rest of the count's delegation think of Yuri's death? *No,* she thought with a chill, *his murder.*

A little shiver ran down her neck. Like a whisper in an

empty room, the question breathed across her mind. Had he been silenced for contacting her? Whoever the murderer was, it was likely he knew she had met with Yuri and that he had warned her about the baron.

She remembered her uncle's response in the carriage. He must have already been informed by officials at the Hudson's Bay Company about Yuri's death, for how else would he know? He was depending on her willingness to visit New Archangel, and the murder of one of the count's delegation was not something he'd wish her to know about.

Savana frowned at the brief article. Yuri had said the danger might be to both of them. She folded the paper, staring at it. Perhaps the real danger was from Count Aleksandr. Would he not be in a perfect position to hire an assassin? There was also her grandmother Countess Catherine Rezanov, yet her emotions argued against this—after all, it was the countess who wished to see her.

Then who, thought Savana, had not wished Yuri to warn her against going to New Archangel, and for what reason? She remembered what Trace had said about the baron, and yet she had little reason to trust Captain Wilder.

Zoya walked up behind her so quietly that Savana jumped. "Your tea is getting cold, my dear. Is anything wrong? You look so troubled."

Zoya's iron gray hair was weaved into two neat circular braids worn at the sides of her head. Her thin frame was lost within a plain gray muslin dress topped with a starched ecru lace apron.

Her name was simply "Zoya," a faithful woman of Russian ancestry who had first served Savana's mother as personal maid before her untimely death at New Archangel. Of her own choosing, she had gone with James Mackenzie and his small daughter to Bellomont House in England while James returned to his work with the Hudson's Bay Company.

Savana considered her as much a part of her family as the Bellomonts, and perhaps she loved her even more. In Savana's lonely years in the cold Bellomont mansion, separated from her warm and generous-hearted father, Zoya had become the grandmother she never had.

The elderly woman was actually too frail to be making such rigorous journeys, as she'd done recently in coming with her from London to San Francisco, and Savana worried about her, yet Zoya had insisted.

"How could I allow Nadyia's daughter to visit Baranof Castle and not accompany her? And permit an old woman's sentimentality," she had said in London, "but I grow old, Savana dear. I would finish out my last days on earth near the church I attended with your mother. My brother Nikolai is still there serving the bishop. And he keeps a precious garden where many go to meditate." And so Zoya had managed the tedious voyage with remarkable stamina.

Savana now stood from the chair. "Zoya, when you served the Rezanov family did you ever hear of a man named Yuri Bering?"

Zoya's brow puckered as she added hot tea to the half-empty cup. "No. Should I have heard of him? Have you met him since your arrival?"

Savana couldn't tell her that she had. "He was a member of the Russian delegation," was all she said. "He's been found dead in a warehouse in San Francisco. The paper said he was murdered."

Zoya set the teapot down on the earthen brick to keep warm. "Murdered!" she whispered.

Savana pulled up a chair for Zoya to sit down, but before she could question her further, a rap on the chamber door interrupted. "I'll get it," said Savana and went to answer.

A tight-lipped officer informed her that the baron had returned to Fort Ross and wished to express his loss in not being on hand to welcome her himself, but if convenient, he wished to speak with her alone before the dinner reception. He would be waiting at seven in the commander's private office downstairs.

"Tell the baron I shall meet him as requested."

When he'd gone, Savana dressed meticulously in her

white satin gown. The close-fitting bodice had a fairly low décolletage, with fitted *gigot* sleeves, and ankle-length skirts puffed out with crinolines.

"I could wish you were dressing for some young English gentleman to admire, rather than the baron," said Zoya.

*An odd remark,* thought Savana, working her smooth flaxen hair into coiled and looped braids about her head. "You do not like the baron, yet you refuse to tell me why." She studied Zoya in the vanity mirror.

"I have never met him," said Zoya evasively. "So how could I dislike him? You are mistaken."

Savana didn't know whether to believe her or not. She might have insisted on more information, except Zoya could be pressed only so far about the Russian family before she would become uncommunicative. She had tried too many times at Bellomont House while growing up, and Zoya would soon complain that such discussions made her too upset. *"The memories are not all happy ones, Savana. It is better to forget,"* she would say.

Savana wasn't about to allow the opportunity to learn the truth slip through her fingers this time.

"I must go down tonight, Zoya. Uncle is counting on me, and you forget I see all this as my opportunity as well. So much depends upon our friendliness with the baron. The treaty is important."

Zoya had heard it all before, and Savana could see she was not in agreement, nor impressed with the necessity of trade treaties.

"I wish you would not go down tonight," was all she said.

Savana had hoped Zoya might have remembered Yuri, but now wished she'd kept his death from her.

Savana turned to her with a smile. "I don't want you worrying about me. Why don't you retire early, Zoya? You look worn out from all this travel. Remember, we've a long journey to Fort Vancouver."

Zoya sat quietly in the high-backed chair and remained

silent as Savana left the room to keep her appointment with the baron.

Savana pressed her hands hard against her white satin skirt over stiff petticoats so they wouldn't rustle as she came down the wooden steps. It was unusual to meet the baron for the first time without a proper introduction, but Savana was willing to set aside custom to discover the reason for the meeting.

At the bottom of the stairs she stopped. A door to her right was ajar, and in the late afternoon shadows the lantern light shone softly under the crack.

She suddenly felt uncomfortably tense as she grappled with the realization of meeting Peter Sarakof for the first time. She fought back all the negative things she had heard about him and knew she must judge him for herself, not by the foreboding gossip of Yuri, Captain Trace Wilder, or even the disturbing silence of Zoya.

It was only fair, she decided, to give the man the right to prove his enemies wrong. Savana gave a light tap on the door, but before she could push it open farther, it was pulled aside by a military attaché who bowed his head briefly and stepped aside, allowing her to enter. He went out, closing the door behind him.

She glanced past the commander's desk, stacked with papers, toward Baron Peter Sarakof standing at the window. His gaze fell upon her.

"I am Savana Rezanov Mackenzie," she said with a steady voice.

# 9

## THE RUSSIAN BARON

Baron Peter Sarakof's polished black knee-boots sounded in confident steps across the hardwood floor as he walked to meet her. His pale, wintry eyes did not hesitate to take her in from head to toe, missing nothing, and Savana felt the chilling glance as more than a physical appraisal. She sensed the analysis of her will, her character, as though he searched like a hunter for some vulnerable spot on which to set his sites. The thought swept through her like the bitter wind from the gray Pacific which rattled the panes in the commander's office.

That he was primarily a man of military bearing came across in his stance. His white uniform coat flaunted decorations that she was unacquainted with, and his trousers were black with a thin white stripe down each leg. Her eyes strayed away from him to where a short Russian pistol in a holster lay plainly in view upon the desk. Beside it, a fur-lined cloak characteristic of the snow-packed winters of Russian America was thrown across the desk, and a scabbard with sheathed sword beside it.

His gold hair waved across a wide forehead, and a short mustache was groomed above a straight, hard mouth that lacked humor until he unexpectedly smiled, which highlighted the deep cleft in his chin.

She could see how the baron might be in some trouble with the women in St. Petersburg in the court of the czar, and against her will found herself blushing slightly.

He was younger than she had expected, perhaps in his late thirties, and an arrogant confidence flanked him. She felt his dominance immediately as his eyes held hers, probing for any weakness. His was a will that surged like crashing waves over those less able to stand.

He bowed precisely, extending a strong tanned hand, and Savana extended hers in an elbow-length white glove. He bent over it.

"I bring you greetings from your grandmother Countess Catherine Rezanov," he said. "She expects you at the castle in New Archangel and looks forward with anticipation."

He spoke precise English, and his Russian accent went well with his dignified appearance. Savana offered a slight curtsy. "I look forward to meeting her, Baron Sarakof."

"Peter," he corrected with a smile. "We are destined to be good friends, Savana—I may call you that?"

"Yes . . . of course. I also look forward with anticipation to meeting the countess. When my uncle, Sir Douglas, told me of her desire to see me, I was both surprised and pleased."

"You must understand that the countess has long wished to see Nadyia's daughter; however, it was most unfortunate that she was under the mistaken impression you had died as a child."

She had not heard this before. Could it be true?

Before she could respond, he continued gravely, "There are those in the extended family who would not wish you to reconcile with the countess. There is a large Rezanov inheritance destined for the covetous purses of lesser relatives.

You pose a threat to their hopes."

The information came as no surprise. Savana had struggled with past resentment over the idea that the family dared to judge her so coldly without having met her—nor did they even wish to.

Uncomfortably, Savana hastened, "I assure you, my desire in seeing the countess has nothing to do with an inheritance. I mean—I wouldn't want you or the countess to think that I—" Under his remote gaze she stopped.

"Forbid such unworthy thoughts another moment's concern. It is the wish of the countess to remember her granddaughter. And like you, she has more noble concerns than passing on her daughter's inheritance."

"I wish nothing," Savana assured him again.

Turning to the desk and lifting his fur-lined cloak he produced a small gift-box tied with gold lace. "The countess has asked me to present this."

Savana hesitated. "Oh, but I couldn't—"

"She would be most offended if you refused."

She offered a smile and took the box. It was clear by the way he waited that he expected her to open it in his presence. She laid the box on the desk and untied the ribbon.

With a silent breath she lifted the heavy strand from its velveteen enclosure. Diamonds reflected up at her: huge, glittering, and cold. She imagined the necklace itself must be worth more than all her father had left her in the London bank from his years in the Hudson's Bay Company. There were earbobs as well—each a cluster of diamonds that dangled and flashed like an icy waterfall. At the bottom of the box was a folded piece of linen paper stamped with an official mark from St. Petersburg. Savana opened it and read:

*Savana,*
*These belonged to my daughter Nadyia—your mother.*
*It is my wish that you have them. I am sending the jewels*
*ahead to Fort Ross by the able and trusted hand of my*
*nephew Peter in order to assure you of my profound interest.*

*The diamonds are a cherished Rezanov family heirloom that befits the celebration of my heart in finding you at long last. So much remains to be spoken between us that must wait until we meet face-to-face. I have found in Peter a loyal ally as well as a beloved nephew. He will have much to tell you. Do pay heed. It is important.*

*Countess Catherine Rezanov*
*New Archangel*

Overcome for a long moment by the implications, Savana looked again at the message. The countess accepted her as her own blood—her *granddaughter*. What then was she to make of the story that the Rezanov family had rejected the offspring of James Mackenzie and had sent her away by the hand of Zoya?

So much must wait until, as her grandmother had written, they would meet and speak of these matters face-to-face.

Her jumbled thoughts raced. "Her gift is far too generous."

"The countess does not think so. Nor do I—not that I had much to do with her decision once she asked my opinion. She is a gracious and intelligent woman. I see much of her in you."

She looked at him. "She speaks well of you in her letter. I assume you are close to your aunt."

"I spent many summers with her in St. Petersburg when I was a boy. She married my uncle after the death of her first husband in the war, who unfortunately died fighting France. She has resumed the Rezanov name at the wishes of her only son, Count Aleksandr."

Savana was startled by the revelation that the ruling count of Russian America with which Britain hoped to make a treaty was also a relative—her mother's brother. Did Sir Douglas know?

He must, she decided. Why else would he have insisted she journey with him to New Archangel? Yet, he hadn't informed her, and she wondered why, when Peter did not try to keep the information from her.

"Then—do you mean to tell me the count is my uncle?"

The amber-colored depths of his eyes flickered with some inner hostility that brought a slight twist to his lip. "He is," he stated. "Although it may be he does not wish to see you . . . for selfish reasons of his own. I am sorry to tell you so."

She refrained from showing her disappointment. After all, she was under no sentimental delusions. Until the letter from her grandmother, she had not entertained the thought of any family acceptance.

"I would not force myself," she said simply. "As a matter of necessity, I don't expect to remain at Baranof Castle longer than necessary for Sir Douglas to negotiate with the Russian-American Fur Company."

His eyes held hers. "I hope that you will wish to remain in New Archangel indefinitely. The countess will wish it also."

The meaning behind his suggestion was not lost, but she pretended to miss the obvious. "I naturally wish to learn all I can about my father, James Mackenzie."

At the mention of her father his expression faltered. He looked quickly at the diamonds. "May I?"

She hesitated, then relented, not wishing to appear ungrateful. He removed them from the box and stepped behind her to fasten the necklace. Savana added the earbobs.

He smiled, and a bright glitter sprang to his gaze. "They have never adorned any woman more beautiful."

He was quick with his compliments, she thought, but reminded herself that the countess depended on his loyalty. There were so many questions that needed to be asked she hardly knew where to begin.

The baron interrupted her jumbled thoughts. "In truth, Savana, I did not ask to meet with you before dinner tonight to only give you the gift from the countess. There is something else. Perhaps you should sit down." And while Savana watched him, uncertain whether or not she wished to trust

105

him as the countess's letter advised, he drew up a cushioned chair and Savana sat down, her white satin rustling, the diamonds flashing light.

"It is a serious matter," he said.

He now had her full attention. "Is it about the countess?"

"No, James Mackenzie."

There was something in his voice and in the way he watched her when he mentioned her father that baited her expectations. "What about my father?" she asked quietly.

"From the moment I met Sir Douglas in St. Petersburg last year and understood the granddaughter of the countess to be alive, I was able to convince her of our error in having believed certain members of the Rezanov family concerning your death—and your father's. Fortunately, she was able to see through Count Aleksandr's wishes that it should appear so—" He paused to let his words settle, as though they brought him unhappiness.

Sir Douglas had visited St. Petersburg? When? And why would her grandmother's son, Count Aleksandr, wish to make his mother believe she and her father were dead. . . . She stopped, and her eyes swerved abruptly to the baron's even gaze.

"My father?" she whispered and stood quickly. Peter took hold of her shoulders as though she might fall.

"What are you suggesting?" she breathed, not daring to hope.

"It concerns the whereabouts of your father, James."

Savana's eyes searched his, her heart thudding. "What about him?"

"You must say nothing of this to anyone, including Sir Douglas, but the countess and I believe he is alive, a prisoner in Siberia. Any success I may have in getting him safely to Baranof Castle depends on the strictest secrecy.

"I expect to be sent to St. Petersburg once we return to New Archangel. The countess will give me information for the czar. Your grandmother," he said, "has willed me to say nothing more until I bring you to her. She will then explain everything."

Savana's emotions stumbled over the astounding news. Her beloved father—alive!

In a moment of profound gratitude and awe, she silently gave thanks to the Lord. She was thankful too that Peter was on her side, and her hand moved to rest on his arm.

"Baron, I'm overwhelmed with gratitude. I—"

His hand closed over hers and she tensed slightly, realizing the intimacy of their gesture. She wished to pull away, but he seemed grave and unaware of the moment. There were voices outside the door and it opened with a wide sweep—

"Ah, Baron! There you are," said Sir Douglas.

For a moment she thought she saw two men in the outer hall, but when she turned toward the door, she met only the amazed face of her uncle.

Sir Douglas Bellomont stood without speaking, apparently recognizing the diamonds as a family treasure, though just why he would, she didn't know. He recovered his official demeanor, although his shrewd eyes had difficulty tearing away from the necklace.

"How positively clumsy of me not to knock first. Baron, Savana, I do apologize."

Savana pulled her hand away and glanced at Peter, but he showed not the slightest sign of the embarrassment she felt.

"Think nothing of it, Sir Douglas. Enter, please," he announced. "Your niece and I have been admiring the Rezanov diamonds. A gift entrusted to me by the countess. I am certain you and I both agree they have found the rightful owner at last, and," he said with a bow of his blond head toward Savana, "a most gracious one."

"Indeed, indeed. Well, my dear, congratulations," said Sir Douglas, walking up to her, his gaze meeting hers with secretive delight. *The treaty at New Archangel for England is within our grasp*, they seemed to say.

"A most beautiful picture you make, Savana," he said. "How like your mother you look. You agree, Baron?"

"The countess will be delighted and most surprised."

The diamonds seemed exceedingly heavy on her earlobes and around her slender throat. Sir Douglas offered an encouraging smile and turned to the baron.

"I understand you're looking to buy wheat for Count Aleksandr."

She was now merely the silent spectator as the two strong men, each with differing goals for their nations, discussed the matter of the wheat. Naturally, she knew her uncle's motives. If he could deliver a shipload of wheat to the Russian colony at the time he and Savana arrived at Baranof Castle, it would afford him the leverage to convince Count Aleksandr that England could meet their dire needs without any help from Boston.

"Unfortunately, there is not a kernel of wheat in all the area," said Peter with restrained temper. "A bizarre circumstance. And the feeble production of Fort Ross once again proves a disappointment, Sir Douglas. I arrive with a ship and find little to acquire except cabbage! New Archangel needs wheat, badly enough to pay a premium price. You have a supplier?"

"I do, Baron. A most fortunate act of providence."

Savana noted the cool gleam of suspicion in the baron's eyes.

"And how is it, Sir Douglas, you have what I could not locate at any of the Spanish seats of authority? My emissaries have returned from as far south as Santa Barbara, and they say this has been a bad year."

Sir Douglas smiled. "The Hudson's Bay can be relied upon, Baron. We have, or rather, I have a supplier, for the right price. He will sell it himself and handle its shipping."

"Rather unusual, but if this is his offer, I should like to hear from him myself. When can I meet him?"

"I've taken the liberty to arrange the meeting tonight. He is here to dine with us at the commander's gracious invitation. He's anxious to answer all your questions, and he waits now with your officer."

Peter looked pleased with her uncle's efficiency. "You are an enterprising man, Sir Douglas. It is no wonder that London has chosen you to represent them north of the Columbia. If your supplier is here, I shall meet him now, before we dine."

Savana saw her uncle's pleased expression as he went to the door and stepped into the hall. There were low voices, then her uncle returned.

"May I present the partner of the Rancho del Rio, Trace Wilder."

Savana turned. *There could not be two men in all San Francisco with that name.* Her gaze veered to the man entering the room, bringing with him a disciplined energy that set her on edge.

Surely this could not be a cocky dock worker . . . nor the wayward American cousin related to Sir Douglas. Her gaze flicked over him. There was no mistaking the man with the flint blue eyes and dark brown hair, though why Trace was now masquerading as a partner with Don Diego eluded her. It became clear at once that her uncle was privy to the deception. Trace now looked a Virginian gentleman in black broadcloth and white ruffled shirt, but no matter how well dressed and glib-tongued he might be, his earthy looks convinced her that he was a man to be reckoned with. She recognized that beneath his tailored demeanor there was the same flavor of danger that had made her suspicious of him on the wharf.

His arm remained in a sling. *At least that much of his act was genuine,* she thought cynically.

She remained uneasy as his presence brought an iron will into the room that matched Peter Sarakof's. If she mistrusted him—and for good cause, she told herself—she could not, however, fault his newly polished manners.

Trace's behavior appeared to be as precise as that of the Russian baron's. Why was he doing this? For more money, no doubt. He did everything for money, she thought coolly. *Does he know Yuri is dead?*

Trace had not seen her yet, or had he? Had he been the man she had momentarily glimpsed with her uncle outside the door? Had he witnessed her hand on the baron's arm? The scene, she knew, could easily be misconstrued, and she touched the diamond necklace.

She stood still, scarcely breathing, hoping against hope he wouldn't notice her as Baron Peter Sarakof broke the astute silence. He was looking at Trace with cold eyes and what Savana judged to be quick anger. Did he already know Trace?

She recalled what Trace had said about the men who had attacked him. Was there any truth to his accusation that the baron was involved?

A frozen smile formed on the baron's mouth. "Ah! It is the 'American' born in 'England' who has now taken out 'Mexican' citizenship! We meet again, Captain Wilder!"

"Am I to assume, Baron, we meet on more favorable terms this time, since California is neutral territory?"

At the tone of his voice the baron's eyes dropped to his slinged arm. "An accident, Captain Wilder? Nothing serious, I hope. It would be a grave loss if you could not manage your own vessel."

"It will heal, Baron. And we'll meet again."

"Perhaps not as client and seller, Captain."

"I'll look forward to it."

Savana had been unconsciously holding her breath, tensely watching them. Trace believed Peter to have been involved with the men who had attacked him. But was there something more personal between them?

Her uncle too looked alert, as if his shrewd gaze were judging two warriors. Evidently the dislike between Trace and the baron came as a surprise to him as well.

"You gentlemen have met before?" asked Sir Douglas flatly, looking at Trace with concealed anger. "You did not mention you knew the baron." He took out a cigar and placed it between his teeth, continuing to eye the two men.

"Baron Sarakof and I met in the waters off the Stikine where he commands the patrol boats for Count Aleksandr."

Sir Douglas paused with a slight frown at the news, then lit his cigar, but Peter smiled thinly at Trace.

"Nor did you tell me, Captain Wilder, that you and your friend Fletcher were trading partners with Señor Diego in California."

Trace smiled unpleasantly. "Nor did I tell you that Diego is an important official in the Mexican government in Santa Barbara. A matter of utmost importance if you and Count Aleksandr at New Archangel want our wheat. I thought you would know the manner of men with whom you were dealing."

"I do not make claims to such knowledge, Captain Wilder. Had you informed me of your position when we unpleasantly encountered one another off the islands belonging to Russian America—"

"I beg to differ. The islands and waters are in national dispute. The matter is not settled. At least two, maybe three other nations do not accept the czar's monopoly on trapping and trading with the Indians."

"—our confrontation at sea may have proven less controversial," concluded Peter.

Trace's brow lifted as if to parry the remark. "Did I not inform you, sir, that I had worthy business to attend in New Archangel with the count?"

Both Savana and Sir Douglas looked sharply at Trace. *He had business with the count!*

"It was you, Baron Sarakof, who turned me back. And now you are more anxious to trade? This is a matter the count will find confusing."

Peter's square jaw clenched and his amber eyes raked the American, sizing his opponent. "Perhaps I should have looked more carefully at your ship's papers before turning you back, Captain Wilder."

Trace smiled. "If it is wheat you want, Baron, perhaps

not," came the reply. "I do not like Russian officials snooping in my cabin." Then he added with a smooth tone that might have smelled like bait to a hungry wolf, "I have the wheat you came to San Francisco to buy for Count Aleksandr. I am willing to try to do business this time . . . on certain conditions."

Savana wondered what he had in mind, for it was clear to her that he was now not only representing her uncle and the Hudson's Bay Company, but his own personal interests as well. Had he agreed to work for England in order to meet the baron again?

Sarakof walked over to the commander's desk and coolly removed a Turkish cigarette from his cloak. Sir Douglas was quickly at his side, providing a lighted match. The baron's gaze was fixed on Trace, but Trace looked at the Russian pistol in its holster beside the sheathed sword.

"I find it odd, Captain Wilder, how you alone have the monopoly on wheat."

"Do you? There is money to be made. The count pays a good price. Diego and I bought early from the other growers, knowing you would arrive." He smiled. "We were right. As for our run-in near the Stikine—I'm a charitable man, Baron. I'm willing to let it go this time."

"This time?" Peter bent his head toward the lighted match Sir Douglas held.

"I am not always so charitable," said Trace.

The baron's eyes hardened. He drew on the end of the ill-smelling cigarette.

"I am charitable now," said Trace. "Though, it will require more than Russian roubles."

"I suspected as much. And the answer is no. It is quite out of my jurisdiction. Fletcher will stand trial."

"Then there will be no wheat." Trace turned to walk out.

"Wait!" Sir Douglas's brows rushed together in frustration. "What goes here, Trace? You told me nothing of this personal quarrel between you and the baron. You cannot simply walk away from our bargain. You now work for the Hudson's Bay Company!"

Trace paused. "Then I suggest, Sir Bellomont, that you convince the baron. Until then—"

"Wait," said Sarakof.

Trace turned, calm and unrelenting.

"I am in dire straits, as you well know. We must have that wheat at New Archangel before winter sets in. There are no other markets. It's too late in the season to buy from Peru."

Trace stood, his expression unreadable. *He knows what he is about,* Savana thought with subdued admiration, even if she didn't agree with his national aims.

"What are your terms?" asked Peter.

"The release of the Boston ship *Washington,* with its captain and crew."

Savana remembered what he had told her about a "run-in" with Sarakof's patrol boats. Evidently Trace had not been trying to mislead her. She noticed Peter was silent and musing, watching him.

"Your friend and smuggling ally, Fletcher, fired on one of my gunboats. He must stand trial."

Trace gave a laugh. "You also must be in dire straits along the Stikine. Do you worry yourself over the danger from a merchant schooner with a leaky bottom? What threat could Fletcher have been to your patrol boats with their Russian swivel guns? He might as well have used a bow and arrow."

"Nevertheless, he was in Russian waters."

"Neither Boston nor England accepts what you wish to call 'czarist territory.' "

"Then you suggest your Boston friend had rights to trap and trade with the Indians?"

Trace shrugged. "Boston or British, the Joint Occupation Treaty is in effect in Oregon."

The baron's amber eyes were like molten glass. "May I suggest that you and Fletcher are American agents."

"I am a citizen of Spanish California!" Trace feigned dismay. "How could I be an agent? Unless you mean to suggest that Mexico now lays claim to Oregon Country as well?"

"Very clever, Captain. Then of course, you are not interested in Oregon Country for the American government?" Sarakof scoffed.

Trace smiled. "As Sir Bellomont will tell you, I serve England—and myself. The Wilder plantation was destroyed in Virginia. I've resettled along the Sacramento River with an ambition to make enough money to grow our own wheat and raise beef. If you're not interested, Baron, there are other buyers—"

"Assuredly he's interested!" gritted Sir Douglas over his cigar.

*Well, Uncle's recently hired "British" seaman is showing his true colors*, thought Savana, watching Trace and Peter as they locked horns like competing stags.

Trace was watching the baron rather than her uncle, and there was something more in the suggestion of his voice when he said quietly, "The count, I understand, is without leniency when it comes to Boston ships trading in the channels and coastal islands."

The baron's mouth tightened. "The Russian-American Company and Count Aleksandr wish no further trouble with the Boston traders, nor with the Hudson's Bay Company. I am, however, under orders by the czar to see that my patrol boats guard our trapping and trading at all costs."

"I've heard you intend to end free trading not by political negotiations between governments, but with a noose for Boston men, or a journey to Siberia."

At the mention of Siberia, Savana remembered her father. . . .

"There have been disappearances of American ships," said Trace. "Some of those mariners were my friends."

Savana tensed. So there was more to Trace's interest in New Archangel than indifferent service to either Washington City or the Hudson's Bay Company.

The baron apparently disagreed, or pretended to, and he examined his Turkish tobacco with utmost curiosity. "The islands are a veritable maze, often shrouded in fog, as you know, and have been used to your advantage in the past. One must be quite an expert to navigate. No wonder ships become, as you say, lost. And maps of the islands are nonexistent."

Trace's smile was dangerously cool. "The shipmasters I speak of have cruised the channels and traded with the Indians the same as I. They were in familiar waters."

"I shall not ask whether you have been there recently. As you say, you are a Mexican citizen and I shall accept that. Something important has come up and I set sail tomorrow. It is wheat I am anxious to discuss."

"You shall have it. Diego's wheat is as plump as morsels of gold."

Savana was intrigued by the discourse. Did Trace actually have a partnership with Diego?

"Then I am assured we can reach an agreement."

"I have made clear my conditions, Baron."

Peter's face set hard. "I shall speak to Count Aleksandr about your American friend and his crew."

"And the ship."

Peter's mouth twisted and he took him in coldly. "The ship, as you earlier suggested, was no more than a leaky bucket and worth little. Nevertheless, I shall see if it's possible to have it returned."

"If not, Fletcher and I will accept equal recompense in roubles."

The discourse ended with a stony silence. As Trace turned to leave, his granite blue eyes fell on Savana standing silently in the corner of the room. He showed no surprise, though he looked directly at the diamonds, then met her gaze. She felt her face turn warm. *He believes I've compromised to receive these.*

They looked away as if by mutual agreement, but Peter must have noticed something more in Trace's look than she did, for he asked abruptly, "You have met the granddaughter of Countess Catherine Rezanov?"

"I've met Miss Mackenzie," he replied. He turned to the baron. "By the way, Baron, five Russian thugs jumped me in my room. You wouldn't know where they've disappeared to, would you? Your ship perhaps?"

Savana's breath paused as she glanced from one man to the other. Peter's face flushed with anger. His nostrils flared. "If you weren't without the use of your dueling arm, Wilder, I might call you out for that."

"It will heal, Baron."

"Good. I shall remember."

At the official dinner, Savana noted that Mrs. Warrender and Roslyn had been selected to sit beside Trace, and she wondered who had arranged the seating.

She also noted, as she ate her Russian dish of skewered lamb and sipped her sparkling water, that they didn't lack for topics of conversation. Mrs. Warrender was attentive to everything Trace said, and when the dinner was over and the music began, he had claimed her daughter Roslyn for the first waltz.

Peter was in negotiation with Sir Douglas over the delivery of the wheat, and the Russian officers of the delegation from New Archangel milled about, drinking their vodka and speaking Russian.

*Strange,* she thought. From their festive mood it appeared no one was concerned over the death of their comrade Yuri. One would think his sudden death would be a viable topic for the members of the count's delegation. Was it because of their loyalty to Peter? Maybe Yuri had been the one member of the group who had opposed him. She had considered the possibility of casually inquiring of Peter about Yuri's death, but an opportune moment had not come.

She wondered what urgent business was bringing the baron back to New Archangel, and whether it might suggest anything unusual. What of her own voyage north? Whose ship would be bringing Mrs. Warrender, Roslyn, and Reverend Withycombe to Fort Vancouver?

Mrs. Warrender and Roslyn were now nowhere in view, and Trace stood in the shadowed doorway leading into the other section of the commander's house. Savana calmly decided that her questions of travel were valid enough to inquire of Trace.

The oversized Russian officer who loitered at Savana's elbow was becoming odious company, his heavy face turning florid and sweaty under the vodka. She quickly excused herself and slipped away, hoping he wouldn't trail persistently after her.

"Oh bother," she murmured to herself, for as she glanced at the doorway where Trace had stood only a moment ago, she saw that he had disappeared.

Savana glanced over her shoulder to see the Russian officer looking for her, so she rushed ahead through the doorway into the cubicle and stopped abruptly as she confronted Trace.

"Oh," was all she said.

"Looking for me?" came his casual suggestion.

# 10

## CONFLICT AND SUSPICION

Savana looked into the unyielding flint blue eyes that challenged her, managing to retain her casual dignity. She offered a smile. "Well—if it isn't my uncle's American cousin—Señor Wilder—or maybe Boston Agent Wilder?"

His manner remained undisturbed and he returned her smile. "My dear cousin Savana, does it matter? As it is among those destined to become cherished and intimate friends, you may call me Trace." He then looked pointedly at the diamond necklace. "Rezanov diamonds . . . a wedding gift from our bold and daring baron. So soon?"

Her eyes flickered coolly. "You're not suggesting, Captain, that I'm willing to marry Peter for diamonds?"

"Ah, so it's Peter now, instead of Baron."

She smiled sweetly. "He too believes that he and I are among those 'destined to become cherished and intimate friends,' and insists I call him Peter."

Trace offered a disarming smile. "And what might I gain from you if I insist?"

She smiled ruefully. "A good price for your wheat."

"Well, that's a beginning. I suppose I shouldn't complain, since I can't offer diamonds."

It was time he learned where they came from, though she suspected he was making much of the matter of the jewels to show his distrust for the baron and any action the baron might make toward her.

"The jewels didn't come from Peter; they belonged to my mother, Nadyia. My grandmother sent them," she said, and couldn't keep the satisfied, wistful tone from showing in her voice. He must have caught it at once, for he gave her an inquiring look.

"The countess, I was told by Bellomont, has requested you to come to Baranof Castle to meet her."

"Yes," she said. "It came as a total but pleasant surprise. I was under the impression that no one in my mother's family cared to meet me."

He watched her. "I see this change brings you pleasure."

"That my grandmother lives and wants to see me? I find it a great satisfaction. For years I've longed for just such an opportunity. I've appreciated all the Bellomont family in London has done for me, of course—they've been kind while I was growing up—but my mother's family . . ." She stopped, somewhat embarrassed at sharing a personal reason for wanting to meet the countess. She was yearning for acceptance, family ties, love—and Trace must have caught her feelings at once.

He was watching her, and he obviously didn't share her excitement. "And the baron brought you the countess's request, along with the Rezanov diamonds? A letter from the countess was enclosed?"

She read the troubled curiosity in his eyes. "Yes," she admitted uneasily, not wishing his mood to spoil her own. "Peter brought them to me at her insistence."

As he mused over her words, leaning against the wall, he

looked out at the baron and the other Russian officials. Savana read the restrained displeasure in his face. It caused her to reach and touch the cool diamonds at her throat, watching not the baron but Trace. *What does he think, that Peter is lying?* Savana's fingers tightened. She would not be rejected again!

She deliberately turned her inquiring thoughts to Trace. The disagreement between him and the baron about the man named Fletcher held her attention, for the new information about his interest in Russian America and his concern for a friend cast Trace in an entirely different light—one that might warrant admiration, if she allowed it. And yet—if he actually were a Boston agent, Fletcher might also be working with him in Russian waters.

"You made quite a scene with Baron Sarakof tonight," she said in a low voice, glancing over her shoulder into the dining hall cleared for dancing. "For a time I thought he might call you out in a duel."

"You were concerned for my welfare, I hope?"

She was, but allowed the question to slip by unanswered. "You seemed to want to anger him." She looked at him inquiringly. "Now do tell me, Trace . . . about Fletcher. Are the two of you truly partners in the rancho with Don Diego, or is 'rancher' another of your disguises, and maybe Fletcher's too?"

His gaze was scrutinizing, as though weighing her motives. "Are you asking because you want to know, or did the baron ask you to find out?"

"I suggest Peter already knows a good deal about you and doesn't need me to ask. I am simply curious to know if you're a California rancher." She reminded him casually, "In San Francisco you said you hoped to rebuild your father's plantation in Virginia."

He had also mentioned a girl in St. Louis who planned to come to Fort Vancouver to work with missionaries, but she refrained from mentioning this, not wishing to appear interested. If Trace took her questions seriously, he now apparently chose to be lightly evasive, but for what reason, she could not surmise. "And what am I offered for this coveted secret information on the mysterious exploits of Trace Wilder?"

"Then you are actually a partner with Don Diego in ranching? Does your friend Fletcher also share in the rancho?" she persisted.

"You haven't told me who put you up to finding out about Fletcher—Bellomont?"

It was Savana who now turned evasive, realizing she may have given herself away by showing too much interest. She smiled. "So now you don't trust my uncle any more than Peter."

"When it comes to trust, my dear, I thought I made that clear the night when we rendezvoused beneath the mist-kissed trees. I have few reasons to trust either man. Bellomont would do anything for his beloved England short of throwing himself to hungry lions—not that he wouldn't sacrifice either of us to accomplish his goal. Anything for a treaty."

She resented his estimation of her uncle. It was true that Sir Douglas was a patriot, but he held deep affection for her and would do nothing to see her intentionally harmed.

"So you know all about the treaty England hopes to make with the Russian-American Fur Company."

"I didn't know it was a secret," he said smoothly, and when she looked at him doubtfully, he smiled. "Bellomont informed me. The Hudson's Bay Company hopes to push the Boston traders out of Oregon, despite the Joint Occupation Treaty."

"And, of course," she lightly mocked, "you're going to offer your loyal service to help England."

"For the right price." He scanned her with a faint smile. "You look dubious, Miss Mackenzie. Could it be that, unlike the Hudson's Bay Company, you don't see that I have much loyalty to offer Mother England?"

She arched a golden brow. "As you so succinctly put it

in San Francisco, Captain Wilder, if my uncle believes in you, why shouldn't I?"

He laughed quietly. "Come, Savana, admit you don't trust me any more than you do a rattler."

"I'll admit I find it strange that with the end of the recent war you'd wish to serve the cause of England in the Pacific Northwest. You are, after all, an American."

"But warmly related to the Bellomont family in London," he suggested.

Savana couldn't tell if he were being facetious or not.

"You're right," Trace went on, "it does appear as though the war is never quite over. It could easily erupt again at any time. So much remains to be settled."

"How fortunate that you at least believe Oregon Country belongs to His Majesty," she said with a rueful smile.

"Or the czar?"

"So you still think I'm working as a Russian agent. For Peter, I suppose?"

"I admit that, like you, I have suspicions, but I would be disappointed if such were the case."

"Would you? Well, perhaps I shall keep you wondering, but I'm quite certain you have your own national cause, even if Uncle Douglas believes you're a valuable man to the Company."

"It's my wheat that is valuable," came his smooth voice. "It will afford Bellomont a warm welcome in Count Aleksandr's castle."

"And you approve of the treaty he hopes to make with the count, even though it's against the Boston traders," she said.

"I've already mentioned my feelings on the Northwest Territory."

"Maybe. You haven't said where your loyalties are."

"They're with Trace Wilder. Anything else shouldn't make a difference. I've the wheat to sell to the Company. And the Company wishes to sell to Sarakof. Nothing else matters except how quickly I get paid."

She wondered if she believed him. What her uncle seemed not to see, or perhaps didn't want to, was whether or not Trace had motives other than money and the release of his friend.

It was true that he looked to be a man loyal to no one but himself and his friends, she thought. And his cool questioning of the baron earlier that evening had boldly implied personal reasons for sailing his ship into Russian-American waters, but could there be more?

"Maybe someone else told you about the treaty Sir Bellomont hopes to negotiate before we ever arrived in San Francisco. Andrew Jackson perhaps?"

He folded his arms and his smile left. "Never mind me. It's Sarakof's motives you need to spend more time dissecting. You might ask yourself why he wishes to keep his past in St. Petersburg so secretive before he sweeps you away on his bleak gray ship to Baranof Castle in the wintry paradise of New Archangel."

She had gotten little of the information she wanted, and his uninformative responses to her questions were annoying. Nevertheless she hoped she had kept her feelings from showing. "I regret to disappoint you, Captain Wilder, but I've no mind or mood to be swept away by any man on any ship to any paradise, wintry or tropical. I told you on the wharf that I pay heed to the warnings of Aunt Hillary when it comes to not trusting certain men."

"You will find me in wholehearted agreement, Miss Mackenzie. Then may I suggest you pay closer attention to the valorous baron from St. Petersburg?" His gaze dropped to the diamonds winking about her throat. "Ask yourself what was so threatening to his ambitions that he needed to revert to such desperate measures as stealing Yuri's letter to keep you from learning about his character."

She hesitated to bring Yuri into the discussion knowing it would give more credence to his warning—and to Yuri's. He'd told her his life was in danger. Now he was dead.

She had first entertained thoughts that Trace might have

been involved in his death, but after what she'd heard tonight, that notion no longer appeared plausible. Whatever else she thought about Trace, she didn't see him as a murderer.

"Does the baron know you've met with Yuri?" he asked.

Under his sober gaze she felt herself being drawn to trust him against her will. She glanced again toward the dining hall, where the baron and her uncle were in view.

"No," she confessed quietly. "Neither does Sir Douglas." She wavered on the edge of sharing her disquiet over Yuri's death.

"It's best for you he doesn't."

Her gaze came to his and she sobered. "Yuri was found dead."

He observed her expression thoughtfully. "Yes, he was murdered."

The blunt statement would normally have caused her to shiver, but she sensed that he weighed her response, and she wished to appear calm.

"You read it in the paper? Who do you suppose—?" But she paused, realizing her question gave him the perfect opening to point to the baron's men, perhaps the same ones he claimed had attacked him.

"Did Sarakof ask you if you'd received any information from St. Petersburg?"

"No. And to rush to the conclusion that he was involved—"

"You can't convince me he wasn't. What concerns me is whether or not he suspects Yuri warned you against him. You say he didn't mention St. Petersburg? Or hint of Yuri?"

"No, nothing, but I'm not surprised. I think you may misjudge him because of your disagreement over Fletcher. After all, any man trusted by the countess and anxious to—" She stopped, but he was alert and straightened from where he'd been leaning into the wall.

"Anxious to what?" he asked pointedly.

Savana was irritated with herself for giving too much away.

"Anxious to help you?" he persisted in a relentlessly calm voice.

She must not mention the possibility of her father being alive, not after Peter had urged her to silence. Trace's gaze was penetrating, and she looked away with a quick attempt to turn the conversation in another direction. She said with mild accusation, "No one else knew I'd met Yuri in the warehouse, except you. Only three of us were on the foggy wharf at dawn. Yuri, myself . . ." She looked back at him. "And you."

"There was someone else," he stated quietly. "A fourth person. The one who killed Yuri."

"You don't know that for certain," she whispered. "Peter wasn't there; he couldn't have been."

"The baron? No. He wouldn't stain his hands with outright murder. If he must involve himself he prefers duels—ones that are arranged beforehand to insure his 'luck.' "

Savana's eyes searched his. He wasn't the slightest bit squeamish about making bold and blatant charges.

"He'd have one of his men get rid of Yuri, just as he hired men to move against me."

"I don't know whether to believe you or not," she breathed, her eyes flickering over him. "You may have your own cause, your own motives in turning me against him."

"I do," he stated quietly.

She glanced at him, and he said, "I don't care to see you endangering yourself to whatever plans he has brewing. Your uncle is either foolish or completely selfish to allow you to journey to Baranof Castle. I'm not certain which it is."

She felt the sting of his words, yet they sobered her.

"You forget, Captain Wilder, I've a will and purpose of my own. If I didn't choose to visit the countess I could always return to London, or remain with Mrs. Warrender and Roslyn at Fort Vancouver. I happen to agree wholeheartedly with Sir Douglas in the cause of His Majesty. And I shall do all I can to see to the success of his negotiations with Count Aleksandr—who happens to be the countess's son."

He seized on the information and looked toward the baron thoughtfully. "So Count Aleksandr is your uncle. Quite interesting. I wonder why the baron finds it necessary to rush back to New Archangel instead of voyaging with you and Bellomont? Did he explain?"

She, too, wondered and stirred uneasily. "If I knew his reason, I doubt if I'd tell you. Your mind is made up. You don't trust anyone, do you?"

"I've good cause to not trust Sarakof. My opinion, however, doesn't seem to matter much."

"Should it? I hardly know you."

"You hardly know Sarakof, yet you trust him."

"I haven't said I trusted him. I'm willing to give him the benefit of the doubt."

"By the time you discover the truth it may be to your detriment."

"Are you trying to frighten me, Captain Wilder?"

He leaned against the wall, watching her thoughtfully. "Now, I wonder what he may have promised you tonight when he gave you the diamonds? Something to win your confidence, no doubt."

She thought of her father, and under Trace's scrutiny her lashes narrowed.

"What did he promise you?" he persisted.

"It's not your concern, Captain."

"Unfortunately, for you."

"You are an arrogant man," she breathed, and when he didn't bother to deny it and only watched her thoughtfully, she rushed on. "Peter has shown himself to be a friend, and I'm willing to give him the opportunity to prove his enemies wrong. Despite all your charges of infamy, he's done well toward me."

"Your generous nature, madame, I find commendable, but nevertheless too sentimental and chummy. You will pardon me if I'd rather snuggle up with a grizzly. It was Sarakof who sent men searching for Yuri's information."

"What proof do you offer?"

"He must have gotten the letter from St. Petersburg," he stated. "Now he feels confident enough to have met with you tonight and promised his gallant protection to the dying end."

His manner was smothering and she grew defensive. "And I suppose you'll call him out when you're able."

"Depends on whether he releases Fletcher and his crew."

"You're wrong about Peter. I know it."

"So he already has you charmed. He moves quickly, doesn't he?"

She looked at him sharply. "And what do you want, Captain Wilder, more trouble? What happened to you in your hotel room wasn't enough?"

He looked at her evenly. "I haven't decided yet. I'm thinking about it. About what I want, that is."

She flushed and turned her head so quickly to look toward the lighted room that the earbobs swayed like rainbows of ice.

A tense moment inched by in which she was totally aware of his appraisal.

"You'd look lovelier without them," he commented.

She smoothed her silken hair to see if the braids were in place, keeping her eyes on the dancers in the dining hall. "I wish you wouldn't speak like that."

"You don't like men to say you are fair?"

Although she couldn't prove he was an opponent to her uncle's cause, or her own, and his warning against the baron might only be construed as an interest in her safety, she felt it necessary to hold him at bay. The attraction between them was dangerous.

"I don't like *you* to say it," she informed him.

"Thanks," he drawled flatly. "Next time I won't bother. I'll let Peter do it."

She looked at him, keeping her voice low. "It must be frustrating, Captain Wilder, to be forced to maintain the disguise of a gentleman. I shudder to think what would have

128

happened in the commander's office if you'd had the use of your arm."

Trace smiled. It was an unpleasant smile, but his voice remained deceptively mellow. "I'm in your debt, Miss Mackenzie."

Bewildered, thinking she misunderstood his response, she scanned his face.

He explained. "You've kept me from the added error of believing you to be a young woman of grace, as well as beauty. I won't make the mistake again. Good night." He offered a light bow and withdrew.

Savana felt the lash of his sudden rejection more painfully than she would have expected. She looked after him, a flush of color rising into her cheeks. An odd sense of loss settled over her. She turned away, deciding to retreat to one of the upper rooms for an emotional reprieve before having to perform socially for the rest of the long evening.

The baron intercepted her in the hallway. "I've requested this waltz for you, Savana. It was written by a Russian composer in St. Petersburg." He smiled and held out his arm. "May I have the honor, my dear?"

Savana saw Trace snatching his hat and cloak from the hall and walking toward the front door. She tore her gaze away and took Peter's arm.

*It's just as well,* she thought. *He's dangerous in more ways than one.*

Trace saw his father's cousin and stopped, hoping his unpleasant mood did not show. At the moment he didn't want any of Bellomont's pompous chat about the glorious cause of the British Empire.

"Ah, Trace my boy, there you are. I was afraid you'd left."

Trace glanced toward the dance floor, where he could see the imperious baron and Bellomont's niece, her every move-

129

ment immersed in the waltz, graceful and beautiful in white satin.

"I was just leaving, sir."

"If you wouldn't mind, I need a breath of fresh air. I'll walk with you to your horse."

He wondered what Bellomont wanted now. That he doubted his zealous allegiance to England was part of the game. It would be inconceivable for him to think otherwise, considering his father's role in the war and America's interest in Oregon. And yet it was crucial that Bellomont believe he was crass enough to shrug off duty and national sentiment for the need of money.

The night was cool and damp, yet refreshingly so after being cooped up inside the Russian commander's house all evening pretending his good will. He was anxious to get back to his cabin on the ship—his quarters now that he had left his hotel room in San Francisco. Thinking about the fire fed his anger as they walked along, too slowly for Trace's impatience.

At last Bellomont stopped and removed a cigar from his tailored jacket. "You didn't tell me Sarakof was a personal enemy."

He must make Bellomont believe him an adventurer, a man out to make good for himself who was willing to walk away from his past in Virginia, away from the war and what it had done to his mother, to Yancey, to himself. . . .

"In my business I make a lot of enemies. Sarakof is only one of them. There are good furs up in the North if a trader knows where to get them. I do, and I aim to get my share. Sarakof and I don't see eye to eye."

A match flared up in the darkness, followed by a foul smell of tobacco.

"This Boston friend of yours named Fletcher. If he's been arrested for buying illegal furs, your involvement is not likely to go over well with Count Aleksandr."

It was true about Fletcher, but the situation also gave Trace a believable cover for his interest in Russian America,

130

and his willingness to serve Bellomont and the Company cause. Where Bellomont was not likely to fall for a change in allegiance, he could understand switched loyalties for a personal grievance, and Trace had more than enough to muddle the issue of his motives.

"You play dangerously, my boy. Is it wise?"

Trace allowed himself to show no emotion except the realization of personal plans. He shrugged indifferently.

"I don't seek danger. If it stands in the way of what I want, and what needs to be done, then I'll deal with it. Look, we both received what we wanted tonight, didn't we? Whether I bring my wheat into New Archangel waving the Stars and Stripes or the Union Jack makes little difference to me. You're able to prove to the count that he can depend on Hudson's Bay instead of Boston traders to deliver his goods. And I? I have safe passage into Russian territory. As soon as Fletcher's released, along with my merchant ship—I'll be on my way." He could feel Bellomont's mental scrutiny weighing his every word. The glow on the end of his fat cigar flared red as he drew in.

"I quite understand, of course. You would naturally be tempted to try to take back a load of furs to San Francisco. Doing so, however, might place Savana and me in a somewhat sticky spot at Baranof Castle."

Trace caught the sly introduction of Savana into the conversation and was cautious. He believed Bellomont had a keen eye and had noticed his attraction to his niece. He had thought he had behaved indifferently enough, even going so far as to not request a waltz. He had avoided her altogether until she had come looking for him. She too was being as cool as he, but there was little doubt in his mind that she had noticed him, perhaps more so than Sarakof. The baron had the advantage of position and Bellomont's own endorsement.

He decided to play his hardness for all it was worth, hoping to put Bellomont off the trail.

"I've told her she's making a mistake in going, but she has a mind of her own. She has some notion of learning more about Mackenzie's disappearance. I can't be responsible for a woman with a hard head and a sentimental heart. I'll get you both there safely. And when I've done so, I will consider my job done. Of course I'm going to try for a load of furs. They'll bring top prices in China."

Sir Bellomont was quiet, and Trace knew that mentioning James Mackenzie was a gamble, but he was sure Bellomont must already suspect his niece of avid interest in the mysterious subject of her missing father. To bring it into the open only took him off guard.

"Very well, Trace, but the chance you take with the furs is all your own, and I'll not speak for you if you're caught. I'll be obliged to insist indignantly to the Russian authorities that I know nothing of your intentions."

"I wouldn't expect you to do otherwise," said Trace smoothly. "But I don't expect Sarakof's patrol boats to find me."

"What part of the islands will you be seeking your furs, if I may ask?"

Trace smiled. "That, Sir Bellomont, is private knowledge. Only a few men other than myself know of it and we intend to keep it that way."

Bellomont chuckled with unexpected pleasure. "You've a keen mind for business, and I appreciate your gumption. Beware of the baron is my advice—his animosity is as cold-blooded as your own, and he'll have his patrol boats out watching for you to make an error. If you do, my boy, he'll be on you as fast as a shark smells blood. He isn't a fellow to easily forget an embarrassment. And your bold showdown tonight, coupled with your accusation about his men attacking you, has rankled him indeed."

Trace believed his father's cousin was beginning to believe him a crass-hearted adventurer. He added his final blow. "It was either Sarakof's order, or your own."

Sir Douglas Bellomont jerked back at the sharpness of his words. He lifted both bushy brows. "Good heavens, man! My order? When I need you to deliver wheat and head up the expedition to the Stikine?" His brows then thundered down over his strongly formed nose. "My dear Captain Wilder, I fear you think me a blundering fool."

Trace hid a smile. "No, not that, sir. You are as clever as Sarakof."

Bellomont mused for a moment, considering a response. "As you say, sir, you need me," said Trace silkily.

Sir Bellomont appeared to waver between affront over the pragmatic motivation and ironic humor. He settled instead for a half-chuckle.

"Well, you're honest enough, Trace. You're a bit too much like your father. Zachary was made of steel. When he made his decision to fight for Boston against the king, he stayed by it to the end, even when he knew he was wrong. I can forgive a man like that with such convictions."

It was all Trace could do to control the surge of fire he felt lighting his emotions. His father never believed he was wrong in fighting for America, nor would he have wanted his cousin's forgiveness.

"It's a shame Zachary didn't live long enough to return to England," said Sir Bellomont. "I would have known pleasure in bringing him in to bow before His Majesty. Well, I've his son—at least one of them. And you're the kind of man I need to attempt the expedition. Nevertheless, my boy, be careful of the baron. He's a duelist of some reputation in St. Petersburg."

"So I've heard. I'm surprised you knew."

"I make it my ambition to know. We've got agents in every palace and jungle in the empire, doing their job well."

*Then he must have at his disposal some of the same information on the baron that Yuri was sent to give to Savana,* decided Trace. Sir Bellomont knew about the baron's lack of character, yet would risk his niece to the man's company. Sarakof had plans of his own for Savana, but what were they?

The answer waited at Baranof Castle. And Bellomont was baiting a tiger with a lamb.

Trace felt he could say nothing to Bellomont about the

133

danger he was forcing on Savana, since his concern might alert Bellomont to interests other than what he had claimed. But he decided he must raise the question, framing it with indifference.

"The believability of your niece in the role of a naive damsel fresh from London will be of profound benefit to His Majesty at New Archangel."

"Bluntly speaking, without her the Company will likely fail in its attempt to open a new fort on the Stikine."

"Yes—what could surpass being able to produce the granddaughter of the countess? You have a winning hand, Sir Bellomont. The wheat and Miss Rezanov Mackenzie, and she fully backs the cause of the Company in the Northwest."

"She is the granddaughter of the countess, after all, and one would expect her to be valuable to both England and Russia. But there are hazards as long as she ranks of more importance than an upstairs maid."

Trace thought he knew Bellomont well enough now, and there was no more to be said. He was a dedicated servant of the king and willing to sacrifice Savana if necessary. And Savana's misconception about the baron allowed the perfect trap. *What is it? Who is behind it?*

What did Sarakof expect to receive from his relationship with her?

He wondered what her grandmother the countess was like, and whether or not she might not be the one person who could protect her in the end. That, of course, would not be known until Savana arrived at New Archangel—the very thing he had hoped to avoid.

"I've often thought that women make better spies for their country in certain instances than do men," said Bellomont. "We males have such obvious flaws—temper being one of them. A woman's beauty will most always see her through."

Trace had felt anger toward Bellomont; now he felt disgust—but he couldn't show it. "Having already stated my concerns to you in San Francisco about bringing a woman on the expedition, I'll be about the business of loading British wheat," said Trace.

"Good," said Sir Bellomont jovially. "And when might we expect you at Fort Vancouver?"

Trace had intended to go ashore at the fort in order to make contact with his friends Jason and Daniel Lee at the mission compound. There he could discuss President Jackson's hopes of an overland route into Oregon, bringing American settlers. But he must be careful. His association with Lee could alert the British.

"Aside from the injury to my arm I could be there in a few weeks."

"Chief Factor McLoughlin will be anxious to send you on the expedition to explore the Stikine. Say thirty days?" pressed Sir Bellomont.

"No longer than that."

"Then I shall expect your arrival at the British fort."

Trace asked indifferently, "Did Sarakof explain why he was called back to Baranof Castle sooner than expected?"

"A message came by the captain of a Russian merchant ship on its way to Peru. It seems Count Aleksandr has suddenly taken ill. The baron must leave first thing in the morning."

The news was not good. Count Aleksandr was the prime czarist official at New Archangel. If anything happened to the count, or if his illness demanded his return to St. Petersburg for treatment, then Sarakof would be in command. At least until the czar sent out another man, or the count recovered—if he did recover. He suspected that there was trouble between Aleksandr and the baron. He believed the sudden illness was exactly what Sarakof wanted. Would Aleksandr return to St. Petersburg, or would he decide to remain at the castle to keep Sarakof from assuming command?

What better way for the baron to retrieve his fallen armor than by negotiating an important treaty with England in the count's absence? And Bellomont would also get what he wanted in the bargain—the end of the American traders in the Pacific Northwest. America's nearest port would become Boston if the Russian-American Company banned them from trade at New Archangel.

Perhaps Savana's grandmother, the countess, was the one person he could go to at Baranof Castle to protect Savana from the schemes of Sarakof and Bellomont. Visiting the Russian territory would become perilous should the baron unexpectedly replace Count Aleksandr.

Trace now believed that the count's life was in danger. He must warn him against Sarakof, and there was little time, since the baron was setting sail tomorrow.

# 11

# THE RELUCTANT SPY

Zoya was up waiting for her but shared none of the excitement Savana felt over the unexpected news that Countess Catherine Rezanov wished to see her. Wanting to nudge her out of her mood, Savana was tempted to also tell her about Peter's belief that he could locate her father. Remembering his request for secrecy, however, she told Zoya only of the letter from the countess.

Savana expected to see the elderly woman smile, and put her thin arms around her as she shared her happiness. Instead, Zoya, pale and tense, gathered her robe about her long nightgown and eased herself wearily into the chair where the Russian Bible Savana had given to her one Christmas remained open to Psalm 139. The words "Even there shall thy hand lead me and guide me" were underlined.

Zoya stared at the diamonds glittering in the lantern light as Savana stooped beside her, anxiously searching her eyes.

Savana touched the stones at her throat. "Do you recognize them? You must have seen Nadyia wear them on many occasions."

Zoya reached to silence her, and her fingers were cold as they clamped tightly about Savana's hand.

Her odd behavior alerted Savana. "What is it? What's wrong?"

Zoya shook her head. "Too much is wrong. If I could think as well as I did twenty years ago, perhaps I would remember."

Savana smiled. "You're not that old. And you've no trouble remembering to lecture me about a hundred small things. Do you recognize them or not?"

"Yes, yes, I suppose they were your mother's diamonds."

"Only 'suppose'?" asked Savana, unsatisfied.

Zoya rubbed her forehead. "The Rezanov diamonds . . . but that is not possible. They . . . they were brought to St. Petersburg years ago after your mother died. The countess returned with them. Unless . . ."

Savana hung on her every word. "Unless what?"

Zoya looked at her somewhat confused. "I cannot see anyone in St. Petersburg sending them to you by the hands of the baron."

Savana caught the hidden scorn in her voice when she mentioned Peter. "But you can't deny *this*," and she handed Zoya the letter from her grandmother. "You saw the letters the countess wrote to my mother at Baranof Castle. Is this her handwriting?"

Savana watched her nervous reaction. After a perplexing interval of silence, Zoya handed the letter back, shaking her head. "Dear me! I do not understand how it can be, but yes, it looks like the countess's handwriting, but remember, my eyes are not what they once were. Even if it is so, and she has sent the Rezanov diamonds and the letter by the baron, it speaks of trouble. We should have remained in London."

"The journey to New Archangel is an opportunity I can't refuse, Zoya. Visiting Baranof Castle will allow me to learn more about my mother and my father's forbidden work with

138

the Aleut. How could I refuse such an offer?"

"That is what troubles me," Zoya had protested. "They knew you would not refuse."

Savana turned, searching the elderly woman's face, wondering at the strange remark. "They? Who are *they*?"

Zoya shrugged and looked away, as though she had said too much. "Your mother's enemies. Your father also had his, perhaps more than Nadyia. It was he who troubled the waters with his encroachment into the Russian-American Fur Company's policies with the Aleut."

"That is what I must find out—what happened to him and why. I won't rest until I know the truth. And if the baron gives me opportunity, I must use it." Savana fingered the diamonds and stood, looking down at Zoya as she sat in the chair. "What do you know of the baron and his family?"

Zoya's remote gaze looked away. "The baron I have not met, nor do I recall the Sarakof family at St. Petersburg."

She wondered if Zoya were telling her all the truth. What was she keeping back?

"Did my mother or the countess ever speak of him?"

Zoya shrugged again. "Perhaps. When the countess visited from St. Petersburg they discussed many things, including relatives. The Russian family is much like the Bellomonts and Mackenzies; some were more important politically and close to the czar; others stood on the fringe, hoping to be invited closer. And if not invited, well, some planned more ruthless ways to climb the steps."

Was she speaking of Peter? "Are the baron's family considered outsiders by the Rezanovs?"

Zoya remained without expression. "Miss Nadyia never spoke of them, and if the countess spoke of her husband's nephew Peter in my presence, I do not recall. Your mother had her own concerns when the countess arrived a month before you were born."

Savana could see that Zoya deliberately remained locked within a silent past that she had helped to create, for what reasons Savana could not guess.

She carefully removed the diamond earbobs. *Something else to worry about*, she thought. *How will I keep such a treasure safe?* The gems sparkled in her palm. *Perhaps these are false.*

What an odd thought. It was Trace Wilder who had fed her suspicions, and remembering the unpleasant scene in which he had walked away from her, she wondered. Peter had informed her during the evening that Captain Wilder and his roguish friend Fletcher were not only poachers in Russian waters, but men of ill repute. Remembering that he was willing to switch loyalties for money added to Peter's credibility. *Even if Trace's father fought on the erring side, he died nobly*, she thought. *But what is to become of Trace?*

The next morning Savana received a brief message from her uncle telling her he wished to speak to her in private before they returned to San Francisco to board the *Beaver.*

She dressed and went downstairs, thinking she would find him at the breakfast table. Reverend Angus Withycombe was there alone and greeted her in a friendly fashion. Savana wondered what benefit he would be to the cause of England at Fort Vancouver. It was likely his position as an Anglican minister would afford him opportunity to gather information on Jason Lee.

Sir Douglas also said the Hudson's Bay Company in London was displeased with Chief Factor McLoughlin. Rumors circulated that he was "too helpful and friendly" with the arriving American missionaries. Perhaps Withycombe, sent to serve at the fort chapel, was really there to watch McLoughlin.

Savana inquired about the absence of Mrs. Warrender and her daughter, and Withycombe looked up from his journal.

"Miss Roslyn's under the weather, poor child. We may need to delay our departure, I'm told."

The thought of any postponement was disheartening,

since Savana was anxious to set sail. "Who mentioned a delay? Mrs. Warrender?"

"No, Sir Douglas."

She was surprised. "Roslyn appeared well last night at dinner."

"These trials do come upon her suddenly enough," he said. "She'll jump out of it. She's anxious for her wedding to take place at Fort Vancouver."

Savana frowned. "I hope she feels better by luncheon. We're expected to leave for San Francisco by then. Zoya and I are all packed. Have you seen my uncle?"

"He's out back somewhere continuing his morning hike. Sir Douglas, the jolly fellow, was up before the first bolt of foggy sky," he said dourly. "He kept me awake by pacing the floor all hours of the night. I had the misfortune of being given the smallest and shabbiest room of them all—the one below his. You might ask him," he said stiffly, "that if he must pace the floor over the outcome of Oregon, to do so in his stocking feet instead of his frontier boots."

She covered a smile. "I'll be certain to tell him," and seeing a basket of bread rolls on the table, she snatched one for her breakfast. They were still warm and sprinkled with plump, moist raisins, perhaps bought from some mission vineyard.

She came down the wooden steps that led out into a garden, where in summer, tall vines trailed across and down a roof-lattice.

The early morning was fresh and still, and this section of Fort Ross was as yet undisturbed by the colonists, usually up and doing chores. She caught a glimpse of a servant, an Aleut Indian brought from New Archangel. There were a number of them serving the Russians she'd been told, and she wondered if they were here of their own choice. Thinking of the Indians brought to mind her father's past labors among them and how he might have been sent as a prisoner to Siberia for his missionary work.

She wouldn't grieve for his treatment now. *He is alive,* she told herself again brightly, her heart singing with joy. And Peter had plans to aid the countess in ending his prison term.

The yard was yet dotted with pockets of fog, but the ocean wind was blowing them away and shaking the dead-looking vines that she guessed to be either grape or berry. She could see little in front of her except the branches which would slumber until awakened by the warmth of the short growing season.

She walked ahead toward the bare plateau that over-looked the Pacific Ocean, taking in deep breaths of the salt-laden wind. Sir Douglas could be seen walking along the cliff's edge, his rough knee-length coat flapping and his face toward the ocean. She called a cheery greeting and joined him on the windy oceanfront, noting his thoughtful scowl.

"Reverend Withycombe was right, after all. He said you kept him awake pacing."

"He did, did he? Well, the man's a noted complainer. How he'll fare at Fort Vancouver in service to His Majesty is no secret to the likes of me. He'll be squalling like a tomcat to get home to London after a month of living on salted salmon. Never mind Angus, I must talk to you about Fort Vancouver; a matter has come up of some concern."

She thought she knew what concerned him, and wrapped her arms around herself wishing she'd brought her cape. "If it's the delay caused by Roslyn's illness, I hope it doesn't mean we'll need to stay at Fort Ross longer than we planned."

"No, no, I've arranged other plans for you. Rather sudden changes, actually. I hope you won't mind."

He glanced at her, and she noted the thoughtful glint in his eyes. "What changes?"

"It's necessary you sail to Fort Vancouver without me."

The news came as a total surprise. "I don't understand. Without you?"

"You won't mind terribly, my dear, will you? At my age I'm ghastly company for a young and charming niece, whereas our dashing American Captain Wilder will prove a more interesting conversationalist—a gold mine of information for the British cause."

"Captain Wilder!"

She tensed, her eyes searching his leathery old face with its wily smile of good humor. His bristly brows shot up in a characteristic look of dubious surprise. "You're not afraid of the man, are you?"

"Afraid?" she found her voice. Was she? "Hardly that," she said defensively.

"Splendid, because I've arranged for you to voyage aboard his ship to Fort Vancouver. He'll be sailing a few weeks behind me, due to the healing of his arm, but that suits our cause fine. It will give me time to take care of a few matters at Fort Vancouver until you arrive. The Peter Skene Ogden expedition to the Stikine must be worked out with McLoughlin. And," he scowled, "I need to talk with Withycombe. He'll be there to discover the cause for McLoughlin's friendly interest in Jason Lee, but I've a notion Angus will do more harm butting heads with McLoughlin than he will be of aid to the Company." He looked at her. "Once you arrive at the fort, we'll sail on to Baranof Castle."

She continued to watch him, her tension growing. The last thing she wanted was to sail with Trace.

"I don't see why it's necessary to voyage aboard his vessel when I could just as easily sail with you and the baron."

"I won't be voyaging with Peter," he said. "Zoya is being sent ahead on the *Catherine* to prepare your stay at Baranof Castle. And I need you on the *Okanagan*."

The news was doubly disturbing, for she didn't wish to part with Zoya. She assumed the *Okanagan* was the name of Trace's ship. "Need me, for what?"

He reached for his cigar and, seeing he hadn't brought one, shoved his hands into his trouser pockets and began to walk the cliff's edge. Savana walked beside him, feeling the raw ocean wind buffeting her.

"Uncle, if you don't explain I shall burst."

"It's necessary for England that you voyage with Trace.

143

You're the one person who may have opportunity to unmask him."

She stopped. *Unmask him.* . . .

He looked at her insidiously. "He's as cool a gentleman as I've come up against, and I don't like it. You are another matter, my dear girl. He may appear aloof, but I've seen the way he's looked at you. Now, now, I'm not asking you to set aside your future relationship with Baron Sarakof by being friendly with Trace. It's information I need, and you can ask the sort of questions that I cannot."

"I think he's already said what he's about," she reminded him stiffly, feeling her face turn warm as she contemplated her uncle's suggestion that Trace found her becoming. "Money. He wishes furs. To trade. He admitted as much."

"And to me as well only last night. That may all be true, and I'm willing to give him the benefit of the doubt. There are men from Oregon in San Francisco now, one of them an American named Ewan Young. They're looking to buy cattle to bring back—I suspect for future American settlers. I received disturbing news late last night. A possibility that these cattle are owned by Wilder."

"He's said nothing to me. He talks in circles and seems to enjoy doing it. It's a game with him."

"Then learn what his game is. I think you're the woman who could do it."

She was about to flatly refuse on the basis of her Christian principles when Sir Douglas said thoughtfully, "That's what bothers me about Wilder; he leads me on a hound's chase after a rabbit that isn't there."

She couldn't help but smile. "There aren't many who can do that."

"No, and I don't like it," he said with a scowl.

"Then if you don't trust him, aren't you risking a good deal by this wheat venture?"

"Bah! I would lose the entire possibility of the pact with Russia without his blasted wheat! And there's more," he said and began walking again, this time more briskly.

Savana walked beside him in troubled silence. Things weren't going right. Did her plans ever work out the way she had hoped?

"Trace is friendly with Jason Lee," he said. "Too friendly for my peace of mind. I want you to find out aboard his ship what he and his brother have to do with the American missionaries at Fort Vancouver."

She voiced her surprise that Trace would associate with a missionary.

"The sun never sets on the British Empire, my dear. There is a reason for that. The British were made to rule. It's in our blood."

"You sound horribly arrogant, Uncle, like Governor Simpson and Lady Francis at Red River Settlement. The half-breed wives of his Company officials were deemed unsuitable company for his English bride."

He waved a hand. "Never mind that. . . ."

" 'A bit of brown' he calls the Indian women—"

"Savana, if you hope to learn your father's fate and discover what the Americans have planned north of the Columbia, then you must guard your tender emotions from becoming enmeshed in moral and social justice. You're not here on a crusade. All that can wait for the appropriate time."

She looked at him, troubled. "Just as long as that time truly comes. In London you didn't tell me I would need to spy on missionaries."

"Missionaries? Rubbish! Jason Lee is an American agent! We've England's interests in Oregon Country to think of. It is loyalty to His Majesty that must inspire us both. Your interest in the work of Jason Lee is essential."

"Why should he trust me? I'm not a missionary, nor am I an American, and Trace knows it. He'll see through my questions at once."

"I've taken care of that. No need to be concerned. You'll tell him you've been sent by the British Foreign Mission Society."

She stirred uncomfortably. "He knows why I'm here and

it has nothing to do with missions—"

"In a way it does," he interrupted. "James was involved with the Aleut."

"The Aleut have nothing to do with the Americans' work near Fort Vancouver."

He waved a hand and again impatiently searched for a cigar that wasn't there. "No matter. You'll tell him you've been sent to journal the success of their methods with the Indians."

"Uncle, that's coming very close to betraying the Lord's cause!"

"It isn't, my dear, it isn't. For one thing Lee and his brother are only a front for President Jackson to win Oregon. And Trace is little better. The scoundrel is out to best me where Oregon's concerned—if he can. If anyone is masquerading as wolves in sheep's clothing it's the hypocritical Americans!"

"But—are you certain of this? How do you know Jason Lee has more on his mind than teaching Christianity to the Indians?"

"I am most certain. The American President won't admit it, but sending agents to the Columbia posing as missionaries affords excellent opportunity to spy on us. We, Savana, shall beat Jackson at his own game."

"This has nothing to do with New Archangel—"

"It has everything to do with it. Whether it's Jason Lee at Fort Vancouver, or the Boston traders selling goods to the Russians, it comes out the same: We're in a race to win Oregon. And America is the one we must defeat."

Even if she agreed with his reasoning, the battle seemed hopeless. "If you're correct, then Jason Lee is only the beginning," she protested. "There will be other agents."

"There are, indeed. In particular, two men who pose a threat to British expansion in the Northwest. And that's where you will come in. I'm expecting a message from one of our agents in Washington City. I should have received it in San Francisco. I believe he was intercepted on the wharf by an American agent."

She tensed. *The wharf . . . could Trace have thought Yuri was that agent?* But Yuri was Russian. Still—what better cover for an agent to appear Russian?

"We suspect President Jackson has received financial backing from Boston investors to build Independence, Missouri, into a supply town. They'll use Independence for launching a future exodus of American immigrants by wagon train to settle Oregon."

"By land! Isn't that impossible? It's never been done before. How could they possibly cross the mountains?"

"Maybe not impossible at all for the right wagon train master. He'll need an excellent scout. If the wagon train is successful, it will mean Oregon will fall to Boston by default once they arrive to settle by the thousands. We must stop it from happening."

"That's madness, Uncle; what can I do to stop a wagon train?"

"From Trace you can learn much. Find out if Reverend Lee has come with secret plans to set up a provisional government once the wagon train is launched. Discover if he's there to help route the first band of settlers from Independence to the Columbia. And more importantly, I want to confirm the names of the two American men who are working with Lee."

Her heart pounded. "I could never accomplish all that!"

"For England?" He slipped an arm around her shoulders. "You can, and you will. Those two Americans know the Great Plains and the Rockies. One is on friendly terms with the Indians and will be the lead scout for that future wagon train. One of them has traveled through Oregon Territory several times. If they can be stopped, it may give England just enough time to move in our settlers from Canada and beat them at their own game."

Savana felt very cold and stood looking at him as the ocean wind ruffled her hair. She thought she knew what Sir

Douglas was thinking, for the same thought was rampaging through her own mind. *Obviously the two men are Trace and Yancey Wilder.* Yet she could not bring herself to speak their names aloud.

"I have my suspicions about one of those men even now, but I could be wrong." He looked at her shrewdly. "I need to play along with him for the present. You're the bait."

"Uncle—"

"Don't worry. If I didn't know he was a gentleman, I wouldn't let you board his ship." He chuckled. "It's Wilder who is in trouble—I've confidence in you, my dear."

*What about me?* she thought. *Is not the risk mine?*

"Once I'm through with him, Russian America will offer many interesting prospects for seeing to his demise."

Her eyes swerved to his. "What do you mean?"

He chuckled. "Don't look so pale; I'm not speaking of his death. No, nothing like that. You'll sail on his ship, Savana. You'll learn everything you can about what he and Yancey Wilder are up to in the Northwest, and with Jason Lee. By the time you arrive at Fort Vancouver and we sail to Baranof Castle, you'll have done a double duty. A noble work for your country."

Her loyalties belonged to England, and she felt no qualm at spying for the king against Boston. But spying on the missionaries? Whether they were Americans or British—her pretense seemed a dreadful thing to resort to. It was treason of the worst sort—not to His Majesty King George, but to the King of kings.

Did not the loyalty uniting Christians in their labors for their Master go beyond nationality and politics?

Savana felt the wind softly touch her and glanced up into the gray sky where rain clouds had unexpectedly gathered and sprinkled her face with tiny cold droplets.

"It's not as if you're betraying your faith," he said kindly, as if reading her mind. "It is the so-called missionaries under Lee's banner who have laid the groundwork of deceit. And Trace is using their cover for his own government. You'll do well, Savana. And it won't last long. Only a month aboard his ship. Then we'll be off to Baranof Castle to meet the countess and see what we can discover about your father's disappearance. Who knows, my dear? This may all have a blessed ending, after all."

*A blessed ending?*

# 12

## DIVIDED LOYALTIES

When they arrived back in San Francisco, they waited several more days before any word came about their plans to embark for Fort Vancouver. Savana began to wonder if perhaps Captain Wilder was deliberately delaying his response to Sir Douglas about taking her on as a passenger. Though she had not seen Trace since the official dinner at the Russian fort, she had learned from asking about the headquarters that there was a problem in loading the wheat. What may have caused the delay no one seemed to know. But Sir Douglas was involved in smoothing out the cause for concern with Señor Don Diego, and she heard that progress was being made.

Nor had she heard from the baron since the night of their meeting when he had given her the Rezanov diamonds. She later learned that he had not departed as he had first intimated. He and Sir Douglas had traveled on horseback to

Monterey—a rather odd set of circumstances, thought Savana, wondering.

It came as no surprise when Uncle Douglas arrived a week later to inform her that she would indeed voyage on Captain Wilder's ship the *Okanagan*, along with Mrs. Warrender and Roslyn. Her uncle was obliged to sail with Reverend Withycombe and the baron aboard the *Catherine* as far as Fort Vancouver, where her uncle would then wait for Trace to arrive with the wheat. From there, the three of them would voyage from the British fort on to Baranof Castle.

"What about the perfectly good British ship the *Beaver*?" inquired Angus.

"Ah, she's set sail for Honolulu, my good man. There's sickness aboard, says the captain. They're in quarantine. But don't be alarmed, Mrs. Warrender. Your daughter has none of the symptoms of the crew. The doctor assures us she's getting stronger every day."

Savana wondered if he were telling all the truth, but her uncle's expression was benign.

Reverend Withycombe was frowning over the change in plans. "What about the wheat?"

"The deal is settled and Baron Sarakof is satisfied. Captain Wilder is in the process of overseeing its loading now. He'll be sailing from San Francisco Wednesday morning."

Savana followed her uncle to the door and asked quietly, "What did you discover about Captain Wilder at Monterey?"

Her uncle's eyes flashed with ill humor. "If he's involved in this cattle drive and American plans to settle Oregon, he's covered himself well. The Mexican governor at Monterey insists Wilder's a citizen as he claims, and a partner with Diego in shipping. A bit much if you ask me, but the governor could not be bribed into telling what he knows." His brows hunched together. "I may be wrong about Trace, after all."

"I'm not convinced," whispered Savana. "The fact he does so well to erase his trail tells me we need to be more cautious of him than I thought."

With Roslyn steadily improving, Savana reluctantly boarded the carriage with the others in the party as planned and rode to the wharf. The morning was chill, and the familiar fog hung over the hills and bay on their last morning in California.

Stepping from the carriage onto the wharf with its suspicions and memory of Yuri, Savana looked back toward San Francisco with a final goodbye. Russian Hill, named for the sailors who died exploring the coast and were buried on the hilltop, was draped in mist. Russian Fort Ross would soon be sold to Sutter, and the Russians living there would find their way to New Archangel or choose to settle elsewhere in the Pacific Northwest. Imperial Russia's foothold in California was fast crumbling, and even Mexico was locked in a duel with the United States over the destiny of Texas. The Pacific Northwest would be different, she thought. This time England would not lose.

Savana turned her back to the past and looked forward to the Columbia River and farther north to Russian America and Baranof Castle. As she did, her gray eyes fell uneasily upon the fair ship *Okanagan* that was to bring her to the British fort on the first half of her voyage.

As her eyes moved over the ship they came to rest upon Captain Trace Wilder, dressed as she had first seen him that morning when he had so *magnanimously* rescued her from the falling pelts.

He stood watching her, the gray drizzle wetting his black hat and pea coat. She drew her white hooded cape protectively about her, feeling the cool wetness on her face. How would she ever discover his true mission?

Was he as innocent of the clandestine as he insisted? For a moment she found herself earnestly hoping that he was indeed an independent privateer and rancher, partner of Don Diego.

# 13

# THE CAPTAIN OF THE *OKANAGAN*

Captain Trace Wilder retained a bland expression as he watched Savana board. He believed he understood the motive behind Sir Douglas Bellomont's unexpected arrangements to have his niece sail aboard his ship as far as Fort Vancouver, while he pretended an urgent need to depart with the baron aboard the *Catherine*. Savana was under orders to try to learn whether or not he was an American agent. Both she and Bellomont were right in their assessment of him, of course. He was an agent for President Andrew Jackson, and the task set before him was formidable.

He smiled faintly to himself as he leaned against the rail watching her. What she didn't know was that he wasn't going to allow her to disembark at British Fort Vancouver, nor was he going to bring her to the baron.

She was his prisoner for the present, and would remain aboard his ship until his own mission was accomplished.

He straightened, scanning her. In the meantime it might

be interesting to enjoy her company. In order to learn what she could for England, she would need to change her tactics and become much more friendly with the "Boston clod." A few pleasant dinners together in his cabin and a stroll or two around the deck would be enjoyable. Of course she was going to be furious when she discovered he had seen through her plans all along and was enjoying leading her on, but this was one British spy that might be setting a trap to catch him. He would allow himself to be caught—in due time, of course.

His contact at New Archangel had informed him that Count Aleksandr did not approve of Baron Peter Sarakof as head of the Imperial Navy there. There'd been trouble over the seizure of a French merchant vessel and the jailing of the crew. France was making a robust fuss over the incident, and Count Aleksandr had been called to answer for it, something he did not like. Did Sarakof know this, and was he making his own plans to protect himself against Count Aleksandr?

Circumstances had worked out better than he had expected. If Savana were aboard to learn his plans, it was equally true that he intended to discover from her what it was that Sarakof expected of her at Baranof Castle.

He had first thought Savana to be a complication that he didn't want added to his mission. But the flaxen-haired girl, as lovely as a white rose, as frosty and unreachable as the snowy-capped glaciers, might hold the key to more than his legal entry into Russian-American waters.

His eyes narrowed as he watched his steward and several husky Hawaiian crewmen hustling to load the women's trunks. Mrs. Warrender and her daughter Roslyn would be secretly transferred to another agent's ship going to Fort Vancouver on the north bank of the Columbia River, but Savana would remain aboard the *Okanagan*. The baron was a dangerous man. Trace had made up his mind that he wasn't going to turn the lamb over to the drooling wolf until he had at least pulled his teeth and defanged him.

In the meantime . . . there was much to learn from Savana. But he must let her make the first moves—after all, he thought with a faint smile, she was on a secret mission for King George.

Trace wondered whether or not he could break through that stilted British reserve. He'd like to discover whether she was in love with Sarakof, or if the marriage had been family arranged. He felt a prick of irritation. She thought him an unpolished clod in comparison to the insufferable Russian baron. Just how much did she know about him? Was her loyalty to England or to Russia? Or was it to some other cause—learning about her mother and father?

Because of his assignment he had already learned a good deal about her. She was twenty—considered old by England's standards for not being married—but the Bellomont family had big plans for her and Baron Sarakof. Her father, Sir James Mackenzie, was a legend among the French voyagers in Canada. He had led his own brigade of trappers for the North West Company before it sold out to the Hudson's Bay Company after the debacle at America's first foothold in Oregon, a fort by the Pacific called Astoria. America had lost it to England in the recent war, but the Boston men had turned around and won the battle at York.

He'd been told by Senator Baxter that Savana's father had been considered a maverick by the Bellomont and Mackenzie families, and as a lad had left his home in Scotland to work for the Hudson's Bay Company. His sister had been sent to school in London, where she had become close friends with one of the English Bellomont daughters, and had ended up marrying Sir Douglas.

MacKenzie had raised Savana for some years, and then had come to realize that his daughter could do better in England. He had sent for his sister, who had come to see the child first—to "make certain she's not a half-breed."

The flaxen hair and gray eyes had convinced her that her maverick brother had fathered a daughter by a fair woman of Russian blood at New Archangel, a woman related to the countess. Little Savana deserved better in life than Mac-

Kenzie could give her, so Lady Hillary had brought her to Bellomont House.

Senator Baxter had informed him of all this in St. Louis the night before Trace departed to fulfill his mission. He thought he knew more about Savana's mother than she did, but even he didn't have all the truth. The key to the puzzle was missing. What was it that the baron knew?

Mrs. Warrender's pleasant voice interrupted his contemplations as she called to him from across the deck and, realizing that he'd forgotten his social duties as captain, left the upper deck and came down the short steps where Mrs. Warrender stood with her daughter Roslyn and Savana.

Mrs. Warrender was her usual self now that her young daughter was well on her way to recovery, a polite, genteel woman who thought him a dear friend. Roslyn, whom he had heard would marry some Company teacher at Fort Vancouver, watched him with a gleam in her eyes that he pretended not to notice—as all gentlemen did. Savana stood looking as frosty as ever, gazing out at some noisy sea gulls as though it were a rare sight demanding her full-orbed attention.

"Ah, my dear ladies," he said smoothly. "Welcome aboard the *Okanagan*."

"How good of you to give up your cabin to us, Captain Wilder. You're quite certain you're not put out by us?"

He restrained a smile. Of course he was put out, and didn't look forward to sleeping with the overcrowded, ill-smelling crew below, but she wished to receive his gentlemanly denial. "My privilege, Mrs. Warrender. I hope I can make your voyage as comfortable as possible. I'm afraid the three of you will find it a little cramped, however."

"We'll make do, Captain. There'll be no selfish complaints from us. Come, girls, the men have brought our trunks to the cabin."

Roslyn smiled at him and swept by in frills and feathers, following the more sedately dressed Mrs. Warrender. Trace looked pointedly at Savana.

"What? No word of sweet appreciation, Miss Mackenzie?"

She paused, somewhat uneasily, and while he read nothing but propriety in her expression, he noticed the faint color in her cheeks as their eyes held disconcertingly, and she managed a friendly smile.

"Yes, I—umm—look forward to sailing with you, Captain Wilder."

He pretended gravity and offered a bow. "I assure you, Miss Mackenzie, the feeling is mutual."

She seemed to analyze his expression, and he lifted a brow, trying not to smile.

"How many days until we rendezvous with my uncle at Fort Vancouver?"

"Oh, perhaps two or three weeks. Depends."

She tensed slightly. "On what, Captain?"

He glanced casually at the sky. "Oh, the weather, the wind—" and he looked at her. "And a few other things."

Her eyes narrowed slightly but she was quick to smile. He smiled too. "Nothing to concern yourself with."

"Good. I should hate to keep Sir Douglas waiting at Fort Vancouver for my arrival."

"Yes, that would be a tragedy."

Her eyes came swiftly to his, searching uneasily.

"The wheat," he said with a grave expression, "must reach New Archangel in the name of His Majesty."

"Yes . . ."

A brief silence hung between them and he tried to divert her thoughts. "You can, of course, Miss Mackenzie, make do with the wearisome company of a passel of Yankees till then?"

The cold, damp drizzle that had been falling when they arrived at the wharf had given place to a steady downpour that began to run off his hat and down the back of his neck, and he must have unexpectedly frowned, for a faint smile touched her lips as she drew her white fur cape about her.

"I shall survive, thank you. I think, sir, it is you who are more likely to be inclined toward boredom, which makes me wonder about you."

A glimmer of alertness showed in his flint blue eyes. "Oh?"

"Yes," she said sweetly. "A man who cannot only sail a ship but also lead a cattle drive with equal agility is curious indeed. What else do you do?"

He smiled wryly at the mild accusation in her tone and the look of humor.

"Dare I read from your inquiry the faintest suggestion of friendly curiosity toward the mysterious Yankee, Trace Wilder, Miss Mackenzie? Or may I assume that you question my ability as captain of the *Okanagan*?"

"Perhaps you assume too much, Captain."

"I assure you I sail a ship better than I handle ornery long-horned steer. I sailed the waters of the Northwest Coast long before I ever became partners with Diego."

She laughed. "I suspect your partnership with Señor Diego is a mere convenience, which you can relinquish with sudden ease. Am I right?"

He smiled pleasantly. "You're getting wet . . . and we haven't even left the harbor yet."

"So I am. You will excuse me, Captain?"

"Until dinner. Unfortunately it's not French cuisine. I think the Colonel has something very British cooked up for you and Mrs. Warrender."

"Perhaps Paris cuisine another time, Captain."

He held her gaze. She managed a smile and then, without another word, turned and went to the cabin.

He looked after her thoughtfully, frowning a little. She wore spiked armor beneath that soft fur. Trying to break through promised a task more unpredictable than facing down the Russkies' gunboats.

If Savana's curiosity on the subject of Trace Wilder and

his brother Yancey seemed to be going nowhere, she was gratified that Mrs. Warrender and Roslyn were also interested, undoubtedly for different reasons. But if his three passengers were interested in Trace, it could also be said that he managed to return the compliment, and Savana wondered how it was that in the end, the answers to his questions seemed always to revert back to her, and what she avoided explaining was offered by Mrs. Warrender.

During the dinner, the degree of his courtesy toward them alerted Savana that he was being deliberately so, and she tried to guess his motives. What did he expect to find out about her?

"So you've come from London, from Bellomont House?" he asked.

"Yes," she said simply, and looked at the silver fork. It was of exquisite design. A strange commodity aboard a vessel that carried furs. "I saw your family portrait there," she couldn't resist saying. "Your grandfather had it removed during the war."

Mrs. Warrender made an awkward attempt to change the subject, but Savana refused to be detoured. "Aunt Hillary showed it to me. It looked to have been painted on a Virginia plantation. Yancey held the reins of the most gorgeous horse I've ever seen."

She watched his response, but if he felt any irritation it wasn't visible, though she noted something flicker in his eyes.

"He loved that horse. Called him Yankee. You'd appreciate that name, ladies."

Mrs. Warrender gave a small laugh as did Roslyn, but Savana did not.

"Unfortunately the British soldiers took him."

"When they burned the plantation?" she asked pointedly, hoping her bluntness would break through his guard.

"Yes," he said, nothing in his voice, "after they burned it." He held her gaze. "Yancey never forgave them—but then, he was a year younger than I, and more hotheaded."

"But you have," she said smoothly, "*forgiven* the British."

"Savana dear, would you like more tea?" asked Mrs. Warrender.

"How could I not forgive the past when it's now represented by three lovely English ladies?" he stated silkily.

"How kind of you to say so, Captain," said Mrs. Warrender. "War is such a dreadful thing. May God grant we never have another one between us. England and America share so much in common—"

"Especially interest in Oregon Country," interjected Savana with a smile, and was surprised when he laughed. For some reason she was not upsetting him but affording cynical amusement. He immediately turned back to his own questions, watching her with that faint smile on his mouth.

"So you've come from Bellomont House, where you saw our accursed family portrait, did you? And Zoya, she voyaged with you as a companion?"

She hesitated. "Yes, Zoya."

"But she's not with you now. She remained at Fort Ross?"

"No. She went on to New Archangel with the baron."

"Rather odd."

"She was needed to prepare for my visit. She speaks both Russian and English."

"So does Sarakof," he reminded her.

She smiled. "But Peter doesn't tell the Russian maids how to prepare my room, or a hundred other small but important matters concerning my visit with the countess."

"Zoya is a relative on the Russian side of your mother's family?"

She hesitated again. "No. She was my mother's maid before she died."

"I see. Then she went with you to Bellomont House?"

"Yes, she practically raised me in London."

"And Sir Bellomont was made your legal guardian after your father's death?"

She noticed that he spoke of her father in the past tense, even though for her the question remained unanswered.

"No, my father's sister, Lady Hillary."

"Ah yes, dear Lady Hillary and her worrisome concerns."
Trace watched her. "You've been in the Northwest Territories before?"

"Yes. After my mother died and Zoya brought me to my
father, we left New Archangel for Red River Colony. I lived
the first ten years of my life there."

"And now she's come to marry Baron Peter Sarakof,"
said Roslyn. "And to aid Sir Douglas in the cause of England."

He smiled. "You're very patriotic, Miss Mackenzie. Will
you be sorely disappointed if Oregon ends up with an American flag flying in the wind?"

"It is my ambition, Captain Wilder, to see it doesn't. But
actually, it's New Archangel I'm interested in, and my father's work there before he disappeared. He worked with the
Aleut."

"A noble cause. And you've arrived here after stopping
at the Hudson's Bay Company post in Honolulu?"

"Honolulu, yes . . ." Her eyes came to his, and they were
distracting.

"How long do you expect to stay at Baranof Castle? Not
that I mean to pry, Miss Mackenzie."

"I don't know yet until I meet with my grandmother.
What of you, Captain? I suppose your friend Mr. Fletcher is
the reason you've decided to work for the Company and
England?"

"He's part of the reason. I think I mentioned the need for
money."

She wondered whether to believe him. "Do you really
have a partnership with Diego?"

He smiled. "Among other dealings, yes."

She wondered what else he could mean. Again, Mrs.
Warrender made an attempt to steer Savana away from her
pointed questions, but Savana noticed she did nothing when
Trace questioned her. *Strange, I could almost think she was a
Boston sympathizer,* Savana thought.

The blue Pacific waters rolled to the horizon, which was dull gold in the late afternoon when Trace came on deck. The *Okanagan* must not reach Fort Vancouver, so he set his course for Portland and farther north toward New Archangel.

A good wind was kicking up whitecaps around them, and the *Okanagan*'s bow pointed toward the cold northern seas as though anxious for the mission ahead.

Trace, wet with flying spray, stood at the wheel beside the Nez Perce Indian named John Wesley, watching the ship move along under a full head of sail. Trace's sea boots and oilskins were glimmering wet, the sky was gray and dense with rain clouds, but the wind was their friend.

"How does this trip compare to maneuvering in the Stikine?" asked Trace.

Eighteen-year-old John Wesley, who had been educated at the Methodist mission school in the East and was a friend of Yancey and now Trace, grinned.

"Flying-fish sailing, Cap'n. I have fallen in love with her." And he patted the wheel, his black eyes twinkling. "I'll get one of my own someday. And fill her with skins to sell to China. Then I plan to buy a bigger ship."

"You're never satisfied," said Trace and smiled. "Soon you'll want to capture a Russian patrol boat."

"Good idea, Cap'n. Maybe Fletcher will help us when you get him out of the Russky salt mine."

"I'm certain he'd love the opportunity."

"I'll help too." He touched his dagger.

Trace smiled. "Better stick with salmon and beaver."

Trace went below to study the charts again, glancing at Colonel Pelly asleep in his bunk, his old body swaying to the light roll of the schooner. Pelly had gone with Trace's father in the war to attend his needs, and in his devotion had nearly died seeing to Zachary's wounds during and after the onslaught. His devotion was now offered to Trace. There'd never been a time while growing up in Virginia that he couldn't remember the old Scotchman Pelly being around the plantation, and as a boy, Trace had thought him to be ancient. He was perhaps sixty, but as sharp in memory as an eagle. His white hair was clipped short, and his wide mustache was oiled and curled upward.

Because Pelly had followed his father to war, Trace and Yancey had affectionately dubbed him "the Colonel."

Trace sat down at the desk and studied his charts—a prize that any East or West Indiaman would have sighed over if they had them.

If the wind held they would make good time—well ahead of his ally, Captain Dembe, who secretly carried the wheat for New Archangel.

Hours later, when he came down to shake John Wesley awake, the mate opened his eyes at once, alert as a tiger ready to spring.

"How are the wings of heaven, Cap'n?"

"The wind's holding. We're making knots. But looks stormy." Trace took off his oilskin. "It's raining, and we're drinking spray, but the wind is for us."

John Wesley was quickly on his bare feet, slipping into a deerskin tunic and moccasins.

Colonel Pelly held steady as he poured the three of them heavy black coffee. Trace tasted it and spat it out. "What is this, Colonel, boiled-down chicory?"

The Colonel grinned. "Dandelion leaves, roots, and sorghum. Ain't none better in all Virginny."

"Tastes like rat poison."

"Never satisfied. Nothing like your pa—thankful to the good Lord for everything, includin' my coffee when there weren't the real thing to be had."

"I'll wait." Trace pulled off his wet shirt and tossed it on a nail, anxious for his turn to sleep.

"You figurin' on trouble at New Archangel?" asked the Colonel.

"The cap'n likes trouble," teased John Wesley. "That is

165

why he gave his cabin to three females. Even one brings trouble, but now he's got three troubles!"

"There won't be any trouble if Count Aleksandr is wise enough to listen to our information."

The Colonel chuckled. "Ol' Crackerjack Bellomont won't be liking his wheat delivered under the Star-Spangled Banner. Wait till he finds out how you made him eat possum! He won't like being fooled none."

"If I can deliver the wheat and delay the treaty with the Hudson's Bay Company, I won't be seeing Bellomont," said Trace.

"You better hope so if you aim on keeping Miss Mackenzie happy with you."

Trace looked at him but said nothing. He knew she would be furious when she found out he had no intention of delivering wheat under the British flag to New Archangel, and that his working for Hudson's Bay had been a bluff. The wheat was on Captain Dembe's ship, and by now Dembe would be nearing their rendezvous and expecting to meet up with him near New Archangel.

John Wesley went up to the wheel and Trace fell wearily onto his bunk.

"And when you deliver that good ol' American wheat to the count, what then?" asked the Colonel, looking uncomfortable. "You got any ideas to see us avoid that Russian baron named Sarakof and his patrol boats? It won't be jes' Sirrah Bellomont that'll be as ornery as a riled bear. How you goin' to get us outer there, huh?"

Trace closed his eyes and saw nothing but the wide sea rolling before him. "We unload the wheat as quickly as Count Aleksandr permits, buy whatever supplies are to be had, then lay a course for Fort Vancouver to Jason Lee. We'll wait for Ewan Young to arrive with the California cattle and make plans for the wagon train."

"All this we're going to do I 'spect, 'fer Baron Sarakof gets his patrol boat to watching us. I say we're in a heap of trouble."

Trace smiled. "Don't worry, Colonel. I can handle it. You just make certain Bellomont's niece remains quietly aboard ship."

The Colonel cocked an eye at him. "And what you going to tell her when you bring her back to Fort Vancouver? She'll be madder than a wet hen chased by a hornet, if you ask me."

Trace turned his head on the pillow and looked at him. "She'll thank me before it's over. Sarakof has plans to use her to his own ends. I don't know just how yet, but I aim to find out before it's over."

"That won't help your hide if Sarakof gets you. Then what? I ain't chipper enough to go hunting you up in Siberia somewhere, and Yancey is likely to get himself hung trying."

Trace frowned and rolled in his bunk. He covered his eyes with his pillow. "One thing at a time, Pelly."

# 14

## PALE-HEARTED MOON

Outside the hull, just beyond her ear, Savana could hear the whispering wash of the sea, rustling by with its strange secrets, its untold tales. They were about two weeks out of San Francisco, and except for brief discourses at dinner, she'd not been able to learn much from Trace.

It was toward evening, and she felt restless in the cabin with Roslyn napping and Mrs. Warrender asleep in the chair. She slipped her cloak over her shoulders and left the cabin in hopes of finding the captain alone. Usually one of his crew was with him, either the grinning, handsome Indian named John Wesley or the shrew-eyed old Southerner, the Colonel. Perhaps tonight would be different since the ship seemed strangely quiet. She believed they were nearing the Oregon coast, perhaps Astoria. She had heard that Astoria was a Boston fort begun by the American John Jacob Astor, a man who had made great wealth in his business ventures and who was now in New York.

On deck, she found the wide expanse of the sky a silvery gray with the last of the day's light, and there was an unusual glow in the ocean—what the Colonel had told her was "phosphorus" in the water. There would be no stars tonight, or if the wind blew the clouds away, only mere silvery glint between broken clouds. She felt oddly content with the deck moving beneath her feet and the Oregon coastal wind tugging at her cloak and chilling her face.

She made her way to find Trace, hoping he had not yet gone below. She had asked John Wesley earlier that morning when the captain's watch would begin, and the young Indian had told her he had the night watch this time. Colonel Pelly would host the dinner table and serve his Virginia ham and chick-peas—delicacies he had been saving for a special occasion.

Savana was certain the Colonel would be disappointed if she were not thrilled. The old Colonel seemed to smile at her a lot, as though he guessed some interest in Trace Wilder that she was trying to cover up.

She waited quietly as John Wesley gave her a seat and urged her to keep her hands on the bar at all times.

"Water is rough. A storm is on its way, I think. Are you cold?"

She smiled. "No, I'm . . . I'm all right, thank you. I'll just sit here awhile if you don't mind. I won't bother you, will I?"

He smiled, his black eyes dancing. "Bother me? Uh-uh. You sure bother the captain, though. He'll be coming soon, but don't tell him I said so. He'll throw me over the side and tell me to swim back to shore—he has bad humor, Miss Mackenzie."

Savana laughed and found herself liking the young man even more. She had been told he was a Nez Perce Indian from Oregon Country along the Columbia, and that he had gotten his seasoned experience working with Trace for the past four years. He was dressed in an unlikely outfit—the loose, ruffled white shirt of a dashing California vaquero along with fringed buckskin trousers and moccasins from his tribe. He wore no beads or Indian charms, but there was a lone feather braided into his sleek black long hair.

Savana began to think that all of her expectations of what Americans and Indians were really like were erroneous. His black eyes sparkled and his grin contradicted the stoic personality that she'd been told to expect from Indians. Neither was he silent, but he talked incessantly, which Savana found to her advantage.

"Tell me about Captain Wilder."

"There is too much to tell. He has many faces."

"That doesn't surprise me. How did you get the name of the famous English Methodist minister?"

"I chose it."

"You did!"

"Why not? I have other names too. My first birth name is Illutin. I chose a Christian name for my second birth. Cap'n said Jason Lee is a man like John Wesley, and because Jason Lee told me of the Lord, I took the name of Wesley. Jason Lee taught me that God is not the Lord of one people, but all of Adam's wayward children. You see, I was raised in the mission school after many people in my tribe died from an epidemic. Great White Eagle doctored our people at the fort. Trace was there too, bringing back pelts from the French Canadians. And Trace doctored me. He said I should have a second name because I lived again."

She mulled all this over in her mind and wasn't certain what to think of this new Trace Wilder. It had been much easier to dislike him. "Great White Eagle?" she asked.

John Wesley grinned at her. "It is what the Indians call McLoughlin who runs Fort Vancouver. We all call him that."

"And you came to California with Captain Wilder to work at the rancho?"

He shook his head with disdain. "No, we both love the sea. I voyaged with him from the Bay to Vancouver to China to Vancouver again . . . sometimes to Alaska."

She asked too casually, "What does he do in Alaska?"

He laughed. "You ask him that. He claims I talk too much—that I'm destined to be a preacher like my name. Trace says they all talk long."

Savana smiled, and they were interrupted by footsteps. She turned her head and saw Trace coming to stand his watch. Her eyes narrowed slightly as he shrugged into a dark blue wool sweater, which complemented his muscular build, and a blue woolen sea cap. He carried his oilskins under his arm.

*Most becoming,* she thought with a twinge of guilt, although she behaved indifferently, sitting straighter, chin lifted like true Rezanov nobility.

He apparently hadn't noticed her as he walked along the deck, studying the black, glistening water as the waves rose and then slid away beneath the hull.

"See anything?" he called to John Wesley.

"No sign of any ship, Cap'n. We are a tiny fish alone, lost in a world of water, dancing upon the sea with a heart beating like a drum to the rhythm of the singing waves and talking wind."

"Poet! You must be thinking of a sweet squa—" He stopped when he saw her.

Savana stood, holding to the rail to steady herself, brushing the hair away from her face with her free hand. "Hope I'm not interrupting. I grew restless in the cabin and wanted fresh air."

Trace made no direct reply but walked aft and took the wheel. John Wesley moved aside and grinned, his black hair whipping like canvas in the wind. "You came just in time, Cap'n."

"Sea's getting rough and it's likely to get rougher," he told John Wesley. "Anything of interest out there?"

John Wesley pointed. "Thought I saw a light ahead of us . . . maybe it was only an early star."

"Hang around in earshot. I may want you again."

172

"Aye, Cap'n."

Savana caught the odd exchange. She watched as Trace stared out to sea, and then as if troubled turned his attention to the wheel. John Wesley quietly slipped into the nearby shadows.

Savana sat down again, hoping the flush in her cheeks was attributed to the wind and cold. To take the initiative in being friendly with a man was foreign to her, and the captain of the *Okanagan* was enough man to undo her feminine confidence.

She listened to the sea and, as John Wesley described it, "the talking wind." A pale moon came and went behind the clouds and shone above the foremast while the northern sea rushed past in the half-darkness. Spray blew against their faces. She knew she must say something to get the discussion going her way even if it was audacious—anything to take him off guard.

"You asked if John Wesley had seen anything. Are you expecting a Russian patrol boat?" she said lightly, and her words evoked the response she expected. His head turned toward her, and he reached up to pull his hat lower.

"You're going to get sopping wet if you keep me company for long. Maybe you better go below while it's still safe."

"My, aren't we pleasant tonight!"

"I've seen better nights at sea."

"You must not have slept well. Are you sorry you gave us your cabin?"

"I'd prefer my own bunk and the solitude of my cabin, yes, if that's what you are suggesting. I hope you're sleeping well?" he asked wryly.

She was conscious of an unexpected annoyance when she saw his faint smile, as though something about her amused him. She smiled sweetly. "Actually, quite well."

She stood beside him at the wheel, hands clasped behind her. "Do I afford you amusement? Pray tell why?"

"It's always a delightful surprise when I can guess what

goes on in a woman's mind. And your mind, as they say, is an open book."

She looked at him defensively. "I suppose you do a great deal of reading the minds of women? A waste of precious time, I would think."

"Perhaps more like playing Russian roulette. Trying to guess what a woman wants is a dangerous game, but intriguing."

Her color deepened and she looked out to sea. "I doubt if you know my mind, Captain Wilder, least of all what I want."

"You're wrong."

She refused to look at him, the tone of his voice causing her heart to beat faster.

"You want information," came his smooth reply. "And you want it badly enough to set aside your English upbringing."

"I beg your pardon, but I haven't set aside anything. Least of all being English."

"I beg to differ. We both know that a young woman devoted to her English upbringing would be scandalized by going anywhere without a female chaperone whose jackal eye is on the prowl for the appearance of rakes and boors."

Savana felt her flush deepen.

"I can only imagine what dedication to His Majesty and to your dear, dear uncle Douglas caused you to decide to come meet me under the fading moon."

"Maybe you're wrong. Maybe you underestimate yourself. Maybe I came because—" She stopped as her gaze locked with his, the intensity bringing embarrassment.

"I wouldn't try that approach if I were you. You might be asking for more than you bargained for."

The ship rolled to the side and he caught her with one arm, her cheek brushing the rough wool of his sweater.

He casually kept his other hand on the wheel. "If you're going to stand here, better hold on to the rail with both hands."

She stepped back and held on tightly, but if he were as disturbed as she, he didn't show it.

"What is it Bellomont asked you to find out?"

She glanced at him sharply.

"By the way—you won't need that derringer you've got hidden in your pocket."

Her hand touched the pistol. "I thought I might need it in Indian territory. And it's a Russian pistol."

"So Baron Sarakof does understand the iron backbone in his fragile flaxen beauty."

"He didn't give it to me, but if he heard you say that—"

"No? Where'd you get it?"

She turned to stare out at the sea. "Zoya, when she knew I'd be voyaging alone—with you, an American," she said with a deliberate slight.

"Yet you were wise enough to not tell Bellomont about our meeting on the wharf. Did you tell your Russian maid?"

"No," she admitted quietly, then warned, "which doesn't mean I won't inform Sir Douglas at the right time, and Zoya too for that matter, just as soon as I believe it's beneficial to my personal interests."

"What did Bellomont ask you to find out from me? Did he advise you to use your feminine wiles on my poor innocent heart? I'm ashamed of you, Savana. Trying to take advantage of my masculine weakness—like Delilah and poor Samson."

The ship lurched, and this time she held firmly to the rail with both hands to avoid falling into his arms again. She smiled. "I'm afraid I'd make a poor Delilah. But I think you're horrid to accuse me."

"When you're trying to trap me into giving information you want for Sir Bellomont? Or perhaps it's Sarakof you're trying to help."

"You have a way of rearranging my words to make them what you want to hear. My uncle has good reason to doubt your loyalty to England. And remember, you were on the wharf the morning of Yuri's death."

"Is that why you have the pistol? Maybe you think I killed him. Yet you're aboard my ship."

"I hardly think you'll kill me and throw me overboard, Captain. But you were the last man to be seen on the wharf that morning."

"But I wasn't the last one to see Yuri alive." His brow lifted. "You were. Maybe you shot him with that sweet little Russian pistol."

"You couldn't think that of me—"

"Why not?" He smiled coolly. "Women are extremely dangerous—especially ones with innocent eyes and regal airs."

"I didn't shoot him. He was killed with a dagger."

"Ah, then you do know how he was killed."

"The newspaper said he was killed by a dagger—in Diego's warehouse," she reminded him. "And how was it that Yuri waited for me in *your* partner's warehouse?"

"There's no mystery there. Yuri was a member of the delegation from New Archangel. He was contacting Diego about the possibility of buying wheat. Evidently he also decided it afforded him the perfect spot for his clandestine meeting with you."

"All right. But I didn't kill him, and you know it."

"No, but I'd stake my life that Sarakof found out that Yuri was meeting you at the warehouse and ordered him killed by one of the men who jumped me. He didn't want Yuri's information to fall into your hands and frighten you away from New Archangel."

"Perhaps it's you who's trying to frighten me."

"He needs you to accomplish his own plans. Don't you think it's wise to begin wondering what they might be?"

"Peter! You're suggesting—"

"Has he mentioned his ambitions to you by any chance? Anything about St. Petersburg?"

"If he did, do you think I'd be so unwise as to inform you?"

"No," he stated flatly. "But I happen to be the one man you can trust."

She smiled. "Your confidence borders on arrogance—but then, I've been told all Americans are rather brash."

"And do you still think I'm dangerous?"

She hesitated, for in a certain sense she did, and yet she no longer could make herself believe that he had attacked Yuri. In eliminating his involvement, however, she wouldn't believe it was the baron, not when he served her grandmother and was anxious to help her locate her father's whereabouts. She might tell Trace about Peter's offer, but she had promised she would not. Nor was she inclined to believe that Trace would accept it anyway. He disliked Peter and nothing he did would ever appear in a noble light. She must wait to see the countess before she truly made up her mind about Peter Sarakof.

"I don't know," she responded evasively.

"You could be prejudiced about us poor 'colonial clods.'"

"I suppose you'll never forget what I said on the wharf."

"I might. Under the right circumstances."

She grew uncomfortable and turned to leave.

"Am I dangerous, then, to an opposing national cause or to something more personal?"

"I mean, Captain Wilder," she said with an edge to her voice, "that Americans can drive a hard bargain."

"Yet you're aboard my ship. That doesn't say much for your uncle, does it? What is it Bellomont expects you to find out while aboard the *Okanagan*?"

"You were right—I'm getting soaked by being where I shouldn't. If you'll—"

"He's risking you to Sarakof—a dangerous trap." He looked at her. "It would help if you'd explain what you hope to accomplish at the castle, other than meeting your grandmother."

"Good night, Captain," she said quietly and turned to leave. He caught her arm.

"Don't go . . . I like your company."

Every fiber in her soul told her to leave him, not only because of the risk of being discovered as to the reason she was aboard but also for the preservation of her emotions. She found herself unwillingly drawn to him, and this made her vulnerable.

She stayed and wondered that she did so. It had begun to rain lightly, and far off there was a brilliant white flash that lit up the sky, followed by a low rumble. For several minutes they watched in silence as the distant storm approached.

"You're getting wet," said Trace. "We can talk inside. I'll call John Wesley to take the wheel."

"No, I like the rain. I like it here—the waves, the wind. And whatever we wish to discuss, Captain, we can say it here."

"I think not, Miss Mackenzie," he said too politely. "You see, I have something you'll want that belongs to you."

Something in his tone commanded her full attention.

"Your handbag," he murmured, lifting his mug of coffee but watching her as he finished its contents in one drink.

"My handbag?" she said surprised. "Then you *do* have it," she accused stiffly. "It took you all this time to return it?"

"Unfortunately, it's in my quarters." He smiled smoothly.

As though from out of nowhere, John Wesley reappeared.

"Don't worry about what Mrs. Warrender may think," said Trace. "I come from a long line of Virginia gentlemen who would duel for a lady's honor." He bowed lightly and gestured her past.

Savana swept by, carrying her tin cup of coffee. "Did you

ever visit Bellomont House as a boy? Before the war?" She followed him up the short steps to the round room.

"Yes, once. At Christmas." He opened the door for her and she hesitated, then stepped inside.

"Did you like it?" She looked at him in the shadows while he turned up the lantern.

"No. I thought it stuffy and pretentious. You haven't lived, my dear Miss Mackenzie, until you've wakened up early Christmas morning on a Virginia plantation! But perhaps it's best not to talk about the past. It can't be snatched from the wind."

She thought of her own past, and the mother she had never met. Now a grandmother who would be a total stranger. Not only had they little in common, but their culture was a world apart.

The light flared and settled into a warm golden glow, and Savana stood in the round room, filled with the muffled sounds of wind and sea. She glanced about and saw that Trace now used the room as his office and quarters. A richly polished desk sat in one corner, and as her eyes fell on a stack of charts and papers her heart skipped a beat. . . .

Was there information in one of those desk drawers offering proof that Trace Wilder was working for President Jackson to gain Oregon Country for America?

Trace went behind the desk and unlocked a drawer. Savana's gaze riveted upon its contents. If he bothered to use the lock, it may have important papers. But how would she ever get the key?

She watched him place the key inside his pea coat. There was no way to reach it unless she got near enough and—

Her eyes left the charts as a twinge of guilt pricked her conscience.

He straightened, producing her handbag.

"Yours?" he asked innocently, his flint blue eyes intense under his lashes. "I found it that morning on the wharf. You dropped it." He smiled faintly under her scrutiny. "Fortunately, I left it aboard the lighter instead of bringing it to my hotel room at San Francisco. Otherwise it would have gone up in flames with my trunk. Of course, I've already informed you in detail what the letter said about Sarakof. He's a dangerous man. And he has reasons of his own for wanting you under his authority at the castle."

She wanted to snatch her bag from his hand, for she didn't believe how innocently he had come across it, but she restrained her mood. Why did he keep attacking Peter?

"How kind of you to return it, Captain. As you say, you are surely a true Virginian gentleman!"

His mouth turned up. She opened the bag. Everything was there except the document from St. Petersburg, and she struggled to appear believing and congenial.

"Nothing else missing I hope?" came his bland question.

"No, Captain, nothing missing, thanks to you," she replied as casually as he, but the fact that she didn't actually trust him was not lost on either of them. Yet, what could she say? It was tasteless to accuse him without further proof. And it was proof of his being an agent and working with Jason Lee that she needed. She'd never get the information she wanted by openly charging him of stealing.

It was difficult to still the words of accusation on her lips, but she knew she must.

"And now, you must sample true Virginia cooking," he said. "The Colonel has labored all day to make up his special ham and fritters. I trust you're as hungry as I am."

"Oh yes, starving. How pleasant—just the two of us?"

"Why, yes, Miss Mackenzie. Instead of music we can listen to the howling wind and hope our plates remain on the table." He smiled.

She laughed. "We may need to tie them down. Shall we invite Mrs. Warrender to sample the Colonel's cooking? I think Miss Roslyn is also feeling a bit better. . . ."

His smile was disarming. "They've already eaten and retired."

His congenial mood nearly won her over—but then she remembered something he had said. He had left her bag on the lighter . . . why not Yuri's letter also?

She must be on guard. She must not trust him, and above all else she must not allow herself to forget that his charm was only a front. He too wanted information from her, and he was willing to play gentleman host to get it.

Well. She was willing to test the Colonel's Virginia cooking—and the Virginia gentleman who accompanied it.

# 15

## FOR GOD OR THE KING?

"You're indeed a marvelous cook, Colonel Pelly, but I couldn't eat another bite! I shall soon weigh enough to sink Captain Wilder's ship."

"You haven't tasted dessert until you've eaten Pelly's pecan pie," said Trace.

"Don't tell me you also have Southern pecans aboard, Colonel. You just amaze me!"

Colonel Pelly beamed shrewdly and poured rich, dark coffee into a pristine white china cup and set it before her with grace. "Miss Savana, I declare, you belong in the parlor of a Virginny plantation 'stead of cold foggy London town. An' with compliments like these pouring from your honey lips, I'm ready to be headin' back south jes' as soon as Trace hea' turns this ship round."

Savana smiled sweetly, aware that Trace watched her with lazy amusement. "But, Colonel, what about the California rancho? Surly you could never talk the Captain into selling it and returning to this Virginia of yours!" She looked at Trace over her cup, sipping the strong brew with its nuttylike flavor. "You couldn't desert your partner, Don Diego, could you, Trace?"

Colonel Pelly looked from Savana to Trace, and Trace held out his empty cup to be refilled. "This certainly isn't that disgusting chicory and wheat molasses you've been serving up since San Francisco."

"Been savin' them prized coffee beans we picked up in Brazil. Took me nigh unto an hour to grine 'em up."

Savana glanced from one to the other. "So, Trace, do you own a hacienda near the Sacramento River?" she persisted with a friendly smile. She guessed that he might suspect the cause of her curiosity, but he didn't seem concerned.

"Own the rancho? No. Diego and I are in debt up to our ears," he said flatly. "We're in the process of paying for past mistakes."

"By selling wheat to the Hudson's Bay Company for New Archangel?"

His smile wore brittle amusement. "Yes, and by collecting Russian skins taken from the coastal islands to sell in China." He looked pointedly at her fashionable beaver hat sitting on the chair. "And in Europe."

She wondered at his boldness to admit hunting fur in the waters of Russian America. She noticed that Colonel Pelly had left, murmuring something about dessert.

Savana had reason to doubt Trace's "debts." As he had looked pointedly at her hat, she did so at his Spanish sombrero hanging on a peg where pieces of silver brazenly glinted in the swaying lantern. A poor man in debt did not use silver to decorate his fashionable wardrobe.

"Then you and Señor Diego are partners in the fur trade as well as growing wheat," she suggested.

"Nope. I'm in the fur business alone. Diego grows the wheat—I deliver it."

It was going better now, the way she wanted it to go. She eased into the next question smoothly while enjoying the coffee. She watched him lounging in the chair under the lantern, looking anything except a Virginia planter's son.

"I suppose I heard erroneously then. . . ." and she let her words melt away to tempt his curiosity.

He watched her, and if he was aware of the dangling bait she offered, he only smiled and accepted it—almost, she thought, too willingly.

"Allow me to defend my reputation," he drawled. "What did you hear about the nasty reprobate Trace Wilder?"

"Oh . . . but it couldn't be true," she said quickly, "and well, I wouldn't want to say it because I've decided you are a gentleman after all, Captain Wilder."

"Permit me to insist, Miss Savana. Why, I wouldn't be able to rest my Christian conscience tonight if you didn't allow me to do so."

*Christian conscience.* Was it a lead-in to the American missionaries in Oregon? Was it deliberate?

"Well . . . I've heard that you and your brother Yancey were riverboat gamblers in St. Louis and that you both sold out two years ago and came to Sacramento to raise cows, besides wheat. And that Yancey sold cows—"

"Cattle," he corrected smoothly and tilted back in the chair.

"—sold them to that American in Oregon . . . what was his name?" She furrowed her brows.

"Jason Lee," he offered, his mouth turning.

"Yes, that was it. Reverend Lee and his missionary party from the East. And I believe they're now settling near Fort Vancouver."

"They are—French Prairie. The cattle belonged to Yancey and me. We've sold a small herd to an American named Ewan Young and a few others from the Fort Vancouver area. Young recently arrived in San Francisco looking for cattle to buy to bring to Oregon."

"And I suppose, like the baron and the Russian delegation from New Archangel, Mr. Young was also unable to find cattle to buy except from the Wilders," she said, unable to

185

keep the wry tone from her voice.

He smiled easily. "Fortune runs deep they say. 'Course Yancey and I've no control over the Mexican government. They pay close attention to any cattle or sheep leaving California."

"And you and your brother had the cows just as you had the wheat. What luck," she said softly with a smile.

He lifted a brow. "Not exactly luck. We knew they were coming and arranged to have the cattle ready to support the American missionary group in Oregon."

*He is openly admitting it,* she thought with surprise.

"Jason contacted me a year ago."

She hoped her excitement didn't show. "He contacted you . . . then the two of you are friends."

"Good friends," he said smoothly.

She wondered that he acknowledged this to her so easily when he must suspect her interest.

"I had first intended to deliver the cattle myself," he said. "The wheat offered more interesting prospects." He lifted his mug and drank, watching her response with a flicker of amusement in his eyes.

She set her cup down quietly and watched him, elbows on the table, her chin cupped in her palms. "I'm interested in your cattle."

"Are you?"

She ignored the faint smile. Obviously he didn't believe her, but he must have decided to allow her pretense.

"They're Mexican cattle and about as mean as they come," he said.

"I suspect you handle them quite well. Are you saying you would have delivered them to Fort Vancouver? But surely! Not by ship?"

He hesitated, briefly studying her face. "No, by land."

Her heart beat a little faster. "Oh, but there's no trail! And what of the Indians?"

"There's a trail—through California and right into Oregon Country," he said smoothly.

186

"For horses in single file, of course," she breathed innocently. "Why, I don't see how wagons could ever cross those mountains."

He reached across the table for the pot of coffee, his gaze holding hers.

Her eyes dropped to the table and she rushed, "Allow me, Captain. . . ." and she lifted the pot and refilled his cup. "Then if you don't mind my avid curiosity, how will Yancey deliver the cattle to Jason Lee?"

He took the cup. "Thanks. I haven't said yet that he was. As for the trail you're so 'avidly' interested in, the fur brigades of the various companies—including the American Rocky Mountain Fur—have been traveling it from Oregon down into California for years. Even England's own Peter Skene Ogden has traveled from Oregon through the Snake Country down to San Diego several times that I know of, and so did the American Joe Meeks."

Mr. Ogden, she knew, was the Hudson's Bay man who would be in command of the expedition to open a new fort on the Stikine, and Joe Meeks was the American mountain man, called a pathfinder like the famed Daniel Boone and Kit Carson.

She moved cautiously now. "And do you know the route, Trace?"

"Why, Savana, what a question!"

"But you *do* know, don't you? And I'll wager you and Yancey also know of another route, one that could be used for a wagon train from Missouri. Why, you're so smart. I'll just bet you—" She stopped under his level gaze.

His smile was both amused and challenging. "Savana, I do believe you're flirting. I'm shocked. What would dear Lady Hillary say about such conduct? What of her warning about suspected knaves and rogues? Or do your fluttering lashes mean you've decided I'm a gentleman?"

"Why, I wasn't . . ." she stammered, and felt herself turning warm under his gaze.

"Ah, but you were. And since you're interested enough

to set aside your standards to find out the information you want so badly, I don't have the heart to disappoint you. As to your first question—yes, I probably could lead a wagon train to Oregon, but I'm not interested. I've traveled it once . . . but I prefer privateering on the Pacific Coast. I like the northern waters, the inlets, and secluded bays around Alaska and New Caledonia. It's the best way to trade with the Indians." He tilted backward in the chair, holding his cup and watching her. "As for a wagon train from Missouri—most say it can't be done."

"Jason Lee came by wagon, didn't he? Does he know the route?"

"What does Bellomont wish to know about Missouri? Whether Yancey and I are going to lead a wagon train? Or is it Mother Russia for whom you gather information?"

Savana smiled sweetly. "My, my, am I being accused of acting as a double agent? You've made me into a dangerous opponent, Captain."

"I've always enjoyed challenges."

"You think you have me dissected, don't you? Well, you're quite wrong. I've come to learn about my father's disappearance."

Mention of her father alerted his interest. "Did the baron speak of your father at Fort Ross when he brought you the Rezanov diamonds?"

She avoided an answer. "Now it's you who ask too many questions. Shall I tell you the truth, Captain?"

"Please do!"

"I've come for another purpose as well."

"Have you, now!"

"Yes, I suppose you've recognized my interest in Jason Lee?"

"Why, not at all."

She ignored the amused glint in his eyes. "I've come from London as an unofficial representative of the London Mission Society to write a journal on him and the American missionaries."

There was a perceptible moment of awkward silence, and she couldn't tell if he believed her or not. Her conscience ached and a feeling of hotness climbed into her cheeks.

*He's right*, she thought. *I do make a naive spy.*

"I must say I'm both surprised and pleased," he said smoothly. "I'm relieved as well to hear of your missionary interest. I wouldn't want to become too friendly with a female agent. . . ." His flint blue eyes flickered under dark lashes. "You see, I am very shy around attractive young women, and practically defenseless."

She smiled ruefully. "I am certain you are able to defend yourself from being taken unfair advantage of, Captain Wilder."

"Then I have no cause to fear you?"

*The rogue.* "None at all, sir," she said sweetly.

He sighed. "I am relieved, Miss Mackenzie! Even though I can see why Sir Bellomont might wish to use someone like you to enhance his success for the glorious cause of the honorable Company in the Northwest, I see now you have a much more noble purpose in mind. What could I do, then, but offer you my trusting assistance? And just what would you like to know about Jason to place in your Baptist Mission Society journal?"

She toyed with her empty cup. "Somehow I'm surprised you would know Mr. Lee out here in California."

He shrugged and again tilted his chair back. "As I told you, Jason is a friend of mine. I first met him on his eastern tour to raise support for the Indian missions."

"And you're interested in Indian missions?"

"I once thought I'd like to be a physician missionary to the Nez Perce. Does that surprise you?"

It did, but she wondered why it should, when John Wesley had told her that Trace had turned the direction of his heart toward seeking Christ.

"The war changed your plans—I believe the Colonel mentioned it," she said simply, wondering why she preferred to think of Trace as an enemy agent.

"War changes everything," he said.

She stirred a little restlessly in the chair and hoped he would say no more, but he asked, "What kind of a journal are you writing?"

She drew in a small breath and felt her conscience pricked. *Lord, forgive me.* . . . She wondered if her sense of guilt showed. She concentrated on the journal she had decided to write while at Bellomont House, not on Jason Lee but her father's work among the Aleut, and found herself saying, "Oh . . . on how well English missions and methods are working with the Indian culture. Then, of course, I hope to compare this with Lee and the American missionaries."

He watched her silently, hands locked behind his head. She hastened truthfully, "I did spend a month with the Clapham Group missionaries in London before I voyaged to San Francisco."

The silence lingered and Savana shifted uncomfortably. "At Fort Vancouver, I hope to learn about Mr. Lee and his work."

"Jason and I became friends when he brought two Indian boys with him to the missionary meetings in the East. A Nez Perce and a Flathead. John Wesley knew them." Trace smiled. "And I'm acquainted with a young woman serving with Jason. Her name is Rebecca Baxter. I'm sure she'd be more than pleased to bring you to the Lee compound in the Willamette Valley. The missionaries have opened a medical clinic and a school-orphanage for the Indian children whose parents have died."

She didn't know why, but a tiny sick feeling fluttered in her stomach. "Yes, I'd like that . . . is Rebecca by any chance the sister of the Miss Baxter you mentioned to Sir Douglas?"

His gaze flickered with interest. "Yes."

"How nice," was her inadequate response, but somehow she no longer had the desire to pursue the matter and wondered how she might leave without revealing her feelings.

"You mentioned the two Indians who came east? Then it's true. The story of how their chiefs went to St. Louis?"

"You know about it?"

"I've heard of it in London. Several Flatheads came seeking the American pathfinders Lewis and Clark, asking that someone come to their people to teach them about God and the Bible."

"Yes, whether the story is all true I don't know," he said. "But it started the missionary movement into Oregon with Jason Lee and his brother Daniel. There's Dr. Samuel Parker too, a circuit riding preacher. The cattle we sold to Ewan Young are needed for the missionary compound," he said.

Her eyes casually searched his. She was liking him more and more and must be wary of her feelings. "They say that your friend Jason Lee is not a missionary at all but an agent of President Jackson."

"They? You mean Bellomont?"

She pushed her empty cup away. "Is he wrong?"

He shrugged, becoming remote. "You'll need to ask Jason Lee. I don't speak for him. I speak for myself. If you don't mind my asking, I thought you came to meet Baron Sarakof with the idea of a possible betrothal. What's this about the London Mission Society?"

"I did come to meet the baron, but I'd already made plans to come to Oregon Country even before Sir Douglas made arrangements for my visit to Baranof Castle," she said truthfully.

His surprise and curiosity showed as he studied her. "You had already made plans to come to the Northwest?"

"Yes, I wanted to learn more about my father's disappearance. I was never satisfied with the report of his death in a blizzard. Naturally I would have needed to convince Lady Hillary first."

"And an introduction to Sarakof gave you the cause you needed."

"Yes," she said pointedly, seeing no reason now to pretend. "While I'm at New Archangel I shall learn about the missionary work of my father among the Aleut, and what happened to him."

"Atrocities were committed against the natives by the Russian fur trappers. Your father, I believe, tried to help the Aleut."

She looked at him in surprise. "How did you know?"

"I've been there before," was all he said, then easily changed the subject. "Tell me more about Baranof Castle and your grandmother."

"There's not that much to explain, since I know so very little about her myself. I didn't know she was alive until I arrived in San Francisco. Sir Douglas told me she wished to see me."

His interest showed. "How did he know? Did she contact him?"

"No, Baron Sarakof informed him when he arrived at Fort Ross."

"Ah . . . I think I'm beginning to understand."

"Understand what? I wish you'd tell me what disturbs you."

He started to say something, then paused. "Sarakof's up to something. What it is I don't know yet, but I intend to find out."

She smiled mockingly. "Your assignment from President Jackson?"

"You might have asked Sarakof where he got the diamonds."

"From the countess. I told you, my grandmother thought I'd died as a baby. She knows better now and she wishes to see me," Savana said, unable to restrain the warm sense of belonging that the idea brought her.

He did not look pleased but thoughtful. "I don't want to spoil your hopes of family reconciliation, but after twenty years she's suddenly decided she wants you?"

"I told you," she said defensively, "she thought I was dead."

"Odd. I was under the impression she had sent you by way of Zoya to your father, and that the family had rejected you."

She looked at him in frustration but was surprised that he knew so much about her. She was about to ask how he had come by the information when his next question startled her.

"You're certain she's even at Baranof Castle?"

"Why, of course—" She stopped beneath his sober gaze. She knew what he meant—that the baron might be lying. "Why would he lie? And how would he get the diamonds? And for what cause would he lure me to New Archangel? Peter is on my side."

"Ah, the dear and noble Peter."

"Oh, I know what you think about him, but I believe you're wrong. Anyway, it's worth the risk going there with my uncle, and I intend to follow it through to the end. And what of you! You still haven't explained your actions on the wharf. And like Peter, I too believe you're a Boston agent."

"And if I am?"

She looked at him directly. "If I had proof, I'd inform Sir Douglas as soon as we reach Fort Vancouver. It's my obligation."

He studied her. "And just what do you think I should do with you, Miss Mackenzie, if I've proof you're working for Bellomont—for England?"

Savana looked at him, a small prickle crawling up the back of her neck. Then she gave a small laugh, hoping to sidetrack him. "If you thought that, you'd be clever enough to not let me know you suspected it."

He smiled, and for a moment their gaze lingered. "Maybe not." He stood, setting his chair back. "You wouldn't change your mind and make matters easier on me by deciding to remain at Fort Vancouver if I brought you there? You could stay with Rebecca and learn firsthand about Lee. Who knows," he suggested, "you might unearth some dark plot about a wagon train of odious Americans heading toward the Columbia."

Savana, too, stood to her feet and looked at him wryly. "The idea is tempting. However, my mind's made up.

There's one cause on my heart more important than even an American wagon train. Visiting Baranof Castle to meet my grandmother and learning about my parents. I want to discover my roots, Captain, and establish a relationship I was denied."

His displeasure showed. "You may be in for a disappointment. The past and its hurts is not always mendable. Hungering for a relationship that doesn't exist leaves you open to more pain. You'd be wiser to find what you're searching for in a relationship with your heavenly Father."

She wondered that he was able to pinpoint a longing in her heart that even she had not yet been able to understand.

"Anyway," he added, "I don't trust the baron, and I'll foil him if I can."

It wasn't clear what he meant, and she wasn't certain she wished an explanation at the moment. She turned away. "If you'll excuse me," she said wearily, "I wish to return to the cabin."

Trace came around the table and picked up her hat and cape.

"Thank you, and you can tell the Colonel I very much enjoyed his cooking, but I've no appetite remaining for dessert. Good night, Captain Wilder."

She walked to the door, and he opened it, and as she began to pass through, he took hold of her arm. Her eyes rushed to his. He met her gaze steadily.

"Flannigan!" he called.

A burly crewman appeared from the rain-swept deck. "Aye, Captain?"

"See Miss Mackenzie to her cabin."

She read nothing in his expression as he looked at her and said, "Storm's rising. See that you don't come on deck or you could be washed overboard."

"Thank you," she said flatly and brushed past him.

Once outside she felt the lashing rain and wind and struggled to draw her hooded cape around her, allowing the man named Flannigan to bring her below.

On the morning of the third week out, the *Okanagan* was churning through the rough seas of Cape Disappointment with the sun just above the horizon and gray clouds scuttling in from the north. Trace came on deck and met John Wesley coming down the portside, shirtless in the cold wind, his Turkish trousers wet and baggy. A carefully groomed feather in his shiny black hair somehow managed to stand immaculately straight in the scowling wind. He grinned at Trace and stretched his arms up toward the vast gray heavens like a lazy panther.

"The sea! The wind!" he said, as if that explained everything about how he felt.

"Astoria," quipped Trace briefly, holding the glass steady as he leaned against the rail moving with the lull of the ship.

John Wesley took the telescope and peered through it, then handed it back, his dark eyes scornful. "British flag."

"A sad twist of history, my friend, one we'll need to alter. Someday we'll change the flag."

Trace studied the horizon astern, but there were no sails in sight. Evidently the British ships were wintering in Hawaii as they often did since the days of Captain James Cook, or they were already bound for Fort Vancouver where Peter Skene Ogden was to lead the expedition for the Hudson's Bay Company through Russian-American waters to build the new fort at Stikine.

Trace was satisfied with their voyage so far. It looked as if the *Okanagan* would arrive off New Archangel ahead of Ogden and the British expedition, as Trace had planned. Bellomont would be cooling his heels waiting for him at Fort Vancouver, and perhaps Ogden as well. He knew that Ogden needed no help in navigating the region: Peter Skene Ogden was the prince of the Hudson's Bay Company's explorers.

It might be that Ogden had even gone ahead to New Archangel without Bellomont, although he couldn't imagine Bellomont remaining at Fort Vancouver if Ogden decided to start out before the *Okanagan* arrived.

"Think Captain Dembe will make it to parley with you?"

"I have my hopes set on him. If he doesn't, we're in trouble."

"What of the girl?"

"No matter what, she stays with us," said Trace firmly.

Trace had delayed in San Francisco deliberately, and had been in contact with his American friend Captain George Dembe of the *Yankee Trader*. Quietly, under cover of darkness, the wheat had been loaded not onto the *Okanagan*, but onto Dembe's ship.

Captain Dembe had sailed several days before him, and if all went as Trace had planned they would rendezvous in the maze of little islands where Boston ships often bought furs from the Indians, undetected by Sarakof's patrol boats.

Trace had learned much from the natives. John Wesley knew the hunting grounds well, and on a previous fur expedition had told him of the cloistered spot. A ship could anchor there for weeks and never be spotted. Trace had made it his ambition to know these coasts better than anyone but the Indians. He had also learned from various independent traders who worried less about their nationality than they did about a good fur catch. There were English, Scottish, French, even Hawaiians who had their own ships or schooners, and who knew where to go to avoid the "Russkies."

Now and then a trader was caught by Russian patrol boats and arrested. They were never heard from again and their vessels were confiscated along with the furs. Some of the unfortunate men were hanged, or shot—perhaps those sent to Siberia the worst off.

He scowled into the cold wind stirring up whitecaps around them while the schooner's bow pointed like a statue toward the icy northern seas.

Trace, his handsomely chiseled face wet with wind-driven scud and spray, stood beside John Wesley at the wheel. Their sea boots and oilskins were shiny with water, the sky abovc was gray with more clouds, and the wind was invigorating.

"I'll leave her in your hands," Trace told him. "It's your first big storm. Think you're ready?"

John Wesley stared at him; then his Indian expression took over like an iron mask, no humor in face or eyes. "I can, Cap'n."

Trace smiled, for he knew that the trust he invested in John's abilities had touched the man's soul.

Leaving him at the wheel, Trace went below to the cubbyhole to study his charts again. The ship pitched and he tied down the charts on the rough wooden plank. If the wind held they would soon be nearing Fort Vancouver. Trace was relieved he could soon discharge Mrs. Warrender and her daughter to the safety of a Boston schooner that would bring them up the river to Fort Vancouver. Nonetheless, the Columbia River was treacherous even in good weather, and he knew of several ships from England that had crashed within the last year, ships requested by McLoughlin for the expedition to the Stikine.

He could imagine Bellomont's surprise and anger when he discovered what Trace had done in going on to New Archangel without him, and keeping Savana from meeting Sarakof.

The ship creaked and groaned. Trace glanced down at the floor, wondering how the women were managing. Knowing Savana as he believed he did, she would insist she was doing well even if she was not. He wondered if he should check on them, but decided against it.

"Keola!" he called, and the young Kanaka from Hawaii poked his dark head in through the door.

"Cheer up, Captain," came his unusual greeting, his brown eyes shining with excitement over the storm.

"See how the fair damsels are surviving. They may be sick."

Keola flashed a grin showing white teeth. "Already have. They are very sick."

Trace sighed. "All three?"

"Lady Warrender is like an anchor, strong as iron but sick. And her daughter, Miss Roslyn, is loudly unhappy."

"And Miss MacKenzie?"

Keola smiled. "Brave to the end but just sent word asking for you, Captain."

Trace stood and secured his charts, then shrugged into his wet pea coat and snatched up his Spanish hat. He took the small medical box from his sea chest and went back up on deck as the ship rolled and pitched. Whistling a Scottish tune, he took the short steps up to the quarterdeck and came to his cabin door. Masking a smile, he knocked quietly.

The cabin rose and fell, and Savana was managing to hold down her food, having faced seasickness on the voyage from England. But the moans and retching of Roslyn as well as Mrs. Warrender tempted her to gag.

At the sound of the quiet rap, she swallowed hard and swayed precariously across the cabin. It had to be Trace, and gratefully she swung open the door.

He stood there looking wet but sound in mind and body, and the sight of undisturbed strength when she felt so sick prompted a rise of irrational temper.

"Where have you been, sir! I've requested help for the past hour!"

He swept off his broad-rimmed hat with a little bow. "At your service, madam."

Her eyes fell upon the medical box.

"May I come in?" he asked agreeably.

"It's your cabin," said Savana, weaving aside, noticing that he was able to maintain his balance over the moving floor.

He stopped, glancing about with a wince. Savana felt a prick of guilt for using every available towel, sheet, and basin on Mrs. Warrender and Roslyn.

"What have you women done to my cabin! This is worse than a warship!"

"I've done what I could," she said, mortified. "A gentleman would never make such a comment."

"Then he hasn't eyes in his head," he said, stepping over a basin that slid and slopped across the floor.

"I need towels and fresh basins," she said stiffly, and as the ship pitched, she felt her stomach move up to her throat, then bounce back down again. "Ohh!"

She clutched at the steady desk, turning white. She closed her eyes, swallowing hard. Trace stood watching her with a narrowed look. Then as she stifled a moan, her eyes wide with horror, his glance softened.

"Go . . . away," she managed, pointing a shaking finger toward the creaking door. "Never mind . . . I . . . I'm going to be very . . . indisposed."

Resorting to a cavalier attitude he swept up a basin. "A gentleman never leaves a lady in dire straits; nor does a captain abandon his ship."

Savana collapsed against the desk as the vessel seemed to crest a mountain and then plunge into a valley. He caught her.

"Keola!" came his calm shout.

Keola poked his head in. "Be of good cheer, Captain!"

"Never mind. Fix the cabin, will you? We'll need to move Miss Mackenzie. Then get back here and help the other two. Where's the Colonel?"

"Sick, Captain."

"He cooks a Virginia ham better than Harry, but he makes a miserable sailor."

Mercifully, Savana was no longer aware of Trace Wilder, or his strong arms around her holding her up. For all she knew or cared he could have been her fatherly old doctor in London who wore small inch-thick spectacles and had Benjamin Franklin hair.

Only on the next day when Savana awoke alone in a strange, small room did she remember his competent aid. He had behaved as cool and businesslike as any physician—checking her pulse and leaving her with a swallow of something strong and horrible that burned her throat but also whirled her already-weaving brain into the escape of sleep.

Now, as the morning light flooded in, her head ached, she was dreadfully weak, and she never wanted to look at the sea again. Her one thought was that she must get better so she could help Mrs. Warrender.

Savana stirred, tried to sit up, and discovered she was in the round room. The floor was not heaving quite so badly as it had been yesterday, and she managed to sit up cautiously, stretching a hand to steady herself.

"I thought you'd be the first to stir to sunlight. Keola will bring you something hot to drink. I imagine you like tea. I had some brought aboard before we left San Francisco." Her embarrassment ebbed when the dread moment to look him in the eyes came and passed, and he showed nothing but an aloof expression. Whether it was deliberate, she did not know, but she gratefully accepted it and the color of shame eased from her face.

"Tea sounds quite good, thank you."

"We'll be out of this bad weather by sunset. Don't worry about the others. I checked on them a while ago, and Mrs. Warrender is recovering enough to look after Roslyn."

"How near are we to Fort Vancouver?"

For a moment he stood looking down at her, and then his jaw set. "Not far. It's my turn to relieve John at the wheel," he said briefly.

Was he being evasive or was it only an awkward moment? She had the impression that he didn't want to tell her where they were.

The cabin door closed behind him, and soon the Colonel came in bringing a tray.

"I put a wiggle of mint in the tea," he drawled with a friendly smile. "My mammy used to say it done settles the stomach."

Pelly appeared as affable as always. She relaxed and

thanked him for the tea and settled in the chair by the captain's desk to drink it slowly.

*The desk.* Her eyes rested on a number of charts and papers spread across the desk. She felt a twinge of guilt at the thought of rummaging through his personal letters, but she was quick to tell herself that her personal feelings must not enter into the work she was to do for England's good in Oregon.

She glanced sideways at Colonel Pelly. He too might be a wealth of information since he had been with the Wilder family from the beginning of their arrival in Virginia.

She sipped the hot brew slowly and began to feel invigorated. For a time she watched Pelly singing some Virginia folk song while he readied her food tray. She must move cautiously so as not to alert him to her motives in questioning him. If anyone was bound to be loyal to Trace Wilder it would be this old gentleman, who had served his father and mother before the war.

"I could almost think Captain Wilder had medical training," she commented easily.

He smiled. "He studied fer a short while. But when Mister Zachary died and the plantation was destroyed, there was no use in making plans, or so both Trace and Yance said. They had to earn a living and there was nothing left but rubble. It was too bad what happen to him. More tea?"

"Yes," she murmured, holding out her cup, her hand still weak and trembling. "Thank you. It was sad about their home. He said he's going to rebuild it one day and return to Virginia. I suppose you'll go with him?"

He frowned, his white brows coming together. "Rebuild—? Not a wager he will, not even Yance."

*So he has no intention of rebuilding as he said.*

"They done scooted away from them memories fast as a possum with a hornet on its tail. It's Oregon Trace has a hankering for now. Yessir, Oregon Country and all the way on up to Russky territory. He got a hankerin' fer it bad."

Her heart beat faster. "Does he?" she prodded gently. "I

wonder why. They say there's nothing much there but wilderness."

He chuckled. "That land of the Pacific Northwest be about as green and lush as a man—or a nation—could want."

"And the captain, being a Boston man, naturally would want it for his president," she prodded.

He looked at her over his hawklike nose as though trying to see her through a pair of spectacles that weren't there. Savana's gaze faltered to the cup in her hand and she took a sip. "You make excellent mint tea, Colonel Pelly."

"Yessir, so the family used to say. . . . Trace spurns it, though." He rubbed his whiskered chin thoughtfully. "That cantankerous boy used to throw it in the potted fern that sat by the pillar. And Yance, he were always late coming in from his meanderings riding that fine-blooded horse. . . ." He sighed.

She remembered Callie. "I suppose Trace had many friends while growing up in Virginia."

"Him and Yancey both."

She set the cup down suddenly. "Was the marriage to Miss Baxter arranged when they were very young, before the war?"

"You mean Miss Callie? She's in St. Louis now, a fancy daughter of the senator. Both Trace and Yancey had it good for Miss Callie, but it looks like Trace is goin' to win in the end. Yance got too much fire in him for Miss Callie. She's a sweetheart of a girl, that one."

She set her cup down. "I think I'd rather take a nap now, Colonel Pelly, if you wouldn't mind."

"Sure, Miss Mackenzie. I'll leave this here tray and you eat that cornbread jes' as soon as you can. It'll settle your wits."

"Yes, I will, thank you."

She watched him leave and then stood, her legs weak, holding to the back of the chair. So Callie was a "sweetheart of a girl," was she? And hadn't she heard something about Senator Baxter in Washington City clamoring about America making Oregon a territory of the United States?

She looked over at his desk, her eyes hard. If they were nearing Fort Vancouver then she needed to act soon. Trace was a capable Yankee with clever aims for his government. And she had almost fallen for his disarming smile. She would search his belongings for any proof of what he was about. And she would hand it over to Uncle Douglas upon their arrival at Fort Vancouver.

# 16

## SEALED WITH A WARNING

In the glow of the oil lantern she was confronted by heavy dark beams and shadows. She glanced toward the door and, hearing nothing, moved swiftly to the captain's desk where her cold hands ran over the various charts, maps, and books spread out before her.

Her eyes swiftly took in a small hand-drawn map and she recognized the outline of the Pacific Rim from San Diego to Astoria, Portland, and up past New Archangel. She paused to take a closer look at the coast of Oregon. Astoria was circled, but why? They had no reason to stop there since Fort Vancouver was not far away. Trace had written something. . . . She brought the map closer to the lantern.

*Cap. Langley. Jan. 22.*

Another shipmaster? From what nation? "As if I didn't know!" she murmured. A Boston trader, of course—but why would Trace be meeting him near Astoria?

*What is the date today?* she wondered. She still felt a little weak from yesterday's bout with seasickness and her thinking wasn't clear. They had left San Francisco the first week of the month. . . . *Then it must be near the twenty-second,* she decided.

Farther up north there was an inlet on the coast of Russian America that was also circled, and she found the Stikine River and the written words: *Ogden and Bellomont. Hudson's Bay Company.*

*Then Trace must know all about the secret expedition to try to open a new trading fort for the Company on the Stikine River.* She frowned. Did Trace expect to intercept Mr. Ogden's schooners?

She began her quiet search through the unlocked drawers for anything that might look official, rummaging through papers and letters, and seeing addresses both in San Francisco and Virginia. She hesitated at the sight of an envelope postmarked St. Louis with the name "Miss Callie Baxter" in the lefthand corner.

Savana was tempted to open and read it. She glanced toward the door again. All was silent. She bit her lip, then suddenly shoved the letter back where she'd found it. *Why should I care what she wrote to him? Probably some sentimental nonsense about missing him beneath the big pale moon shining on the Missouri River!*

She continued her search for anything about a wagon train through odds and ends that offered nothing. Foiled, she shut the drawer.

A blue metal trunk stood open and she knelt, briefly searching through a stack of shirts, trousers, and tunics.

Again, she paused uneasily, considering. She stood and glanced about until her gaze landed on the wide-brimmed hat with its glinting silver pesos. Below it hung his black woolen pea coat. . . .

She sped across the floor to the peg and searched the inside of the hat, then the inner pockets of the jacket. Her heart leaped as her fingers felt the edge of a folded letter. She drew it out knowing she had found something of importance and rushed to the lantern, spreading the fine linen paper out carefully on the desk.

Her breath caught. "Washington City. Office of the United States President Andrew Jackson," she whispered, staring at the official seal.

Her heart began to thud. Her eyes darted toward the door, then back to the letter. She began to read. . . .

> *Though Russia was the first nation to occupy Oregon, they are pulling back, much too quietly and peaceably. If either England or St. Petersburg establish a foothold in Oregon or California ahead of us, our dreams of an America stretching from the Atlantic to the Pacific, our Manifest Destiny, will fail to be realized.*
>
> *As you informed us in our last meeting with Senator Baxter of St. Louis, it will be difficult for the Redcoats to occupy the Pacific Northwest, and even harder for St. Petersburg. Your report on the failure of the Russian colony at Ross to supply New Archangel in the north was welcomed.*
>
> *The plan is forging ahead. Oregon will be settled by our own people, first by the hundreds, and then by the thousands. Once the missionaries have built their compounds they can be used as supply centers for future wagon trains. As we move westward we'll build homesteads, towns, and roads. British and Russian claims will be futile.*
>
> *News has reached us from agents in London that the Hudson's Bay Company intends to sign an exclusive trade agreement with the Russians at New Archangel in exchange for opening a new fort on the Stikine with access to Russian waters and total exclusion of Boston merchant shipping in the Pacific.*
>
> *Do all you can to undermine the success of the Hudson's Bay Company in opening the new fort. Any delay for England will benefit our westward move and—*

Savana looked up, hearing a voice outside the door. She wildly rushed to the woolen coat to replace the letter. A light knock sounded and she heard Trace's voice call her name. With shaking hands she replaced the letter just as the door opened. She whirled to face him, and stood, hands behind her, hoping her expression did not give her away.

Trace had stopped too and was watching her.

For an awkward moment neither of them spoke and their gaze locked. She knew she must look guilty, and she felt her heart beating quickly. Savana lifted her chin slightly, then folded her arms.

Trace walked in and kicked the door shut with a thud. She read his expression and the glimmer of irritation in his eyes, despite a faint smile that challenged her. He stood with hands on hips. "You can begin by bringing me my jacket."

Savana drew in a small breath. Of all the audacity. Her lashes narrowed. "I can see you're not the least bit ashamed of trying to trick me."

"Only a trifle embarrassed at the folly of forgetting my jacket. A good and wily agent would never blunder so badly. But then, perhaps I knew you'd search and was hoping you would."

She sucked in her breath, confused. "Hoping!"

"It saves me from explaining. I let the President's secretary do it for me. I hope you read it all and relished your find. Now everything is in the open between us."

"Why, you're not the least bit ashamed."

"No."

"So! *Señor* Wilder is a jolly good friend of Andrew Jackson."

"No," he stated, "my father was. I wouldn't have taken this mission except he asked me—in the name of my father, Sir Zachary Bellomont Wilder. Not that I expect you to understand."

"You're right, Captain. I do not. You're an agent and a spy, just as I thought," she accused. "And you intend to try to stop my uncle from accomplishing his task with Count Aleksandr."

"Yes, that's exactly what I plan to do, Miss Mackenzie—and you're going to help me."

She stared at him. "Me? I will not! I shall inform my uncle—and the baron—just as soon as I reach the fort."

"Which, my dear, is precisely why we are not going to Fort Vancouver. And you'll aid me by behaving yourself in pristine ladylike demeanor for the rest of our voyage."

"The rest of our voyage—" She stared at him. "Are you saying we've already passed the fort?"

"No, but we will, just as soon as I deposit Mrs. Warrender and her daughter on a longboat for the *Philadelphia*, waiting patiently near Astoria. Captain Langley will bring them on to McLoughlin's."

She must have misunderstood him—"What about me? I'm not staying aboard your traitorous ship."

"Oh, yes you will, until I've finished my business at Baranof Castle. After that, I'm going to transfer you to Captain Dembe's ship on its way back to Honolulu. With some good luck, I may join you in the tropics for a short holiday. That is," he drawled, "after I take care of a personal matter with Sarakof."

She stared at him, trembling with frustration. "You wouldn't force me to stay aboard your ship against my will."

"You're quite wrong. I must. I can't afford the risk of having you inform either Bellomont or the baron. But you might as well know. Even if you hadn't found that letter I wasn't going to release you to Bellomont. It's for your own good, of course," he said smoothly.

"You're abducting me!"

"It looks as if I am. Unless you wish to change your prickly mood and decide to cooperate with me."

"Never."

"Then you'll be kept under lock and key until this matter of New Archangel and the wheat is taken care of."

"I was right. You are a scoundrel, a knave, a cad!"

He folded his arms and scanned her. "Anything else? Surely you can come up with a few more."

"I demand to be brought to Fort Vancouver," she stated with new dignity.

"I'm sorry, Savana. No."

A small silence formed between them. She knew that unless she could somehow manage to escape, she was helpless to stop him or alter his plans.

Briskly, she walked over to the chair and stood holding to the back. "What about the wheat?"

"It's not on the *Okanagan*. Never was. I waited in San Francisco until Captain Dembe arrived. The wheat is safely on his ship and I expect to rendezvous with him near New Archangel—ahead of your uncle and the baron."

"Traitor! You're not going to deliver wheat to the colony!"

"Oh, I'll deliver it all right, but not in the name of good King George, but President Andrew Jackson. And I shall inform Count Aleksandr that the Hudson's Bay Company under Bellomont and Ogden intend to violate Russian territorial waters to set up a trading fort with the purpose of undermining Russian fur trade in China. By the time I've explained what the British are up to, the count may be in a dour enough mood to send his gunboats out to blockade Ogden."

Her eyes narrowed. "Why you—"

He rubbed his chin and winced. "The only question is, will it work? You, Savana, are the fly in the ointment. I wasn't expecting to have the added problem of keeping you from Sarakof. Now I must get into Baranof Castle on my own to meet with the count."

"My, aren't you clever," she breathed with sarcasm.

"Not clever enough. I'm new at this game of intrigue . . . not that it matters."

"You're right. It doesn't matter to me. But congratulations, Captain Wilder, so far you've done a swimmingly good job."

His mouth turned up, and he offered a bow. "Why thank you, my dear Miss Mackenzie. I shall hold your compliment for my strategic abilities close to my heart."

"I'm sure your 'dear Miss Callie' will be interested to hear how you abducted me aboard your vessel and held me under lock and key," she mocked.

His eyes came to hers and searched them until Savana blushed, tore her gaze from his, and made a quick dart for the door to escape.

He caught her wrist just as she flung open the door, and he used his boot to bang it shut.

"Give me any trouble and I'll post a guard. Is that what you want?"

"What I want doesn't mean a thing to you! If it did you'd realize what you're doing!"

"Doing?" he asked in a moment of frustration. "For one thing I'm keeping you from making a mistake with Sarakof! Why can't you understand that the man is deadly! He needs you to achieve his selfish aims in St. Petersburg!"

"You don't know that—and by keeping me a prisoner, I'll not meet my grandmother!"

"Do you actually believe he told you the truth?"

Savana's emotions erupted. "It has to be true! It means everything to me! Can't you understand—"

A quick knock sounded and the door opened. "Cap'n, the women are in the longboat now—" The interrupting voice of John Wesley came to an abrupt halt in the doorway. Savana hastily turned away from Trace.

"Sorry, Cap'n. Mrs. Warrender was wondering about the big delay keeping Miss Mackenzie from the longboat."

Savana marched to the cabin window, her heart pounding, her hands clenched in fists at the sides of her skirts.

"I'll get the proof you want on Sarakof," Trace told her before he went out.

Savana didn't reply. She heard the door shut behind him and the unmistakable rattle of a key. She spun around and ran to grab the knob, jerking on it.

"Trace! Let me out!"

The sound of his steps faded. Again she rattled the knob loudly, then pounded in frustration with both fists.

She had become a prisoner aboard the *Okanagan*.

She leaned her forehead against the door, trying to reject his suspicions about the baron.

By the time Mrs. Warrender and Roslyn arrived at Fort Vancouver from Astoria and explained her strange absence to her uncle, the *Okanagan* would be nearing New Archangel. She took satisfaction in knowing that Sir Douglas would not be far behind.

She felt tension twist her stomach into knots. Both Trace and Peter were dangerous men and equally strong, but the baron had the advantage of operating in his own waters with a command of patrol boats at his disposal.

Could Trace be right? Was the baron trying to deceive her? There was always that possibility, but her uncle also trusted Peter and so did the countess. It was only Yuri and Trace who claimed otherwise. And Yuri was dead.

She shuddered and sank into a nearby chair, trying to think clearly. Perhaps it would have been wiser to not have accused Trace. Little good had been accomplished by the combative ordeal she'd just been through.

Her mind weaved in and out of ideas and plans, trying to come up with something that might win her freedom. If only she could escape at New Archangel and slip to shore. But even if she could get out of the cabin, how would she launch a longboat?

She might try to win the friendship and support of the Colonel or even John Wesley, but both men were utterly devoted to Trace. And so was the Kanaka steward from Honolulu. She'd not spoken to the other crew members and there was little opportunity to do so now. Even if she tried, she might be worsening her situation, for she had no notion of whether or not she could trust any of them.

She wondered how Trace would manage to get into Baranof Castle to speak to the count without her uncle or members of the Hudson's Bay Company delegation.

An idea began to tumble about her mind, enlarging as she mulled it over and debated its wisdom. Trace had asked her to trust him. . . . She sat up straight in the chair.

What if she decided to do just that—on the surface? What if—what if she told him he could be right after all about the baron, about the risk to herself in going to the castle alone?

What if she told him she would cooperate with his interests if he would bring her to meet the countess?

No sooner did the thought gain momentum than she sighed and leaned back in the chair. He'd refuse. He was determined to keep her out of sight and locked in the cabin until sending her aboard the Boston ship bound for Honolulu.

There must be some way! She had to convince him, but how? If only he needed her—

*Yes, that's it! Trace must need me to help him accomplish his plans.*

But he'd see through her offer at once—he was too clever to believe she would suddenly experience a change of heart and switch loyalties from England to Boston.

Unless . . .

Unless he could be convinced that somehow he actually did need her at New Archangel to accomplish his goal. And convinced, even reluctantly convinced, that he had no alternative but to take her with him and trust her. . . . But what did she have that he needed enough to relent and bring her to the castle when he was so firmly against her going?

It was late that night when Savana awoke in the dark cabin feeling the rough movement of the ship in the water. The silver moonlight reflected on the small windows and fell across the desk. The timbers creaked and groaned, filling her ears. In a moment of stark clarity the answer to her dilemma seemed to show itself. Her excitement spiraled. Yes, there was a chance he'd need her after all, if he expected to get into Baranof Castle to speak privately to the count. And who could best see that he got past the inner guards and official committee but herself?

She tossed aside the woolen blanket and weaved her way across the floor to the desk, fumbling to turn up the lantern. She opened the drawer and removed a piece of stationery and the writing pen, careful to keep the ink bottle from sliding across the desk. She wrote a brief message:

*Trace,*

*You cannot hope to accomplish all your aims without me. With my assistance you can get inside Baranof Castle and speak personally to Count Aleksandr. We must talk again.*

*Savana*

*That should give Trace Wilder something to think about between here and New Archangel,* she decided, pleased with her move. *All I need to do when he responds is to make certain he agrees to his part of the bargain.*

# 17

## HEART, BEWARE

At daybreak a week later the *Okanagan* sliced ahead through a churning sea with heavy gray swells reflecting the rain clouds hovering low. The sun was just above the horizon when Trace came up on deck in his wintry sweater, cap, and boots. John Wesley swung down from the shroud lines, his straight black hair whipping in the icy wind.

"Cape Burunof astern!"

Trace squinted against the wind that swept down from the purple-shadowed mountains crested with snow. He rested his elbows on the rail and leveled the telescope, trying to get Savana out of his mind.

He studied the horizon astern, but there were no ships in sight. He was arriving ahead of Bellomont and Sarakof, but he must work swiftly to accomplish his purpose. Bellomont would not be far behind, and Sarakof might also be somewhere in the area, though he believed him absent from the castle. When the baron returned, the *Okanagan*—and Savana—must be anchored out of sight. He had the place chosen before he left San Francisco. A ship could cove indefinitely at Kootznahoo without being spotted by Sarakof's patrol boats because of the thickly wooded islands surrounding the inlet.

Boston ships were greeted suspiciously in these waters even when carrying goods desired by New Archangel. Now, however, with winter settling in, the count was in dire need. There was already thick snow in the mountains, and the low-hanging clouds promised snowfall in the lower elevations. The wheat was a lifeline for Count Aleksandr, and he knew it. The skeleton face of famine could arrive on the back of the icy winds blowing in from the interior of Alaska, and the Russians at New Archangel had felt its bitterness before. At best the ordinary Russian's diet was restricted. Only the officials on Baranof Hill and guests from the nobility in St. Petersburg received a table of fine, fat things to go along with their well-known craving for vodka.

Count Aleksandr would desperately need Trace's American wheat, so he should be welcome. But how could he manage to get past the petty officials to speak with the count? There were bound to be men loyal to the baron, either willingly or from fear. Trace believed that Sarakof would have already made certain of the loyalty of the castle guards before he could have moved this far against the count's authority. And if Count Aleksandr were ill as the baron had informed Sir Bellomont at Fort Ross, the baron would arrive soon to take command of the government. Even now Count Aleksandr might be isolated from men in the Company who were loyal to him and strong enough to oppose Sarakof.

What if the count were already dead?

Trace didn't think so, not yet. Sarakof still needed Aleksandr for the final stages of his plans. Plans which included Savana.

Trace's eyes squinted thoughtfully as he lowered the telescope. He had told her he would learn what those plans were, that he would give her proof of Sarakof's character . . . but could he? The answers would be found inside Baranof Castle, either with Count Aleksandr or Countess Catherine Rezanov. But how would he get past the lesser officials and the men who served Baron Sarakof into the bedchamber of either Count Aleksandr or the countess?

There would be men in the castle who feared Sarakof too much to think of crossing him unless certain of his defeat. Others would be anxious to cooperate with the baron to benefit their own greed and security within the Russian-American Fur Company, men who would turn against the weakened Count Aleksandr.

"I must get inside Baranof Castle to see Count Aleksandr before Sarakof knows I'm there. Getting past the front committee won't be easy."

John Wesley followed his gaze toward the islands. "You could bring the girl, like she offered. She would be a sure entry. It may be worth the problem to take her. She's a nice girl, I think. If she says she will keep her promise, you can take the risk."

Trace had done everything he could since receiving her message days ago to find a reason to reject her offer. Yet, try as he might, he knew that she was right. If she cooperated with his purpose in delivering the wheat she would prove a valuable ally. They could work together to accomplish not only his purpose but also look into the matter of her missing father.

Trace believed James Mackenzie to be dead, but Savana would never know peace or satisfaction until the truth was before her eyes.

Yet to work together for two separate goals at Baranof Castle she must trust him more than the baron. It was irritating to think she did not. Of course, what had he done in the time he had known her to win her confidence? The truth was, he had been an antagonist, however friendly. He'd thought it wiser for her sake—now he wasn't sure.

His emotions were a jumble of confused and mixed feelings. He had every intention of having her out of his thoughts, yet she kept returning.

"She stays aboard," he said flatly. "And while I'm gone I want Flannigan and Broderick on deck with weapons. They're to keep the crew ready. We may need to set sail in a moment's notice."

"You will have the wheat and Bellomont's niece. You've got good weapons in hand, Cap'n. Which men will you take with you in the longboat?"

"You'll draw less attention among the Indians and Eskimos. And I want the ex-boxer, Calhoun; he doesn't talk much and he's plenty good with his fists. And tell Flannigan no one is to come aboard or leave. If anything goes wrong he's to head for Kootznahoo."

"We will be stranded in New Archangel, Cap'n, if Flannigan needs to slip away without us to the cove."

Trace handed him the telescope and turned to leave. "One thing at a time."

Trace kept the *Okanagan* a safe distance from New Archangel and ordered the anchor dropped at nine fathoms. Giving orders to ready the longboat to bring them to the Russian port, he frowned to himself at what he was about to do and walked to the cabin where Savana remained under guard.

Stopping outside the door, he motioned aside the Kanaka guard, then knocked. She would be pleased that he'd bitten the sweetened bait of her proposal, delivered days earlier. Unfortunately, she held the golden key to his entrance into the castle. He waited a moment, then removed the key from under his sweater and unlocked the door.

She arose from the chair, looking regal in a burgundy satin dress with lace, her flaxen hair smooth and sleek and wrapped about her head like a woven shimmering crown. Her eyes came to his expectantly.

He removed his dark blue knit cap, tossed it on his desk

with a surrender that hinted also of challenge, and shut the door behind him.

"Shall we talk business?"

Savana watched him, cautiously, her pleasure over his co-operation concealed in a smile that formed on her lips. "Then you'll bring me to see the countess?"

He folded his arms as he leaned there, a wry smile meeting hers. "Against my better judgment."

The change in his behavior set her on guard, and she mused whether there might not be another motive prompting his action. After several days without an answer to her written message delivered by Colonel Pelly, she had all but given up hope that he would agree to her compromise. In the days following the delivery of the message her avid questioning of the Colonel about Trace's response had yielded little but the assurance that "There ain't no rushin' a man like Trace, but when he does make up his mind, you'll be able to depend on what he says."

"Why did you change your mind?" she asked Trace warily.

He watched her pensively. After a moment or two he apparently came to some decision that he wasn't altogether pleased about having to make.

"All right, Savana, no more games between us. We'll need to trust each other if either of us expects to accomplish what brought us here." He straightened and walked toward her. "Captain Dembe's ship hasn't arrived with the wheat as I had planned. Something has happened, but I don't know what. I had expected to use it to gain audience with Count Aleksandr. I no longer have that advantage."

She searched his face and then, unable to keep a smile from forming, smothered a laugh.

Trace smirked and folded his arms again. "You needn't look so delighted. Especially with Sarakof soon to arrive—

unless you take satisfaction in the possibility of my being sent to Siberia."

The idea sobered her. "You don't suppose one of Peter's patrol boats found Captain Dembe?" she whispered.

He looked at her, alert.

She withdrew behind a bland expression. "Well, I should hate to see you and your crew sent off to Siberia. I wouldn't wish that on anyone—even an American agent who betrayed my uncle."

"Very generous of you."

Savana wasn't at all sure of her feelings. As a representative of His Majesty she rejoiced that the arrogant Americans had been foiled in their plot, except that she had no wish to see Trace come to harm. While she questioned his summation of Peter, she knew the Russian baron was a strong opponent who would show no pity on Captain Trace Wilder.

Trace lounged in the chair behind his desk, musing to himself, his fingers locked behind his head, his booted legs stretched out before him. "It is also possible that Bellomont learned about the *Yankee Trader* and warned the baron."

She slowly walked up to him. "If Sir Douglas did learn that you transferred the wheat to the other Boston ship, you wouldn't think that I informed him?"

He looked up at her evenly. "I thought of that, but you wouldn't have had time."

Savana wondered that she felt a nibble of guilt. Was she beginning to care about the American interests in the Pacific Northwest, or about the rugged young man before her?

"What if Sir Douglas alerted Peter and he already knows you're here? You could be in danger."

He looked at her from beneath dark lashes, his fingers tapping against each other. "You mean that he was waiting in advance to confiscate the *Yankee Trader*?"

She didn't relish saying it: "Yes, and actually baiting you to enter New Archangel."

"Hmm . . . like an Eskimo baiting a wolf? Just enough frozen bait is placed on a sharp knife to get it to begin to lick—as it cuts its own numbed tongue, the wolf doesn't realize it is drinking a slow death."

"Please," she whispered, rubbing her arms and turning her head away.

"Well, you get the idea." He stood and walked to the desk. "I've been thinking about Sarakof, knowing I'm about to enter his domain. There's nothing he'd like better. Unfortunately, I won't know whether it's safe or not. I must try to accomplish my objective and get out before he arrives."

Anxiety tightened her nerves. "But if it is a trap—"

"The message I received a short time ago informed me Sarakof will arrive tomorrow. That may be just enough time, that is—" and he gave her a searching look—"if you cooperate with me. Did you mean what you wrote in your message?"

*Who's told him that the baron will arrive tomorrow? Is there another American agent about, this one perhaps in New Archangel?*

"If Peter could arrive tomorrow, then you must not try to accomplish your mission, Trace. You know he dislikes you, even if you weren't working for Andrew Jackson."

"Then you're beginning to believe me about his reputation," he stated, watching her response.

She couldn't tell if it was her feelings toward the baron that interested Trace or her national loyalties, but she wasn't about to betray either.

"I've no doubt the baron is an able leader, who for his own purposes can become ruthless. After all, he's in command over the czar's patrol boats, but . . . I wouldn't want you to come to harm."

"What interest could the granddaughter of the Russian countess have in the fate of a nettlesome Boston agent?"

"I've no grudge," she said evasively, "national or personal, that I would wish to see a friend arrested."

"Ah—a friend," he repeated, as though tasting the meaning of the word. "Then this unexpected friendship of yours with an unlikely American agent is the motive for your warning," he said with a balmy tone.

"What else would it be?" She walked away from where he stood and removed her hooded cape from the wooden peg beside the table. She held it against her as she turned again to face him, meeting his keen gaze.

"We mustn't waste precious time, Captain Wilder."

"I commend your efficiency, Miss Mackenzie. I have a plan in mind. Without the wheat, I don't have the authority to convince anyone in Baranof Castle to allow me to speak alone with Count Aleksandr. However, if I arrive as your bodyguard to see you safely to the countess, between the two of us, I think I can manage."

"Yes, to see the countess—may I also ask who sent you the message about Peter's soon arrival?"

He folded his arms. "An agent. But unfortunately he can't do much else for me. Don't look surprised—we have as many prowling the Pacific Northwest as England and Russia; we're just not as sophisticated," he remarked dryly.

As she mused, the icy northern wind buffeted the square-rigger, and the timbers groaned and fidgeted in protest.

"I don't expect you to accept my estimation of Sarakof, since you seem quite enamored with him, but I've good reason to believe he plans to eliminate the count and assume command before Sir Douglas arrives."

Shocked, she looked quickly at him, the suggestion doing little to ease her concerns.

"You can," he stated, "join your Russian sympathies with an American cause in order to save the count's life."

"Save his life!"

"I assume you'd want to do so since he's your uncle."

She stood rigid, weighing his suggestion that Peter could move to kill the count.

"My grandmother trusts him; have you forgotten that?"

He frowned. "No, and that's another cause for alarm. I can't see her trusting him with the Rezanov diamonds or with her granddaughter."

"Perhaps you are too suspicious. I've hoped and prayed too long," she persisted. "If there's the slightest chance either Peter or my grandmother can offer new information on my father, then I'm willing to take a risk."

"Prayer is always wise. The Lord also expects us to use sound wisdom before we commit ourselves to any man's promises. You could be walking into a trap."

She restrained a shiver. "Yes, we both could."

He was silent, contemplating. "And you still want to go?"

She nodded, and her eyes took on a thoughtful glow. "New Archangel is where my father served God to bring Light to the Aleut Indians. He was willing to help a people that he knew his Lord cared deeply about. I want to see them, to feel even for a short time what must have burdened his heart—to carry on his work should the Lord so speak to me."

He walked toward her. "So that's it. You want to stay? It will mean the same fate as your father. Do you think the Russian-American Fur Company will accept your meddling any more than they accepted James Mackenzie's?"

"Then there's my mother . . . she died here giving me life. I must visit her grave! Oh, I know she isn't there—if she had faith in Christ she's with Him—but I want my heart to come in contact with something that belonged to her. And somehow I know she cared strongly about my father's work—or she wouldn't have fallen in love with him. What would have drawn her to him except the same fire that burned in his soul?"

She felt his fingers tighten about her shoulders and she sensed a growing oneness.

"Your love can motivate you to serve Him elsewhere if

He calls you. Must it be here where for the present the door to service is shut by authorities in the Russian-American Company? Why not Fort Vancouver with Jason Lee? You could help in the school, or with the medical work, and more missionaries will be coming if our plans are within His will."

Savana was startled by his confession. "Then you are involved with the American missionaries? Sir Douglas believes you're helping Jason Lee, who is also an agent, the missionary work being just a ruse to bring immigrants into Oregon."

"Jason is not a political agent for the American government, but if Oregon becomes a territory it will owe a great deal to the missionaries. They are the first pioneers willing to stay and build a territory. But they came, like your father in New Archangel, because of a higher motive than love of nation. They are more than American patriots—they are citizens of a better country, obeying God's commission. For Jason, and the others who will soon follow, it's a matter of teaching Scripture and building churches.

"Am I involved? Yes . . . as I told you before, they are friends, and when they needed cattle I was determined to see they had them. There are others who will be coming too, friends of mine from St. Louis."

Savana remembered what Colonel Pelly had told her about Callie Baxter, but a strange sick feeling that lodged in her heart smothered the question from being asked: *Is he involved with the missionaries primarily because of his interest in Callie?*

Savana moved away from him, deliberately changing the subject. "What the future holds for me, I don't know, but it begins here, Trace." She turned and looked at him as he waited by the door. "You are right, we need each other—" and she added more indifferently than she felt, "for the moment."

His expression became masked and the earlier mood between them melted away.

"And if I say nothing of your true motives," she continued, "that doesn't mean I agree with the deception of delivering 'American' wheat instead of British."

"Your silence is enough," he said agreeably.

She felt a prick in her heart. It was useless to pretend further. "Trace, you've been honest with me, and . . . and well, there's something you should know about why I'm aboard your ship."

His mouth turned up wryly. "You needn't explain. I already know. Bellomont is aware of a future wagon train heading to Oregon from Independence. And he suspects Yancey Wilder of becoming its scout. What were you supposed to find out from me—the date of its departure? I can't tell you that. I don't know. As for Yancey, your uncle's wrong."

She couldn't keep her surprise from showing. "You mean your brother isn't the scout? But what about his knowledge of the land? I thought—"

"I agree, Yancey would make the perfect scout. And don't misunderstand, I still hope to go to St. Louis when this is over and convince him to take on the mission, but you don't know Yancey. He can be more stubborn than I."

She smiled ruefully. "Is that possible?"

He returned her smile. "I suspected that Bellomont knew about me and Yancey all along. That was the reason he wished to hire me back in San Francisco. And why I deliberately showed up with an offer to sell him wheat for the Company's use in Russian America. You see, I also wanted to know how much he knew."

"And so I played right into your cause," she said, offended.

He smiled. "Your presence aboard the *Okanagan* has proven interesting to say the least, yet I wasn't depending on you. I sent a message to Yancey from San Francisco warning him."

She noticed the change in his voice from friendly rivalry to disquiet.

"You don't think Sir Douglas would actually send some-one to St. Louis to try to harm him?"

"Why not?"

"He'd never do that to a blooded cousin."

"No? The Hudson's Bay Company will do what it thinks it must to keep America from claiming Oregon. We recently had a war, Savana. What is the elimination of one trouble-some Yankee if it can buy time for England to bring in her own settlers from Red River Colony in Manitoba?"

Again she was surprised that he'd discovered the Com-pany's plans, until she remembered his earlier remark about agents in unlikely places.

"Then it's a race for time," she agreed. "And whoever wins Oregon will do so with settlers. It seems we cross pur-poses, doesn't it? I suppose Jason Lee expects to organize the settlers into a provisional government?"

"I've said I would be honest with you, Savana. It's no good unless we do. I can't answer about Jason. I haven't seen him in the past year, but you know my loyalties, and what-ever you think of them, I still intend to see it to the end. I need you to get in to see Count Aleksandr; and if you wish to leave the *Okanagan*, you'll need to cooperate."

"We have a bargain," she said, "but one that lasts only until we reach the castle. Once you meet with the count, my loyalties will remain on the side of England. If you would avoid the baron, I suggest we leave at once."

"My next suggestion." He frowned. "I don't take any pleasure in leaving you unguarded at the castle, and I don't know when your uncle will arrive to stand by you."

She concealed her own worry, for she dare not ask him to stay and risk himself, nor did she want him to. "I shall be safe enough, thank you. The countess, after all, is my grand-mother."

She went to the door ahead of him where her trunk was packed and waiting, and when he made no move to follow, she turned to see him frowning.

"How long will you need to meet with her to discuss your father?"

"I expected to be here for some weeks during my uncle's negotiations with Count Aleksandr."

"You realize that you'll be under Sarakof's care."

"I do not suspect Peter as you do. As you say, you have your cause and I have mine. Each of us must go our own way."

His eyes flickered. "I'm pleased you feel so warm and friendly about it all, Miss Mackenzie. Then once I meet with the count I shall be on my way. Shall we go? You've a countess and baron to meet, and Rezanov diamonds to wear. I wouldn't want to take more of your time warning you of the risk."

As he bowed her through the door, she brushed past him.

"Sarakof will have his trusted men in position," he said, walking beside her. "He works efficiently. So must we."

# 18

## In the Day of My Trouble

While Trace gave last-minute instructions to Flannigan and Colonel Pelly, Savana was aided over the ship's side and down the swaying rope ladder where she was handed into the *bidarka* containing a harbor pilot and a paddler.

John Wesley and another man she'd not seen before entered a second hide-covered canoe, and a brief time later Trace joined her.

Savana had set aside her concerns to bask in the northern beauty surrounding her. In the distance, the snow-covered Mount Edgecumbe shimmered in the sunlight. In the east—if her earlier research in England proved to be accurate—was Mount Verstovia.

As the boat slipped smoothly down the channel, her breath caught when the stone peaks of Baranof Castle came into view.

"Do you know about the earlier Baranof era?" Trace asked, settling his wide-brimmed hat against the icy glare that surrounded them and following her gaze to the castle.

"It was Baranof who encouraged Russian expansion in the Pacific Northwest, resulting in Fort Ross in California," she replied. "I suppose you think Peter is as ambitious as Baron Baranof was."

"But not as capable. Sarakof is weak when he's alone."

She glanced at him, showing her disapproval, but it didn't disturb him and he remained thoughtful. She wondered if he might try to get Peter alone.

"Baranof was tough-minded and could rule even tougher men," he was saying. "He almost captured Hawaii."

Savana shivered in the icy wind and drew her soft cape about her throat. "You know so much about Russian history, perhaps it is you who should have Rezanov blood."

"It is enough to play your devoted bodyguard, bringing you from Fort Vancouver to meet the countess," he drawled easily. "Shall I add some flavor to my acting and let them think my devotion is out of love?"

She felt the wind cool her face. "There's no need for that, Captain. Besides, you wouldn't want talk to somehow circulate the many miles back to St. Louis and Miss Baxter's ears. She might take it seriously."

No sooner had she spoken than she wished she hadn't, for his gaze found hers and held it until she looked out at the water. She hoped he didn't guess her churning emotions. In his buckskin jacket with the Spanish-style hat, Trace looked more like a handsome wilderness pathfinder than a shipmaster.

Savana noticed men on the landing watching their bidarka approach New Archangel, but she couldn't guess if their manner was friendly or not. Trace took her arm and helped her out onto the wooden wharf. "Wait here a moment."

She watched as he went to speak with John Wesley and the wiry, muscular crewman in the other boat. A few minutes later the two men from the *Okanagan* disappeared into the throng on the wharf, and Trace walked back to where she waited. She noticed he wore a small leather satchel and carried a scabbard with sword. He had also worn a gun since disembarking the square-rigger. Trace apparently saw her questioning look for he said simply, "A paid bodyguard always carries his weapons."

Minutes later Savana and Trace emerged onto the street that led to Baranof Hill.

"The natives have their bazaar along the route," he told her. "These are the Indians Mackenzie tried to befriend. They are from the Tlingit tribe, and they gather here daily to sell their wares to the various traders who might come in from the sea."

She paused. "Why, you've been here before," she said surprised, but he took hold of her arm and ushered her along, steering her through the throng gathering to stare at them.

"I didn't think it was a secret," he said mildly.

"Not a secret! You've deliberately not told me or Sir Douglas."

"Maybe." He looked at her and smiled, then gestured. "Those are baskets of spruce roots. Would you like one?"

"No, thank you."

"You don't know what you're missing. . . . And those are whistles. They carve them from rock crystal. Anytime you get into any danger, Miss Mackenzie, all you need do is whistle and I'll come running."

Savana smiled. "I'll remember that."

As they walked together, both the Indians and the Russians turned to stare. Trace's hat with its decorative silver pesos caught the interest of the Tlingit, and Savana's dress, partially covered by her cape, was elaborate, though she knew they must have seen many Russian nobles visiting the castle.

Savana was captivated with the Tlingit men, some with elaborate face paint and markings, and they were much bigger in stature than she had expected. The Tlingit women, in their exotic native clothing, lined the street in silence. They were all offering some object to sell, yet they didn't try to catch her attention with crying and shouting, but stood with a pride that contradicted the position into which the Russians had forced them.

"The Tlingit were an even stronger people before the white man's weapons and diseases destroyed many of them during Baranof's time. They are still warlike to some degree," Trace said. "They turned on the Russian colony in the beginning and nearly wiped them out, despite the Russians' superior weapons. Given an opportunity, I think they'd delight to do it again."

Savana drew closer to his side as they passed a tall, warriorlike Tlingit who watched them without expression, white markings across his broad olive-skinned face. Just then she saw an equally husky Russian employee of the Company stagger out the door of a vodka tavern. She had heard Zoya speak of the *promyshlenki*, the men who hunted furs for the Company. It was the story of how these men had mistreated the Aleut farther north in the islands that had lit the fire of her anger. The Russians would hold the Aleutian women and children captive aboard their vessels until the Aleut men would bring them as many skins as they demanded. While the Aleut hunted, being forced to kill more and more of the fur animals, the drunken promyshlenki would rape their women. At last the Aleut men banned together to fight them, but the Russians had better weapons and slaughtered them, bringing the Indians into slavery.

Savana's father had worked against this evil practice and had ardently complained to the officials in the Russian-American Fur Company here in New Archangel, but they had done little to stop it. Finally he had sought to bring a report firsthand to the czar.

She told Trace about Zoya's brother, a priest at the Orthodox church of St. Nicholas. "He might have known the priest who journeyed with my father."

"I'll do what I can to ask around St. Nicholas, but it may take a day. First I need to see the count."

Baranof Castle came into view, foreboding yet grand.

"Are you certain you wouldn't rather forget this and go back to the *Okanagan*?" Trace prodded.

"The only chance of that, Captain, is if you tie me up and drag me back to your boat."

"Not a bad idea. . . ."

"But if you do, you won't get in to see Count Aleksandr."

They stood near the terrace before the castle and Savana turned, looking expectantly toward the port where islands thick with pine trees were scattered throughout the channels. Farther behind New Archangel was the vast land of unexplored snow and ice called Alaska.

Inside the front alcove they were greeted by a stalwart Russian with blond hair and a heavy mustache who spoke only broken English. While he looked at them cautiously, Trace forcefully demanded that his ward, the granddaughter of Countess Catherine Rezanov, be admitted at once—and that, as her guard, he would not think of leaving her alone for a second until she was safely with the countess.

The somewhat-intimidated front guard grudgingly appraised Trace, whose weapons were obvious. Bidding them into an inner chamber, he insisted upon proof of their identity.

Trace reached inside his jacket for the letter from the countess and held it for the soldier to read.

"English," he said with obvious frustration.

"Then find a man who can read it."

When the soldier reached for it, Trace drew it back, folded it neatly and slipped it back inside his jacket. "Find someone."

The sharp sound of the guard's heels on the floor reverberated as he disappeared down the long hallway.

Savana looked about her, awed by the sight. Despite New Archangel's wilderness atmosphere, the castle was a work of art—marble statues, exquisite paintings, and drapes and wall hangings of gold and scarlet. Several portraits of the czars—most of whom she did not know—were displayed, as was a portrait of Catherine the Great.

Savana's stomach fluttered nervously as she realized how close she was to meeting her grandmother for the first time. Soon she would learn the intimate, personal details about her mother, Nadyia.

She was aware that Trace stood near, watching her in silence. "I can't imagine being born here," she murmured, turning about. "I don't belong, do I?" she asked suddenly, her eyes swerving to his.

He studied her briefly. "You could comfortably pass for any princess, even the czar's niece."

"You say that rather flatly."

"Maybe I prefer you as simply a 'Mackenzie'—much more approachable than a czar's niece."

They looked at each other for a long moment, then Savana turned her gaze as another door opened and the Russian soldier reappeared.

"Come, please," was all he said, and Savana exchanged glances with Trace as they followed, his hand lightly on her arm. She was glad he was with her to offer quiet but strong support.

They entered what Savana took for some manner of receiving room with ornate divans and chairs. She was aware of the cold, of the shadows in the corners, and of a fire in a wall-sized hearth.

Trace did not know why, but his instincts alerted him. The stone walls seemed suddenly too close, the smell of the oil lanterns oppressive. His hand tightened on Savana's arm and she looked at him, sensing his mood. He was about to draw her from the chamber when he heard a faint rustle of garments from a divan in a shadowed corner.

A man stood, pausing to evaluate Trace.

"Welcome to Baranof Castle, Wilder. I've been waiting for you."

He stepped into the light, and Trace stopped. Baron Sarakof stood smiling smugly.

Trace's hand moved reflexively toward his pistol and Sarakof noticed at once.

"No need for weapons, my American captain. You are a guest. And I have fifty armed men at my disposal. You can make no move unless I authorize it." He gestured toward a chair. "Sit down."

Trace felt Savana's arm tense, but she recovered and made a gracious movement to step between them, and he admired her bravery.

"Why, Baron, we did not know you had arrived. This is most pleasant news!" She swept toward him, a white-gloved hand extended and a smile on her lips. Wearing the burgundy and lace gown with her flaxen hair arranged about her head in a most enchanting way, she was astonishingly lovely, and coming between them as she did, she was like water to a crackling fire.

Baron Sarakof checked himself and automatically withdrew behind his immaculate uniform and soldierly discipline. He bowed, heels coming together, and swept her hand into his, bringing it toward his face. "Dear Savana, you are here at last and how much pleasure you bring me."

Trace couldn't resist: "And to the countess as well. You will inform her that the daughter of Nadyia Rezanov is here."

The baron's pale eyes swerved to meet Trace's and all pleasantness left his face, his square jaw flexing with restrained contempt.

"You may be assured, Captain, that Savana will see the countess." He looked again at her and smiled, still holding her hand possessively. Trace saw her casual movement to withdraw her hand to the side of her billowing skirts.

He wondered if Sarakof had intercepted the *Yankee Trader*. If not, there still remained a small chance.

Trace could not broach the subject himself without alerting the baron. When Savana glanced at him, he believed she read his suggestion that she might get by with an inquiry.

Trace said confidently, "It is my duty as guard to bring Miss Mackenzie to the countess."

Baron Sarakof dismissed the idea with an abrupt gesture. "Savana is quite safe now that she's in my company. She is my concern now, and mine alone."

He smiled in a friendly fashion to Savana, but she too must have noticed Sarakof's brusque manner. She said politely but casually, "Captain Wilder is expressing my wish, Peter. I would like to be brought to her."

"The countess has said she will indeed see you soon, but she is indisposed at the moment. She will entertain you in her private apartment before the ball in your honor tomorrow night. Until then, you must be fatigued from such a trying voyage aboard the *Okanagan*. You will rest and refresh yourself until tomorrow."

Trace measured him. His "suggestion" was a polite way of informing her that she was now under Sarakof's guard.

"Does this imply my services in escorting Miss Mackenzie are no longer wanted?" he asked bluntly.

"Doubtless, they were never needed, Captain. You abducted her. What motive might you have had for bringing her here instead of British Fort Vancouver to join her uncle, Sir Douglas Bellomont?"

"Why, Peter, what an odd accusation," said Savana, laughing off the tense moment. "Abducted me? It was Uncle who arranged to have me sent ahead with Cousin Trace on his ship."

"Is that so? Then perhaps the message arriving only an hour ago from the British fort was in error? Chief Factor McLoughlin felt it urgent to inform us that a lady passenger from the *Okanagan* said you were forced to stay aboard against your will."

"Hardly that," she said with a laugh and walked over to Trace, taking hold of his arm with both hands in a friendly fashion. "I didn't choose to disembark at Fort Vancouver and talked my cousin into bringing me with him. I was so anxious to come to New Archangel to meet my grandmother."

Trace's gaze met hers—he had never appreciated her more.

"Then I am delighted," said the baron and walked up to them, taking Savana's arm, his eyes studying her face. "After our short discussion at Fort Ross, I am most pleased you wish to cooperate with our families' wishes that we come to know each other better. I should show you New Archangel tomorrow before the ball."

"I fear you were right about the voyage, Peter. I am indeed fatigued and should take your advice and rest."

Trace looked on, expressionless. *Well done*, he thought. She had avoided Sarakof's trap. He did not look as though he appreciated her slippery refusal, yet Trace could see that he was pretending to relent with grace. He bowed smartly at the waist and dismissed the subject. "Then you will be shown to your room for the night."

Savana turned to Trace. "How good of you to see to my needs these weeks, Cousin Trace. You will stay as Uncle wishes, won't you? I'm certain he'll arrive soon from Fort Vancouver. There was more business to discuss, I believe, on the next load of wheat from your rancho. And I would also like to introduce you to my grandmother tomorrow night at the ball. You will stay as our guest, won't you?"

He immediately snatched the lifeline she had tossed. "If you are certain I won't be imposing. . . ."

"Quite the contrary," she insisted, and turned to the baron cheerfully. "You do not mind, Peter, if my American cousin stays for the ball?"

Sarakof's expression was one of restrained rage. "It would appear, Captain, that Savana would be disappointed if you left so soon."

"I would not disappoint my cousin."

"By all means, stay—and as you say—the arrival of Sir Bellomont will come shortly. Then, I am certain, all things will become clear."

The baron turned, calling for a guard.

A brief exchange of glances between Trace and Savana ended when the Russian guard entered and bowed toward Sarakof.

"Take Miss Mackenzie to her room."

Trace turned to escort her, but Sarakof's voice interrupted: "Not you, Captain. We have a matter to discuss."

Savana paused, glancing at them, and Trace knew what she was thinking. If they were separated at all, it might mean his arrest despite Sarakof's outward pretense.

"You will excuse your cousin, Savana. He and I must discuss the delivery of the wheat."

*Then Sarakof has not captured the* Yankee Trader, *nor does he know yet that there is no wheat aboard the* Okanagan. *Then where is Captain Dembe?*

Savana's brief glance of relief met his, then she turned, bidding them both good night. Trace watched her follow the guard out of the receiving room. His own tension heightened.

He must discover to what room the Russian soldier brought her. She too was under guard. Just what did Sarakof have in mind?

# 19

# TRAPPED IN BARANOF CASTLE

Savana paused in the outer hall, hoping to hear more of what was being spoken between Peter and Trace, but the Russian soldier was nearing a flight of chiseled steps and expected her to follow.

The sound of their steps echoed within the stone hall where bronze lanterns flickered, casting weaving shadows onto the walls.

Her chamber was cold and the fire in the hearth cast a languishing glow onto the fur rug. In the corner stood a huge bed covered with black and white fur. Four steps led up to the mattress, and on either side of the steps were tall brass votive urns with large candles shining through the cutwork.

Savana stood in front of the hearth and turned to face the soldier. "Where is my companion and serving woman, Zoya?"

He shook his head, mouth turning down at the corners and palms held toward her. "No Zoya."

The door shut behind him and she heard something jangle. A key rattled in the lock, and the echo of footsteps faded down the hall.

Where was Zoya? She hurried to the heavy door encircled with leather straps and iron, and uselessly turned the oversized knob. She was not only alarmed for herself and Zoya but for Trace. They were castle-bound prisoners in Russian jurisdiction. Trace did not have the wheat to barter with, and he was avidly disliked by the baron. There was no doubt in her mind that Trace was strong enough to match the baron, but not against his many guards.

"I must get a message to him." But even if she managed to leave her chamber, she knew the baron might have a guard posted, watching her every move.

She must remain calm. Perhaps she was imagining the worst. Maybe she'd been locked inside for what was considered to be her own safety. She might be misjudging the animosity she had seen in the baron's eyes. If she were racing to conclusions, what motives spurred Peter's actions? Did he simply disapprove of Trace as an American, and wish to be rid of him?

Trace had warned her that Peter was ruthless. There'd been a brief time tonight when she had witnessed an aspect to his character that he'd not revealed at Fort Ross. *And yet*, she mused, troubled, *it is also true that Peter is the only one in the family who can bring me to the countess.* She paced. She must not alienate him by appearing to side with Trace. She must give him no cause to think she didn't trust him.

And where was Trace now? What excuse could she use to get a message to him that wouldn't cast suspicion on either of them?

Savana prayed earnestly for wisdom and protection for herself and Trace, and a measure of calm returned to her thudding heart. They were not alone. Words from Psalm 139, planted in her mind years earlier like seed, now blossomed with hope. *"Even there shall thy hand lead me, and thy right hand shall hold me."*

As calm returned to her soul she began to think that her fears forged phantoms across her pathway. After all, if the ball were planned in honor of her, then she was rushing to conclusions. Peter had even offered to show her around New Archangel.

Again she prayed that she might hear from the Lord as to His purpose for her, but her heart was so fixed upon her own wishes that she couldn't hear the still small voice. Did her future belong to Baranof Castle or to Fort Vancouver?

There was a look of smiling disdain on Baron Sarakof's face. "Arrest the American."

Trace's blade whispered from its scabbard as armed guards stepped in his direction from several locations.

"Your sword will do you little good. You are outnumbered," said Sarakof.

"I will kill the first man who thinks himself a swordsman."

The guards hesitated. "What of you, Baron? Your reputation as a duelist is well known. Or do you need more time to arrange your success? Is it not true that in St. Petersburg you pay hired assassins to do your work for you?"

Sarakof mottled with anger. "I need no help to see you die, Wilder, but now is not the hour."

"And neither is it an hour for me to go like a whipped hyena to a rat-infested dungeon. For what do you think to arrest me? I demand to see Count Aleksandr. You are under his authority."

"I will be in sole authority soon enough." He gestured to the guards.

*The ailing Count Aleksandr must be oblivious to the baron's claim of command over the castle. I must locate and warn him, or the countess.*

Was Trace's attempted venture foiled already? He thought of Savana. She must be nearby. He must do something to at least delay Sarakof for a time . . . anything. Despair welled up within him—guards, wherever he looked. While he could put up a strong fight, nothing would be accomplished in the end but a few deaths—including his own. He must be more clever than Sarakof. . . .

"Your ship, where have you anchored it?" demanded the baron.

For a moment Trace wondered. *His patrol boats should have spotted it by now, just a short distance from the wharf—* He stopped.

If Sarakof had to inquire, then Flannigan may have gotten word from Wesley or Calhoun that the baron was already back. Smart Irishman that he was, Flannigan probably weighed anchor and slipped into the foggy maze of islands near the coast to evade the patrol boats.

While the ship remained undetected, it also meant that he, Savana, and his two crewmen were trapped on foot in Russian territory. There would be no escape from New Archangel unless they could somehow reach his ship by bidarka. Any plan, however, must wait. There were objectives he must accomplish within the castle, but he needed something important enough to stall Sarakof.

He smiled at the baron to show his contempt. Sarakof was a proud man and vain, and did not like it when an enemy refused to be intimidated. Trace sheathed his blade with disdain. "You are not only rash but foolish. If you move against me now, it may cost what you desire most—your position close to the czar."

He saw a brief look of uncertainty in the baron's eyes.

"What do you mean?" Sarakof demanded.

Trace showed cool mockery. "You are not so unwise as to think I'd risk coming here without leaving myself room to maneuver? Your treachery is well known, Baron. I expected you to be waiting here at the castle, and made provisions for myself and my crew."

Sarakof was wary. "A safeguard, Wilder? How?"

"Both my ship and the wheat are secure. Until Captain

Fletcher is released and I speak with Count Aleksandr, there will be no wheat."

The baron waved the request aside. "The count is ill and I am in command. What business you have with the wheat and Miss Mackenzie, you must negotiate with me. As to your ship, Wilder, there is no use stalling for time. My patrol boats will locate it eventually. When they do, I shall see your American crew imprisoned for breaching Russian waters to spy for Andrew Jackson, but if you cooperate now, I shall consider a lighter penalty."

Trace smiled. "Do you take me for a fool? Your word is worth nothing." He folded his arms. "Whether or not you locate the *Okanagan* will make no difference. The wheat is not on board my ship. I took the precaution in San Francisco of having it loaded on a separate ship."

Sarakof's mouth tightened. "You lie."

"The ship's captain is under my order to dump it in the Pacific unless he hears from me. And I will not approve the delivery until Bellomont arrives from Fort Vancouver—and Fletcher is released as we bargained at Fort Ross."

Sarakof flushed with rage and appeared on the verge of striking him, but Trace's level gaze held him in restraint.

How long could he manage to bluff Sarakof?

"The hand of the long Russian winter hovers over New Archangel. If you want that wheat you will call off your guards and allow me to move freely about town. If not . . ."

Sarakof's eyes burned with anger. "I could force you to disclose the whereabouts of the ship. I could make you write the captain and tell him to release the wheat."

"If you think that, you are a bigger fool than I thought. Try it, and you will be sure to lose in the end."

The baron measured him and a flash of temper mingled with defeat. "For the present, Wilder, you are free of my dungeon. But one day I shall see you dead."

Trace lifted a brow and bowed lightly at the waist. "Until then, Baron, I should like a warm room for the night." He gestured an airy hand toward the window. "It is beginning to snow again—looks to be heavy. The wheat grows more precious than gold. And being hired by Sir Bellomont to see to Miss Mackenzie's safety until he arrives, I wish a chamber near hers and the freedom to speak with her should she request."

The baron raked him as coldly as though he were an insect, then lifted a hand toward the guards. "Take the American to a chamber." He looked at Trace. "You had best hope the Boston ship soon appears with the wheat—your life depends on it. Sleep well." He whipped about on his heel and strode away.

Night had fallen over Baranof Castle when Savana, dressed and dozing restlessly in a wing-backed chair, came awake, hearing a key turn in the lock. A light knock followed, and she stood, facing the door.

Her breath released silently when it opened and she saw that it was Trace, still wearing his cloak and carrying his weapons. She wondered how he'd managed to keep them. Behind him she glimpsed the same Russian guard who had brought her to the chamber standing immobile in the hall. Trace entered and shut the door.

There was an inner bolt, and he slipped it into place and turned toward her.

She swept toward him, her skirts rustling, catching herself just in time from taking hold of his arm.

"How did you manage?" she whispered, knowing the baron would wish to keep them separated until her uncle arrived.

He took her arm and propelled her away from the door into the middle of the large, chill chamber.

"It's to our gain that he's uncertain. A tiger tracking unfamiliar territory will move cautiously, but we haven't much time to accomplish our plans. For the moment, he's wondering whether to believe us about Bellomont hiring me to guard you until his arrival. Sarakof won't want to anger your uncle. He wants that treaty as much as Bellomont. As long as he believes us, we've some freedom in which to maneuver, but it won't last long. You can count on the baron already rearranging his plans and making new ones to see to my demise."

She felt cold and wanted to tremble but was aware of his strong grip on her arm. "What are you going to do?"

"I don't know yet. . . ."

She watched as he made a quick search of the chamber for another exit.

"There isn't another way out," she told him in a low voice. "I've already looked."

He continued his search. "Do you still have the Russian pistol?"

"Yes . . ."

"Good. Keep it handy. Where's your maid?"

"Zoya? I wish I knew! I've inquired of the guard, but he doesn't speak English."

"Or wants you to think he doesn't so you won't ask questions."

Trace walked to the window and moved aside the heavy drape to look below into the walled courtyard. Savana saw the snow flitting past the pane. He looked over at her, still holding the drape.

"When was the last time you actually saw her?" he asked.

Savana tried to hold her nagging fears at bay. "The night Zoya left Fort Ross and I returned with Mrs. Warrender and the others to San Francisco."

"Soon after Bellomont made plans for you to sail with me?"

"Yes. She was to meet me here."

"She sailed aboard the *Catherine*?"

The quiet question raised the level of her tension, and she walked up to where he stood at the window. The snow was accumulating on the stone wall, and the lighted torches flickered.

"Yes, but Sir Douglas was with her too," she explained, hoping the idea somehow guaranteed all was well.

"But was she to disembark at Fort Vancouver with Bellomont?"

Savana touched the thick brocade drape that smelled musty. "No . . . she was to voyage on ahead with Peter to ready my stay here at the castle. I fully expected her to have arrived with Peter."

A brief silence held them. She watched him gazing thoughtfully down into the courtyard. Did he see something of interest? Savana too peered below and saw only the snow-flakes growing thicker and clothing the stone wall with a white mantle. . . .

Trace let the drape fall back into place, shutting out the night.

"Can you think of any reason why Zoya might be a threat to the baron's plans?"

"No . . ." She hesitated. His gaze was pensive.

"You must trust me enough to tell me everything you know if there's even a small chance I can help you," he said.

She had little reason to doubt him now, since she already knew his mission for Boston. "Zoya was a loyal serving woman to my mother before her death. I'm certain she knows more than she's ever been willing to share with me, despite the many times I've tried to get her to discuss the past."

"But she was against you coming here."

"Yes, to the very last," she said wearily. "She spoke against Sir Douglas's plans to involve me from the time he first arrived in London and asked me to aid the king and the Hudson's Bay Company. Yet she'd never tell me why she was alarmed. For a time I thought it was only the concerns of an aged woman troubled by the thought of a long voyage across the sea." She looked at him, her eyes searching his. "Now I'm not certain."

"She may yet be all right. Is there a chance she might have disembarked at Fort Vancouver?"

Savana shook her head. "I don't think so. Toward the last,

when we were at Fort Ross she said something about making the most of our visit if I insisted on coming. She has a brother she wished to visit. You don't think—?"

His interest showed. "Here in New Archangel? Does he serve the Russian-American Fur Company?"

"He's a priest at the Russian Orthodox church—St. Nicholas. I mentioned the church when we arrived."

"Ah, so you did, and if I'd been a bit wiser I would have taken you there instead of bringing you to the castle."

"You mustn't blame yourself. You didn't know the baron had already arrived. And I insisted on coming. Anyway, I'm not so certain I'm trapped. It is you the baron dislikes."

His gaze flickered across her face, an irritated look in their depths. "You still think he has motives you can trust?"

She clung to her hope, fully aware that the rope was fraying. "I don't know yet," she said evasively.

"You need to be sure. If not, you might awaken one morning locked not in the castle but in a cabin aboard the *Catherine*, sailing for St. Petersburg."

If she chose to believe Trace it would mean an end to her plans of seeing her grandmother, of reconciling with the Rezanov family, and of locating her father.

A flicker of impatience hardened his flinty eyes. "We're wasting precious time. Tell me about Zoya's brother. Could she have gone there?"

She left the window and walked to the hearth, where little warmth was felt from the red coals breaking off the log. "Yes, she intended to visit him."

"Then perhaps she managed to escape Sarakof and is there now."

She turned her head to look at him evenly. "If she had any reason to escape Peter, yes, perhaps so. Zoya didn't like the baron," she admitted at last, her voice toneless.

She turned to stare into the fire as she heard Trace walk up. It came as a surprise when he took hold of her and turned her around to face him, his hands holding her forearms. She looked at him, the warm glow from the fire reflecting on his face.

"Why didn't she trust him? Savana, you must tell me."

"She wouldn't explain. It had something to do with the family's past in St. Petersburg. She spoke of ambitions and intrigue, of certain members scheming against each other to gain position and inheritance."

"She spoke of the baron?"

"I assume she included him," she said quietly.

"What did Sarakof promise that you would take such a risk? Besides meeting the countess?"

She drew in a breath. "All right, I'll tell you, but you're not likely to accept it. My father is alive," she stated. "And both Peter and the countess are willing to help me locate him. Peter thinks he's in Siberia."

Trace stared down at her. She waited, expecting him to attack the news, but he remained silent. "Go on," he said simply.

"Peter will soon journey to St. Petersburg to report to the czar on the work here at New Archangel and the treaty with the Hudson's Bay Company."

Savana paused and saw interest flicker in his eyes. "With the help of the countess, Peter expects to intercede for my father and return with him from a prison term in Siberia." She could see his anger fed by doubt, and she refused to see her hopes die. "Oh, Trace, can't you see? My grandmother wishes to help me and so does Peter!"

"The question remaining is why? What does he expect to get in St. Petersburg, and how do you fit in?"

"What of the countess?" she argued. "Would she also lie? I have the letter she wrote! Even Zoya admits that it's her handwriting—and what of the Rezanov diamonds?" she insisted. "How would Peter get them if the countess hadn't trusted him as she said in her letter? He's her nephew! She told me to trust him."

"I don't know where he may have gotten them—or whether they are even real. Neither do you."

He was right; she didn't know.

"Did Zoya believe the news about your father?"

"I didn't tell her," she admitted.

"You were afraid she would end your dream."

"No!" she said defensively.

"Did she see the letter, the diamonds?"

Savana remembered how Zoya questioned them. Her jaw set. "Yes, and she admitted they appeared genuine." Savana turned and walked away, her back toward him. "Forget Peter—what of the countess? Why would she deceive me?"

"I wish I knew," he said softly. "Maybe she's not here . . . maybe she's in St. Petersburg. Could she have written the letter delivered by Yuri?"

Savana turned to look at him, and his thoughtful anger unsettled her confidence. "You . . . you don't believe my father is in Siberia, do you?"

He walked toward her. She saw pity in his gaze, and it was more disturbing than his suspicions.

"No. I don't believe he's in Siberia. Even if the countess wishes to see you, your father is dead, Savana. He's been dead for five years."

His bluntness stung, and she reached to slap him in her bitter disappointment. He caught her wrist, and their eyes held. Savana felt her emotions break and fall wounded at her feet.

No! There had to be hope . . . there had to be. . . .

Tears moistened her eyes, and as she sought to escape his gaze, she felt his arms enclosing her, going about her back and waist.

"Savana . . ."

Startled, for a moment she stiffened, but when his lips met hers, something as intense as the lightning above the dark, fathomless sea bonded them together. Her resistance fled on wings.

A loud knock rapped on the door, shaking her emotions.

"The time granted your visit is over," came the guard's

clear Russian accent. "You are to return to your chamber, Captain Wilder."

Dazed, Savana's only clear thought was—*So the guard can speak English.*

Trace looked toward the door, and Savana turned her back.

"I'm sorry," he said softly. "About your father, that is."

Savana didn't reply. A moment later she heard the door shut behind him and again the unmistakable sound of the key. She leaned against the back of the chair, shutting her eyes, thinking of her father, and at the same moment trying to tear the memory of Trace's embrace from her heart.

It seemed only minutes had passed, but it must have been longer when another tap sounded on the door, this one quiet. She didn't know why she thought of Zoya, and she turned hopefully, but it was the baron who stood in the open doorway.

Her expression froze, and before she could recover her surprise, he offered a precise bow. He did not enter the chamber, however, and for this small reprieve she was grateful.

The baron stood in military uniform, his amber eyes scanning the chamber as if searching for Trace. His behavior had mellowed, and he offered a smile.

Savana rallied her poise, for she must not let him think that Trace had turned her against him. It would be detrimental. "Peter, you are up late."

She noticed what looked to be a note of subdued triumph in his eyes and it brought unease.

"I apologize for disturbing you, Savana, but I won't keep you long. It's about Sir Bellomont."

At the unexpected mention of her uncle she managed to retain her composure.

"His ship has been spotted. He shall arrive soon. I thought you would be most pleased to learn the good news, and that it might cause you to rest well."

What would have been good news stunned her. The arrival of her uncle meant that Trace would be in more danger. Soon the baron would know that Sir Douglas had not hired Trace as her bodyguard, and that she had supported him in order to shield him from arrest.

He gave a light bow. "The countess will hold the ball in honor of you and your uncle tomorrow night." He looked at her steadily. "Your grandmother anxiously awaits the chance to meet you."

She looked at the baron in silence. He gave a nod of his head, then stepped back from the door. "Good night, Miss Mackenzie," he said cheerfully.

The door shut. *I must warn Trace of Uncle's soon arrival— but how?*

# 20

## EDEN'S FATE

Trace made his decision suddenly. If he returned to his chamber and allowed the opportunity for the guard to bolt him in, Sarakof might be tempted to keep him there. He spoke to the sullen guard who led the way ahead of him.

"I want to see the countess, or did the baron lie to Miss Mackenzie about her grandmother's presence in the castle?"

His bluntness evoked the response from the guard that Trace had intended, and the Russian cast him a sly look.

"The countess, she is here."

"What of the count? Or has the baron arranged his poisoning?"

He could see that the guard was nervous now.

"If he hears you say this, your life will be nothing," said the guard sullenly.

"And more heads than the baron's will roll if Count Aleksandr learns I've been denied an audience with him. Your own head may end up as fish bait. I have come with important information for the czar. Would you dare keep the son of the countess in deliberate ignorance of my presence? I insist upon sending a message."

The man grew pale and nervous and shifted a glance down the hall. "The plans of Baron Sarakof are his own. I am obligated to perform my duties."

"Duties to the count and the czar himself, or to Sarakof?"

"He is a dangerous man."

"And you have opportunity now to put an obstacle in his path to power. See that my message is delivered to the count and you may be rewarded by both of us."

The guard paused in the shadowed hall where the torch flickered upon the high stone walls.

"What message?"

"Tell him I have urgent news for the good of imperial Russia. News that Baron Sarakof hopes to keep from him in order to enhance his own political power in St. Petersburg. Tell him I also have wheat—a gift from the American President Andrew Jackson. Unless I have audience with him, New Archangel will endure a long, cold winter."

It worked. Early the next morning he was awakened and in a short time brought to the count's private chambers.

Count Aleksandr stood from the chair behind a pine desk, his appearance, like the baron's, suggesting military interests. His recent illness also told itself in the gaunt lines drawn upon his otherwise keen face. His eyes, above an aquiline nose, were inquisitive. His closely cropped gray hair formed a fringe across a high forehead.

His vision fixed on Trace with a measuring appraisal. He no doubt wondered about Trace's bold insistence upon seeing him at the risk of the baron's displeasure.

"I've been informed you doubt the loyal intentions of Baron Sarakof and bring news of importance to the czar."

"I do, Excellency. And I bring wheat from President Andrew Jackson, a gift for the Russian people of New Archangel."

"A gift, you say. Most gracious of Boston. And what am

I expected to grant in return for this gesture of friendship?"

The good humor in his eyes accompanied his cynicism.

"That, your Excellency, depends upon you."

"In what way?" he asked bluntly.

Trace removed an official letter from Andrew Jackson from within his jacket. "On your response to this, Excellency. It is a letter from my President. Our two countries share an interest in the Pacific Northwest that His Majesty the King of England plans to undermine. At this very hour, British ships authorized by King George and the Hudson's Bay Company are moving into Russian-controlled waters near the mouth of Alaska. Under the leadership of Chief Factor Peter Skene Ogden, they will attempt to build a new trading post on the Stikine to undermine the trade of both Russia and America, using the Russian waterway to access Alaska."

The count's wintry eyes hardened. "I know nothing of this daring move."

"Baron Sarakof has kept it from you. He hopes to take your position in New Archangel—perhaps through your sudden illness?—and sign a treaty with the next British governor-general, Sir Douglas Bellomont."

Trace laid the official letter on the desk, making certain the presidential seal reflected in the lantern light. A glance at Count Aleksandr revealed that he was furious at the news.

Trace said easily, "There is yet time to blockade the waterway to the Stikine, Excellency. Your gunboats can keep the Hudson's Bay expedition from entering, trading with the Indians, and from building a British fort in New Caledonia. If you move at once, your gunboats can be there waiting for Chief Factor Ogden. May I be so bold as to suggest you not inform the baron but delegate the command of your boats to a trustworthy man? The baron will likely warn the British in order to protect his position."

The count picked up the letter from Jackson and, opening it, walked to the window to read with his back toward Trace.

Several minutes elapsed before he returned to his desk. The taut expression on his face convinced Trace that his mission had been a success. The count appeared anxious to proceed with his plans.

"I shall move at once to blockade Mr. Ogden. You may return to your chamber, Captain Wilder, and I shall call for you again to discuss the matter of the wheat."

Trace had more on his mind and was not to be dismissed so hurriedly. "There is another matter of importance. Your niece, Miss Savana Rezanov Mackenzie, granddaughter of the countess."

Aleksandr's mouth tightened. "She is not my niece. Nor is she of any significance. It was a grave mistake to have brought her here. You may leave with her, Captain, as soon as the wheat is unloaded."

Trace studied him. "If Miss Mackenzie were of no significance, then the baron would not have lured her here under false promises. Neither would Sir Bellomont have been able to make his plans for the treaty with Sarakof. They both expect to use her."

The count stood perfectly straight, hands clasped behind him. "You need not concern yourself with my cousin the baron. I shall take care of his ambitions," he said with finality.

"I'm sure you have ways to deal with him," said Trace with a note of irony, "but I have an interest in the matter of Miss Mackenzie. I want to know how he anticipated using her to enhance his favor with the czar, and why the Rezanov family felt it necessary to oppose his efforts."

"That is our affair. Your government has warned me of British aims in Russian America, and for that, I am in your debt. However, Miss Mackenzie will play no part in the politics of St. Petersburg, so you need not be concerned for her future." His eyes grew chill. "You may also discourage her from any plans for political or monetary gain."

"Miss Mackenzie—though she has as much blood right to the wealth of her mother as the others—didn't come here to coerce the family into an inheritance."

Trace ignored his caustic smile. "Were it not for an understandable desire to know the truth of her father's fate and attain knowledge of her mother, Miss Mackenzie would most likely have remained in London. The Rezanovs, you will admit, have done little to extinguish her curiosity. A few simple letters in the past while she was growing up in London might have been sufficient. Having never received even that much, it was easy for the baron to lure her here with promises."

Count Aleksandr's demeanor remained relentless. "That is not your concern, Captain, and I must insist you—"

"I'm making it my concern. She's in danger and I want to know why."

His brows lifted in an attempt at mockery. "Danger?"

"That's right. She poses a threat to someone who doesn't want her here, and Sarakof expects to use her. Maybe you're the person threatened."

A shadow of concern showed in his tense expression. "I assure you I am not. I know of no danger to Miss Mackenzie. And yet, I will make certain the baron will have no opportunity to use her to enhance his cause."

Trace had come too far to leave now, and Savana would never know peace until she knew the truth. For her future— for his own—there had to be answers.

"When she arrived in San Francisco she received an anonymous letter from St. Petersburg warning her against coming to Baranof Castle. The letter was delivered by a man named Yuri."

Trace saw a faint gleam of interest in the count's eyes.

"The document warned Miss Mackenzie against any involvement with the baron."

"It was probably not important."

Trace smiled coolly. "Someone went to great effort to see that she didn't read the information about the baron. I was attacked in my hotel room and the letter stolen. I have no proof, but I believe Sarakof sent those men."

The count was listening now, carefully. "You were attacked?"

"By thugs with Russian accents."

"You say this letter was delivered by a man named Yuri?"

"Yes, did you know him?"

"You speak as if something may have happened to him."

"Yuri is dead. Killed on the San Francisco wharf. He was silenced for delivering the message about the baron to Miss Mackenzie."

Aleksandr was noticeably shaken and reached a hand to steady himself on the corner of his desk.

*Then the count did not order his death*, thought Trace. *There's no one left now except Sarakof.*

Aleksandr recovered, and a hint of anger flickered in his expression as he walked over to the window and looked out at the falling snow.

"Your reaction to Yuri's death suggests he was loyal to you. Did you send the document?"

"No."

"Who, then? Surely you know."

Aleksandr turned coolly. "You ask too many questions. An irritating habit of Americans."

Trace smiled briefly. "Perhaps I'm concerned about the girl."

"Then take her from here at once. She is not wanted."

"I would, but she's determined to find out about her English father, James Mackenzie."

He turned away again. "Mackenzie is dead. He was trapped in a blizzard five years ago. There is no more to tell."

"I wish I could convince her of that. The baron has told her that her father is alive in Siberia. He's convinced her the countess is working with him to bring the matter of his release to the attention of the czar. With hopes like that, she's not likely to believe us."

He turned abruptly and walked to the desk, a paleness showing about his mouth. "I am sorry. There is nothing I can do. Your government's information on the Ogden expedition is most welcome. As I said, I shall send patrol boats to blockade his entry into Russian waters and turn them back to Fort Vancouver."

"I've been thinking long and hard about the reason the

baron wants to convince her Mackenzie is alive. He's spoken of a journey to St. Petersburg—I fear he may try to bring her there. What would be the advantage of bringing her to St. Petersburg?"

The count's head lifted. "I am quite certain there is none, Captain."

His insistence and the worry in his eyes told Trace the opposite.

"Believe me, Captain, you need not concern yourself further with my nephew Peter," he said, coldly bitter. "I plan to see that his escapades come to a swift end. Take Miss Mackenzie and leave. She's not wanted here—"

"You've said she wasn't wanted too many times," interrupted Trace. "If I were in her shoes I'd not waste another moment on a family who abandoned her and cut her off as though she were dead. Unfortunately, she is not like me. She's a woman of principle and sensitivity. She wants to meet her grandmother—and her uncle," he added with a meaningful gesture toward Aleksandr. "Though why she would is beyond me."

Aleksandr's face hardened. "Impossible. If she came for money, I may see to a moderate inheritance—"

"She would find that insulting. She also received another letter, this one inviting her to the castle, signed by her grandmother Countess Catherine Rezanov."

Aleksandr appeared startled, then recovered. "Certainly not by the countess, Captain Wilder, but by Peter. The countess would never ask her here to Baranof Castle."

"Then you can understand that she had a just reason to come here, that she hasn't connived on behalf of a Rezanov inheritance?"

"That may be so . . . but it changes nothing. Whoever sent for her, whatever the cause, it must come to nothing. It is a Russian concern. A family matter."

"Granted, Excellency, and I've also told you—what concerns Miss Rezanov is of interest to me as well."

"Then I advise you to bring her to your ship and depart

New Archangel before Sir Bellomont arrives. I shall take care of the matter concerning Peter and Bellomont, including the Hudson's Bay Company. And there will be no treaty for a British fort on the Stikine. Good day, Captain Wilder."

Trace stood watching him, then seeing the man's countenance set like granite, understood that he'd get no more information on Savana. He gave a quick bow of his head and walked to the door. He turned and looked back at Count Aleksandr. "There's the matter remaining about Captain Fletcher and his vessel. I'd like him released. More importantly, so would President Jackson."

"I shall see to the matter in gratitude for the American wheat. Good day, Captain."

The official ball given by Countess Catherine was beginning, and Savana, dressed in white satin and wearing the Rezanov diamonds at Peter's insistence, came down the stairs beside him, his hand on her elbow.

"I'm afraid your requirement that we be late was in error, Peter," she said, trying to keep her anger under control. "It will appear as if I've deliberately affronted the countess."

He gave a careless laugh. "You worry too much, my dear Savana. If I know your grandmother, she hasn't even arrived yet."

"From the way the guests are bowing and curtsying in the receiving line, she has," corrected Savana, heart thumping in her chest.

Peter drew her closer to his side as he looped her white-gloved arm through his possessively and escorted her down the stairs toward the small throng of guests. Savana had the ugly notion that his attentiveness was a deliberate show to impress the guests—and her grandmother.

He leaned toward her and whispered, "You look most charming, Savana. The countess will be pleased. You look very much like Nadyia."

To be told again that she looked like her mother set her on edge. For some reason the idea no longer brought the expectation and pleasure it once had. Perhaps it was the hungry look in Peter's eyes when he spoke the words, or perhaps it was the bubble of suspicion that began to rise within that warned of trouble, not happiness.

With a silent prayer on her lips for strength and grace, Savana descended, aware that she and Peter were now the object of attention rippling through the receiving line.

As she descended slowly at his side, the heads below in the outer hall and ballroom turned their way. Savana glanced cautiously through a number of Russian guests and saw no one familiar. It seemed to her that the mood of those present was altered by her arrival with the baron. *Is it my imagination?* she wondered uneasily and glanced at Peter. He looked pleased, even amused, and her tension grew. Something was very wrong—*but what?*

"Did you not inform me last night that my uncle was to arrive in time for the ball? I've not seen him. Is he here?" she asked with a slight hint of accusation.

Peter smiled at her. "His ship docked this afternoon. I was told an hour ago that Sir Douglas is on his way now, quite anxious to see you and our American friend, Wilder."

Savana said nothing. Her effort to warn Trace of her uncle's arrival had been foiled.

"I've more good news for you," said Peter, glancing boldly about the throng below, a look of satisfaction on his face.

Savana tore her eyes away from the guests to look at him. Peter gave a squeeze to her arm.

"I know how worried you've been about Zoya, so I sent soldiers out today looking for her."

Her alarm sprang like a fox. "Soldiers!"

He laughed. "There's nothing to be alarmed about. Zoya merely tired of waiting for you here, and went to visit her brother at St. Nicholas until you arrived."

Savana felt a flood of relief. So Zoya was at the church

after all. And yet—it wasn't like her to stay away now that she knew of Savana's arrival.

Savana's suspicions had been growing to the dreadful extent that she had almost begun to think that—

"Ah," said Peter with a jubilant note of satisfaction in his voice. "You are correct, Savana. The countess has arrived and is waiting for us. I believe she has seen you now—yes, the receiving line is stepping back to let us through. Come; and don't forget to curtsy."

Trace stood alone watching Savana come down the stairs escorted by the baron. She hadn't noticed him when she glanced about, and he came alert when he realized that Countess Catherine Rezanov appeared to be oblivious to her granddaughter's arrival. The elegant woman in her seventies stood at the head of the receiving line, wearing a distant smile as her guests bowed one by one and exchanged pleasantries. Her white hair was drawn back into a heavy braided knot sparkling with diamonds. Her dress shimmered with gems and ermine trim.

It struck him at once that she did not know of Savana's impending appearance. Trace made a move to intercept Savana before Sarakof steered her to the receiving line.

Too late—the line had parted. The baron stood with Savana, his arm looped through hers. Peter smiled as he looked at the countess, and the sight of his personal triumph revolted Trace.

The countess appeared to be stunned, yet it was the expression on Savana's face that bit into his heart. A look of breathtaking wistfulness turned her lovely features into a smile, but the smile died—

The countess gave a gasp, her thin, veined hand clutching at her heart. Excited voices broke out and several men rushed to steady the elderly woman as she began to sink to the floor.

Peter too rushed toward her, leaving Savana. "Aunt Catherine," he cried.

Trace moved through the guests in Savana's direction. At that moment he could have easily felled the baron with a good blow to his belly.

By the time he reached Savana the countess was being escorted from the ballroom by the baron and some close aides. Trace didn't see Count Aleksandr anywhere. Obviously he had not as yet moved against his nephew. Had it all been a boastful threat, or was he busy ordering his patrol boats to head off the British expedition commanded by Ogden?

Trace came up beside Savana and scanned her pale face. She tore her eyes from the countess's retreating form to look at him. He supposed she read his restrained anger, for her eyes faltered and she turned her head away, the Rezanov diamonds flashing.

He took hold of her arm to lead her out onto the floor.

"Please," she whispered, "I can't . . . I must go upstairs to my room—"

"No. You'll give them more cause to whisper. Anyway, you owe me this waltz," he said, leading her away and drawing her into his arms. She looked at him for an explanation, and he gave a half-smile. "The last time it played at Fort Ross, Sarakof swept you away, to my loss. This time," he said quietly, holding her gaze, "it is my turn."

Savana's mind was still reeling from the horrid image of her grandmother's shock when she saw her with Peter. The sight of her slipping to the floor would forever live in her mind. Now it was Trace's flinty gaze that commanded her unwilling attention.

"I had no wish to dismay her," she murmured, closing her eyes a moment. "Peter should have told her I looked so much like Nadyia."

"I doubt if Sarakof wished to tell her anything."

She read the caustic tone in his voice and looked at him again. "You're not suggesting he didn't tell her I was here?"

His eyes narrowed. "What do you think? If she had expected you, do you think she'd topple into a near faint?"

Savana stiffened. "What are you saying?" she whispered.

"You know what I mean—need I spell it out? Come, Savana, you're a smart girl. You have it figured out yourself, but you won't admit it. You have this fantasy cemented in your heart about the long-lost granddaughter coming home to hearth and family love, and a sweet, gray-haired grandmother standing by the rocking chair to meet you with open arms—no, don't try it—a slap on the dance floor, my dear, will really get the tongues to wagging!"

She blinked back the tears of anger, for he was right. But she refused to grapple with the blunt words. "It was she who asked me here—"

"No, it was Sarakof. She didn't know you were coming. I'm sorry, Savana, but there's no time to lead up to this. We've got to get out of here, and quick, before Sarakof—"

She stopped waltzing, her eyes riveted on the entryway. Her alarm no doubt showed in her face, for Trace too followed her glance.

Sir Douglas Bellomont stood there with one of his Company aides, a big man carrying weapons for her uncle's safety.

"So he's wise enough to come armed," commented Trace dryly. "Smart man. We may all need a few pistols before we make it to the *Okanagan*."

Savana's alarm grew and she clutched him. "Trace, you must leave at once. What if he informs Peter you abducted me?"

Trace wore a faint smile. "Maybe your pristine honor will demand that he call for a duel. The winner gets your lovely hand, of course."

"Be serious. This could mean your arrest."

"I am serious. Are you worried about me?"

"About as much as I'd worry about a rattler among rabbits."

He smirked. "Thanks. I guess I know who the rattler is."

"Please leave—before Uncle sees you," she whispered, urging him from the dance floor, but he drew her back into his arms.

"The waltz hasn't ended yet . . . I like it. Reminds me of cold Russian nights and a girl with frosty gray eyes and flaxen hair."

Savana's heart pounded. "What will you do about Sir Douglas?" she said, surprised her voice was calm and steady.

"You might as well know, Savana, I saw Count Aleksandr this morning."

In surprise that he'd managed to do so, her eyes sought his. The earlier moment between them faded, and he watched her gravely, weighing her response.

She thought she already knew what had transpired between Trace and the count and discovered that she felt neither alarmed nor disappointed. She felt very little national zeal at the moment.

"I warned him about Ogden's expedition to open a new fort along the Stikine. Patrol boats are on their way to block the British ship. Whatever treaty Bellomont hopes to negotiate is not likely to be greeted with favor. The wheat—if Captain Dembe ever arrives—is offered as a gift from Boston."

Savana remained silent for a moment. "Congratulations, Trace. You won fairly enough."

"I wish you meant that."

"I do. You foiled my uncle and the British interests." She smiled. "But only for the present. You underestimate my uncle, and England."

"I'd never be so foolish," he said dryly. "You could turn on me now, you know. All you need do is inform Bellomont that I don't have the wheat after all. The baron could move against me without reluctance."

She avoided his gaze. "And see you sent to Siberia or placed in a dungeon?"

He drew her a trifle closer. "Becoming a Boston sympathizer, I hope?"

"Sir Douglas has seen you," she whispered. "He's coming toward us."

The waltz ended, and Savana and Trace turned as Sir Bellomont walked up. Savana recognized the look in her uncle's eyes and she tensed. The three of them walked from the floor away from the guests, and Sir Douglas removed a cigar from under his jacket and struck a match, all the while eying Trace.

"So I was right all along," said Bellomont. "You are working for Jackson in the American cause."

"You've gambled and lost, Bellomont. You shouldn't have risked Savana to the *Okanagan*."

"And you, Trace my boy, should not have risked the wheat to Dembe's old schooner." He chuckled and his eyes gleamed victoriously.

Savana stiffened and glanced at Trace. He watched her uncle thoughtfully, then his mouth turned.

"You're right. Am I to gather by your jubilant smile that you are the cause for the *Yankee Trader* failing to keep her rendezvous with me?"

"I am! I have the ship—and the wheat. And you, my fine American lad, are out of luck. That wheat will be offered to the baron, who will, with some quick and smart speech, get himself off your hook and back into the good graces of Count Aleksandr. I'll have that treaty yet. And you are in somewhat of a tight spot." Her uncle was obviously enjoying more than his cigar.

Savana knew Trace well enough by now to recognize his restrained anger and his concern, but she didn't think his concern was for himself but her. She made a move to speak, but Trace laid a hand on her arm, all the while watching Bellomont.

"I commend you, Bellomont. You've won round two."

Sir Douglas watched him curiously. "Round two?"

Trace smiled briefly. "Round one is already over. The treaty is foiled, Bellomont. I've already met with Aleksandr. Ogden will be turned back by Russian patrol boats. Even the wheat delivery won't save your treaty to evict Boston traders from the Pacific ports."

Savana looped her arm through her uncle's and managed to smile at him. "You've still got a chance for round three, Uncle—but not until you permit Trace to escape safely to the *Okanagan.*"

Sir Douglas looked at her sharply, his eyes narrowing thoughtfully as he scrutinized her face and came to some quick deduction of his own—one that didn't please him at first. "Well, it seems Wilder was right. I did indeed make a grave error in packing off my darling spy aboard the Boston trader's ship. Now what, may I ask, transpired beneath the stars while your poor uncle waited patiently at Fort Vancouver for your arrival?"

"I'll explain everything, Uncle. You must say nothing about having the wheat until Trace is permitted to leave Baranof Castle."

"I'm to say nothing, am I? When this wily Boston scoundrel has betrayed His Majesty? So you wish to save him from the salt mines, do you? And I would wonder why, but it's plainly written in your eyes. Bah!"

He glowered at Trace, but Savana couldn't tell if the anger was altogether genuine.

"Be gone, then," he said gruffly toward Trace. "The longer you hang about, the more tempted I'll be to have your hide. And when you arrive back at Fort Vancouver we've a good deal of talking to do."

Sir Douglas strode away, followed by his bodyguard.

Trace took Savana's arm and led her from the ballroom.

They stopped in a shadowed outer chamber with a tile floor and heavy drapes of velvet, and a door led out onto the snowy courtyard. Savana shivered from the cold and turned

267

to face him, her satin skirts rustling softly, her eyes clinging to his.

"I won't leave without you, Savana."

She shook her head. "Sir Douglas is here now. I'll be safe. Uncle may be shrewd, and your opponent, but he'd never allow anything to harm me. You've accomplished your duty for President Jackson. You've warned Count Aleksandr. Even with the wheat delivery, there will be no treaty between Hudson's Bay and Russia. You must go while you are able, Trace. For your sake," she whispered. "You have what you want."

"Do I?" he asked quietly. "If I leave now, you'll be left to Sarakof."

"I shall be well enough. I can't leave until I've learned about my father—his work among the Aleut was noble and I wish to know about his sacrifice. I'll visit Zoya at St. Nicholas. I know she'll explain everything now—she must."

"I'll stay."

"No—you must go while you've opportunity. Something could go wrong and you'll be at risk again. I . . . I shall be returning with Sir Douglas to Fort Vancouver when this is over."

"All right. I'll look for you there. And," he said, drawing her toward him, "if you don't come—if necessary I'll go to St. Petersburg to find you."

Her eyes searched his. "I think you actually would."

"To get what I want? Yes."

There were footsteps and she glanced toward the ballroom. "Please go, quickly!" She slipped away from him and hurried toward the doorway. Glancing back, she smiled softly and lifted her gloved hand in farewell. "God be with you," she whispered.

Trace's boots crunched on the packed snow as he made his way through the courtyard. He was frowning to himself as he ducked under a small tree and a clump of snow toppled from the branch down his neck. The gate was ahead. He believed Wesley and Calhoun were nearby. If Sarakof had found them, he was the manner of man to boast about it. Trace stepped into the torchlight and stopped.

Baron Sarakof was waiting ahead of him with a group of armed men. He smiled smugly. "Did you think I would allow you to leave, Wilder?" He gestured toward his men. "Put him in the dungeon to rot." He looked at Trace. "By the time Savana and Bellomont realize what's happened, I shall have brought her to St. Petersburg as the baroness."

# 21

## MY GRANDMOTHER, THE RUSSIAN COUNTESS

Perhaps twenty minutes had passed since she'd said goodbye to Trace, and Savana stood alone at the edge of the ballroom, curiously looking about for her uncle and wondering where he'd disappeared to. As she glanced across the room toward a side door, the baron entered alone and unsmiling.

His brittle amber gaze swept the room until it collided with hers. His face softened, and a gesture of intimate greeting showed in his smile as he made his way across the ballroom in her direction.

"I've been searching for you," he said, coming up and taking her arm. "The countess assures me she's not only embarrassed over her display but feeling much better. She waits to receive you in a private meeting. I'm sorry it happened this way, Savana. It was hard for you as well."

She looked at him. "You're certain she was expecting me in the receiving line?"

"It was my fault, my dear; you mustn't blame yourself. I should have expected this, knowing her as I do. Aunt Catherine is dear and precious to the family, but highly emotional. She most always carries her smelling salts with her." He smiled ruefully. "That should convince you how frequently these emotional faints come upon her."

"Nevertheless, it was a dreadful thing to happen," insisted Savana. "I hope seeing me in the Rezanov diamonds didn't upset her."

"Why should it when she sent them? Put aside your concerns. There's not a thing to worry about."

"Perhaps we should wait until tomorrow, Peter."

He smiled. "She'd be even more upset if you refuse now. She has some notion she failed you by her display."

"Failed me!"

"You know how false notions can plague a sensitive soul. She's sent me to bring you to her, insisting she feels well enough. Aunt Catherine is anxious to give you the news about your father. She's located him and written a letter to the czar pleading for his release. She wants me to leave soon for St. Petersburg with the letter."

"He's alive!"

"I'm happy for you, my dear. He's not well, but as soon as we get him under the care of a good physician, there's hope he'll recover."

"Then I'll go to her at once."

"I've a carriage waiting now. She's left the castle with her attending physician for her private villa near St. Nicholas. She often retreats there. Shall we stop at the church and bring Zoya with us?"

Savana searched his face. "Very well, Peter. First, I'll need to tell Sir Douglas where I'm going. If you'll excuse me—"

"Your uncle is in an important meeting with Count Aleksandr. I saw them leave together for his office upstairs. My dear Savana . . . you do look alarmed. If you like, we can have the American come with us. I know how you trust your cousin. I guess I was a little too harsh with him. . . ."

*He can't know that Trace has already left,* she told herself. He appeared genuinely troubled at her hesitancy to trust him. Perhaps she was being too suspicious. She smiled uneasily. "All right, Peter. I'll get my cape and meet you in the carriageway."

"I'll be waiting." He smiled, turned, and left her there.

Savana looked after him thoughtfully. He did not behave as though he had anything to hide.

*Is my father truly alive?*

The wind felt raw and cold as it blew unhindered over the shimmering white-draped slopes of Mount Edgecumbe and The Sisters. In the east, Mount Verstovia was tinted with blue beneath the moonlight breaking through the clouds.

The horses plodded ahead, and Savana sat tensely on the carriage seat across from Peter while he spoke pleasantly of their journey to St. Petersburg. The longer he talked the more animated he became. This was a side to Peter she'd not seen, and it made her uncomfortable.

"You'll do well there, Savana. Yes, you have the manner and appearance."

She was on the verge of telling him she had no intention of going with him, that she would wait for her father here in New Archangel or even Fort Vancouver, but she could see he'd not accept her decision now. *Lord, have I done the right thing?* she kept wondering, her conscience troubled by the knowledge that she'd been so set on her own plans of visiting Baranof Castle that she'd desperately neglected her spiritual life. Except for a quick prayer and a verse or two from Scripture, her entire soul had been bent toward seeking acceptance and a sense of belonging with the Rezanov family.

She turned unexpectedly from the window to look across at Peter. The swaying carriage lantern glowed dimly, and each time it passed his face she saw his smile.

"Peter, you said her villa was near the Russian Orthodox Church of St. Nicholas. We should have been there by now."

"We are. That's her villa."

The driver drew the horses to a stop and Savana looked out the window at an austere two-story house with lights blazing warm with welcome in the windows.

Peter was out and helping her down, and she felt the snow sink beneath her booted feet. She stared toward the front door, and soon he was escorting her over the walk, up the steps, across the porch. She passed through the door.

Light flooded in upon Savana as she entered the hall where a small flight of stairs led upward. Across the hall a door to the parlor was open, the fireplace cheerily warming the room. There were low voices, and then Peter was guiding her forward into the sitting room.

She stood alone now, while Peter walked forward. The countess was seated on a divan by the hearth, and a man in a dark frock coat sat across from her. The man noticed Peter and then Savana, and he stood, his face hard.

"Peter! You fool!"

The countess turned her head and saw Savana standing in the doorway, robed in a fur cloak. Her aged face paled.

Savana took a step toward her expectantly, hand extended, reaching for the past, the future. . . .

"Countess—Grandmother, I—"

The countess stood weakly, using a jeweled cane, and her pale eyes were icy.

"Do not come near me!" breathed Countess Catherine Rezanov.

Savana froze, the blood draining from her face.

"You *dare* address me as Grandmother? You! The shameful offspring of an adulterous affair!"

The venom in her high-pitched voice struck Savana as sharply as a slap across the face.

Peter stepped between them and his voice hinted of mockery. "Dear Aunt Catherine, is this any way to greet your long-lost granddaughter? This is Savana Rezanov Mackenzie—the child of your daughter Naydia."

Her sharp eyes swerved to Peter. "Lies. I should have you whipped to an inch of your life for this."

"Lies? Nadyia knows better."

The countess trembled. "You fiend. Silence!"

"Silence? We need to talk, Aunt Catherine."

The countess weaved slightly on her feet and Peter took her arm, but she pulled away as if his touch shot her with poison. "Boris . . ." She looked weakly at the oldish man in the frock coat. "My medicine . . . quickly . . ."

The man, who appeared to be her personal physician, was swiftly at her side with a small glass, and she drank, spilling some on the front of her jeweled bodice.

Savana stepped backward as if having entered a den of vipers.

"Take me to my room," the countess breathed to Boris.

Ashen and alone, Savana watched the doctor lead the elderly woman slowly up the stairs. She stared as if in a daze, until they had climbed to the top and disappeared down the hallway. She was still looking after them when she felt Peter's strong hand on her shoulder.

"Do not be hurt by this. Her mood will pass. Let me talk with her alone. She knows you are alive now. She'll soon come to see matters for the better."

Savana's voice came low and shaking with emotion. "Leave her alone, Peter. She's old. You'll kill her! Can't you see she doesn't want me? She never did. . . ."

He left her and walked to the stairs, determination setting his face.

Savana rushed after him up the stairs, catching his arm. "Peter! What do you mean—she knows I'm alive *now*!" Her eyes met his, and she felt as though she'd confronted a stone barricade. "Why would she think otherwise? She sent me the letter and the diamonds at Fort Ross."

Something ugly visualized in his expression, halting her words. The icy fear rising within her chest threatened to cut off her breathing. She stared at him, clutching the banister.

"But they had to have come from her," she choked. "The diamonds, how else could such a gift be sent to me? You said—"

Silence wrapped her in a cold mantle of evil.

"You lied about everything."

He smiled. "You're as upset as Aunt Catherine. There is no reason to be. I've done only what needed to be done, and should have been done years ago. I've brought the two of you together, and soon she will calm down enough to understand the situation clearly. Wait here."

Savana watched him go up the remaining stairs and walk down the hall.

*Nothing has changed. I was deceived to think otherwise.* The silence of rejection, the bolted doors that shut her out, it was all there—more painful than before. And Peter . . .

"She doesn't want me," she murmured. "I'm an intrusion . . . a burden . . . my very presence has made her ill."

Savana swallowed, her throat dry, her emotions too devastated to find release in tears.

And Peter evidently hadn't felt the slightest qualm over his ruse. He'd kept his plans hidden, nourished by his selfishness for weeks, months, perhaps even years. Peter had no feelings for what the sudden shock of seeing Savana would do to an old woman. He had deceived them both.

"He was and is willing to parade me about as a spectacle, one that he thinks will bring him money and position—but how?

"Lord . . . help me. . . ."

Tears would not come. She wished ardently that they would flow, opening the inner door to her soul, bringing release.

Awakened from her thoughts, she heard voices rising in argument. She looked up the stairs, hearing but not understanding.

She found herself hurrying upward so quickly that her breath came rapidly. On the top landing she saw the chamber door standing open and the light glowing coldly yellow, a dead amber . . . like Peter's eyes. She hesitated, her steps wounded, then found herself near the door and heard them, heard the baron's firm voice—

"I did not steal the diamonds. Nadyia gave them to me in St. Petersburg."

"Blackmail! She gave them to you to silence your tongue!"

"A small matter, Aunt Catherine. Her reputation will be safe if I also get what is rightfully mine. I was unjustly driven from the presence of the czar, and I shall return with the power and honor that suits me. And if I don't—"

"You mustn't bring her to St. Petersburg. I'll do what you say. I've already promised you that I'll have Aleksandr sign the treaty with Sir Bellomont."

"For now that's enough, dear Aunt Catherine. But I want much more. Nadyia's husband is nephew to the czar. She'll speak to him about getting me returned to the czar's favor. This time, I want a more powerful position. And if Nadyia doesn't cooperate, I shall inform her husband that Savana is her infamous child. I'll produce her in the palace the way I did tonight if I must!"

"Nadyia will cooperate. You must give us both time, Peter, time to do as you ask. Yes, yes, but you must not bring her to St. Petersburg."

He laughed. "Who knows when I may need to use her again? Savana is my golden key. She will hang like the sword of Damocles over Nadyia's head for the rest of her days."

"You beast!"

"Not a beast at all, but a man. One who must survive and who must fight his way up past the imperial dogs to eat more than crumbs from the czar's table."

"If you betray Nadyia's past to Ivan and the czar—I shall have you killed!"

"Fear not, Aunt Catherine. Would I be so cruel as to go to Ivan and tell him that Princess Nadyia Rezanov Peshkov in her school days at Baranof Castle bore a brat to a Scottish peasant trapper?"

His laughter rippled the chamber.

Savana's eyes rimmed with tears. Her mother was alive, but memory of a baby born in New Archangel twenty years ago brought her shame and threatened her present position as a princess, a niece of the czar!

"Very well, Peter, you conniving devil. I will do as you demand. But I will not see her, is that understood?"

"You need not. I've convinced her Mackenzie is alive. Once she's my wife in St. Petersburg she will be told the bad news of his death. Perhaps a few letters from you will do to solace her craving for family acceptance. After that, it won't matter."

Savana silently backed away and fled down the stairs. *Escape,* her mind shouted.

She threw open the front door and ran into the cold night. It was snowing again, large white flakes that fluttered slowly, softly touching her face.

She stopped, panic seizing her. The carriage was gone.

When the baron had left Trace in the courtyard, his guards had brought him to the back of the castle to place him in the dungeon. Unexpectedly, a firm voice demanded, "Sheath your swords."

The guards stopped and looked about the darkness, bewildered, wondering who had given the order.

Trace seized the moment. He drew his blade and stepped back, but before a battle ensued, Sir Bellomont stepped forward with his massively built bodyguard. Wesley and Calhoun also appeared with brandished weapons.

"What goes here?" demanded Bellomont with an indignant British brogue. "By the king! I shall have you all for this outrage! Do you dare arrest Captain Wilder? The good British fellow who brought the wheat? And a message for the count! Baron Sarakof is under arrest. He's to be brought back to St. Petersburg to stand trial for treason against your czar!

Now don't be stupid fellows and make matters worse on yourselves."

The Russian guards looked wildly at each other, but before they could decide whom to believe, Trace made his escape through the courtyard, the Nez Perce Indian leading the way over the stone wall. Calhoun, a big man and not light on his feet, trailed behind but caught up with them at the wharf.

Trace smiled at them. "Smart move. What about Bellomont?"

"He found us in the courtyard. We saw Sarakof coming with his guards. We've been watching you for days, Cap'n, but couldn't get near you. When we told Bellomont that Sarakof was coming with guards, he moved quickly, like a snow leopard. Tells me and Calhoun, 'I'll save his hide, but you be ready to fight.' "

Trace was surprised that Bellomont would aid him. This was the second time. He looked back toward Baranof Castle. Sarakof would have already returned to the ballroom and was now unsuspecting.

Now was the opportunity he needed. He must go back for Savana.

"Find a bidarka," he told them. "You must alert the *Okanagan*. We'll need to make a run for it. Maybe our luck will hold now that Bellomont is in a congenial mood."

"We already have a boat, Cap'n," said John Wesley. "It will bring us to the *Okanagan* all right, but I saw Miss Savana leave in a carriage with Sarakof. Maybe they went to St. Nicholas like she wanted."

Savana had left with the baron! He must find her! She was at risk.

"If I don't return with her by morning, leave without us. Understood?"

John Wesley exchanged sober glances with Calhoun. "Aye, Cap'n."

# 22

# A REFUGE FOR MY HEART

By now the baron would have discovered she had fled. Would he come for her on foot or horseback? *Please, Lord, don't let him find me. Help me get to the church.*

She stumbled through the drifts of snow. Picking herself up she struggled on. The sky was now completely overcast and small gusts of chilling wind blew against her. She looked behind and heard nothing but the snow falling from sodden branches. Ahead, some pine trees were darkly silhouetted. The air was cold and still as Savana rushed through the trees and came upon a path that curved and swung to the left.

In the distance lights burned in the windows of the church.

"Zoya." Her heart warmed and her steps quickened through the drifts. Yes, dear beloved Zoya would be there waiting. And after all, hadn't she been the only family that had stayed close to her all these years?

Yes, she still had Zoya. And at Fort Vancouver she would

find Trace again. Her confidence strengthened, she made her way steadfastly toward the church where Zoya's brother served as a priest.

When she arrived, the door was open. She entered its cloistered silence. The flames on the candles flickered and weaved as a breath of wind entered with her. She stood looking about but saw no one.

"Hello?" she called. "Is anyone here? I'm looking for Zoya."

Her feet made little sound as she tracked snow down the aisle. The lights glimmered on Byzantine art. Sheep and shepherds gazed down at her.

"Are you Savana?" came a quiet voice from a small room to her left.

A priest stood, his hair white. "I am Nikolai," he said. "Zoya was my sister."

His words thudded into her heart. *No, no, not beloved Zoya too.*

"Where is she?" she asked.

Nikolai walked toward her, his lean face and hollow eyes troubled. "She is dead, Miss Mackenzie."

Savana lowered herself slowly onto the hard bench. Everything around her seemed hard and cold and unreal as the candles continued to weave their fiery glow without shedding warmth. She trembled, and her eyes left Nikolai, as if drawn to the scene of the Good Shepherd. It was Jesus she needed so desperately. His Lordship over her life, her plans, her hopes. . . . Zoya was dead. Her father was dead. No one wanted her—yes, the Lord Jesus wanted her. He'd never fail nor forsake her.

"How did she die?" she whispered, closing her eyes and resting her head on the back of the pew.

Nikolai sat down and for a moment was silent. "I found her in the trees—about a quarter mile from here. She—she must have fallen and hit the back of her head on a rock. . . ." His voice trailed off.

Her gaze rushed to his. They stared at each other, and as

tears formed in Savana's eyes, Nikolai bowed his head.

"I think someone killed her," he whispered, and his shoulders shook with silent sobs.

*Horse hoofs!* They both looked quickly toward the front door. Savana stood, holding to the back of the pew.

"Swiftly. Hide behind the altar!"

The door flew open and Trace stood there. Savana let out a cry and rushed toward him, his arms closing tightly about her.

"All right?" he whispered.

She nodded. Yes, she was all right now. All at once Savana knew that. The terrors and confusions of the past days melted as his arms held her. She had the Lord . . . and she had Trace. She had enough to keep the light burning in her heart and soul. For a long moment she allowed herself the indulgence of relaxing against his shoulder, then he led her toward the front pew where Nikolai stood.

"Where's Sarakof?" asked Trace. "John Wesley said you went with him in a carriage."

"I did," and she told him what had happened, with the glittering light of the candles throwing shadows across her pale face. As she talked, it was as if she were reliving the scene all over again, while Trace stood listening, anger flickering in his eyes.

She stood, her emotions bursting. "And Zoya is . . . is dead," she finished, and couldn't contain the rush of tears. "All these years I've harassed her about news about my mother, my grandmother, my father . . . and . . . and it was Zoya all along who was all of them to me! Oh, if only I could have seen her tonight! If only I had one last chance to tell her she was worth them all! And now it's too late—"

Trace held her tightly by the shoulders. "Don't, darling! She wouldn't want you to do this to yourself. She knew how you truly felt. Why else would she have stayed with you so devotedly all these years?"

He lifted her chin gently and brushed the tears from her face with his thumb. "It's not all over. Some situations in life are so involved that they can't be worked out into small, neat packages with pretty bows on them. Injustices, hurts, misunderstandings—they can't always be solved instantly. Some hurts are never solved in this life. We must leave them with the Lord of Eternity. For now, there is hope in His promises, a healing balm for the wounds of the spirit, a future glistening with His Presence if we yield to His plans."

She looked at him, her heart in her eyes.

He must have seen what flickered in their depths, for he paused as though his breath caught.

Nikolai came from the shadows of the pew. "He is right, Miss Mackenzie, Zoya did know. She also knew about your mother. One of the last things she asked me to do before the day she disappeared was to tell you about your parents."

Savana looked at him eagerly. "Please!"

"Nadyia met James Mackenzie at this church. They were both young, but she was far younger, only a girl. She fell in love with him. She respected his concern for the Tlingit Indians and the Aleut on the seal islands, who were abused because of the greed of the Russian trappers. James was a hot-tempered man when he saw injustice of any sort. James became somewhat of a missionary to the Aleut and nearly got himself killed by the Russian hunters. But he was a brave and sometimes stubborn man. He kept on, and he accomplished much good. To this day there are believers in our Lord among the Aleut, and here in New Archangel we have a number of believing Tlingit. Even some of our services on Sunday are given in their language."

Savana's heart warmed. "And . . . how does that explain how my mother became involved with him . . . I mean," she said uncomfortably, "if I am . . ."

"You are not," he said gently. "They were secretly married. The marriage was very brief. The tragedy, my dear Miss Mackenzie, is the remainder of the story. Zoya knew it, and she only informed me a short time ago.

"Princess Nadyia had a difficult birth. When she recovered she was told you were dead, and that James had been killed on the seal islands in an Aleut uprising. She left Baranof Castle a young girl. She reentered society at St. Petersburg at the wishes of the Rezanov family and eventually married Prince Alex Peshkov, a nephew of the czar. They are, as I am certain you will be pleased to know, in love and contentedly married. Unfortunately, she thought you were dead all these years."

Savana could not speak and allowed the words to settle in her heart.

"What about the marriage record?" asked Trace.

"Unfortunately, the records were destroyed at the family's wishes. My word means nothing, and the priest who married them was killed along with James on their doomed journey to the czar."

Trace looked at Savana, but the look of disappointment was erased from her face. "It's enough that I know the truth, that God knows. . . . I'm pleased Nadyia is happily married. I will do nothing to disturb that." She looked at Trace, her eyes sparkling. "As you say, Trace, some things are best left for the Lord to settle. But the baron—"

"Yes," said Nikolai darkly, "the baron. He believes the dark side of things. Unfortunately, so does the countess. She wasn't here when her daughter married James secretly. She arrived during the last month before you were born. And unfortunately, she believed what she wished. She had large plans for her daughter in St. Petersburg and would not see them interrupted. She sent the baby to James by way of Zoya. Zoya knew the truth, but her testimony was deemed of little value, seeing she was a mere nursing maid."

Nikolai looked at her. "Zoya believes it was Nadyia who sent Yuri to warn you against the baron. Whether she will ever wish to see you, I cannot say."

"It will be hers to choose," whispered Savana. "Perhaps it is better this way, after all. I would never fit into the life of St. Petersburg, nor do I wish to go there to live." She looked at Trace. "Not now. I want to go to Fort Vancouver and meet the missionary Jason Lee."

Trace slipped an arm about her shoulder. "You've just won yourself a bargain. I'll be sailing tomorrow." His expression sobered. "But first, there's something I must take care of."

Savana thought she knew what it was and grasped his arm tightly. "No, Trace, please don't. Let the baron go. If anything also happens to you—"

"Quite true, Captain Wilder," rang the baron's voice from the doorway. "You now stand in the way of the fulfillment of my plans. I cannot allow that, of course."

"Please!" cried Nikolai. "This is a sacred place! You must not fight here!"

"No need to," said Trace calmly. "A duel, Baron?"

Sarakof smirked. "It is you and I, Wilder."

Savana clutched Trace. "Don't trust him," she whispered. "He has no honor. He'll attack first before you're ready."

Trace disentangled her frantic grip and handed her to Nikolai. "Is there another way out of here?" he asked in a low voice.

"Yes, through the back chapel. There's a carriage there, and horses."

"Take her and leave while I have him occupied. Bring her to the British ship the *Beaver*. Then send a message to Sir Bellomont."

"No," choked Savana. "I won't leave without you, Trace, not this time."

"You will. Don't worry. If I don't make it to Bellomont's ship—"

"Enough whispering, Captain Wilder. Step forth and play the man," challenged Sarakof.

"Then I'll meet you again at Fort Vancouver," Trace told her.

Savana reached a hand toward him in a gesture of hopelessness, but Trace lifted it briefly to his lips and turned from her to face Sarakof. "We shall see who plays the man, Sarakof."

Savana followed Nikolai to the tarantass, a heavy boatlike carriage mounted on four wheels with a hood that could be closed in bad weather.

"I cannot leave without him," she persisted.

"He seems able to confront the baron," said Nikolai. "Please, for your sake. If God wills, my child, you will see him again."

*And if not?* she thought. "Oh, heavenly Father, protect him, return him safely to me!"

Nikolai sat on the front end of the tarantass and drove the three horses hitched side by side with four reins. He gathered the reins and shouted, *"Nu rodniya!"*

The horses bolted off, eager to run, and Savana sat on the bearskin rug, hearing the horses jangle and the wheels turning in the snow. The trees raced past, the clouds disappeared from the black sky, and the white stars were winking and flashing in the heavens.

Staring up, her heart squeezed with anguish for Trace; tears wet her face and dried in the wind rushing past. As she squinted up at the heavens she prayed fervently, not with words, but with a welling up of emotions inside that could not be formed into sentences of petition.

As they raced along, disjointed thoughts moved across her mind as prayers. *I'll do what you want.*

*I'll even follow in my father's work if you will . . . anywhere. Fort Vancouver? All my tomorrows I surrender at your throne of grace. . . . Take care of Nadyia . . . .*

"The Father's house," she whispered. "I know I shall one day be welcomed there. In the end, isn't that what truly matters? The Father's house and family?"

*And Trace—I leave him in your hand. He is yours before he's mine. And I wish it so.*

Savana looked out across the snowy field. "Goodbye, Zoya."

Above, the majestic stars smiled on, silently reminding her of the Father's house.

# 23

# THE SNARES OF DEATH

Trace stepped from the church into the snow.

"Over here, Wilder!"

Trace turned toward the voice and into a flash of light and a small explosion. A stabbing pain ripped through him and he felt himself going down. . . .

The baron smiled to himself. He strode up to the body of the American lying in the snow and watched the white turn red with his blood.

"You were a fool, Captain. You had too much honor."

He raised the pistol again, this time toward Trace's head to make the deed certain. His own breath seemed to burst forth from his lungs with a blow between his shoulder blades. The pistol slumped in his hand and he sank to his knees.

Warm blood soaked the back of his shirt, and he was growing weaker.

"No, Peter," came a cool voice. "You were the fool."

Holding a pistol, Count Aleksandr walked from behind Peter and stood looking down at him. Aleksandr's face was pale and damp with sweat.

"The hour you made your decision to poison me and destroy my sister, Nadyia, your epitaph was already written."

Peter tried to speak, but the words died in his throat. He fell forward, the side of his face landing softly in the snow.

Count Aleksandr turned away to Trace and stooped beside him. He saw that Trace was yet alive.

"Boris!" he shouted into the night. "Attend to the American. Then get him into the carriage and to Baranof Castle."

# Epilogue

## WATCH FOR THE MORNING

*British Fort Vancouver*
*Two Months Later*

The walled fortress of Fort Vancouver was built in the middle of a small plain along the Columbia River. Outside the gates and westward, the small town-size community known as French Prairie belonged to retired Hudson's Bay Company workers—most of them French Canadians who were married to Indians.

While Reverend Withycombe fumed over the "traitorous" decision of British Chief Factor McLoughlin's to allow American Methodist missionary Jason Lee to build a compound there, Mrs. Warrender celebrated the decision by throwing a supper party in her newly built log cabin, constructed by the American widower Jake Murphy, whom she had first met in Hawaii. Roslyn Warrender was now Mrs. Hugh Fraser, and happily aiding her husband's work as

Company teacher for McLoughlin's school within the fort.

Savana wondered about the exclusion from the school of the half-breed children of the French Canadians and the handful of Indian orphans who had survived the epidemic that had taken the lives of their parents.

"Rebecca has already made plans with Jason Lee to build a school for them in French Prairie," Roslyn told her.

Just as Trace had predicted, Savana found Rebecca Baxter to be a delightful friend. She had recently married the Company doctor from Montreal, Duncan Cameron.

In the weeks that followed the painful ordeal at New Archangel, Savana sought healing for her inner turmoil by spending much of her time reading the Scriptures and adjusting to the thoughts of a new life that would begin when Trace arrived on the *Okanagan*.

One door had shut; another had opened. It was wise to forget, to forgive, and journey forward into the exciting future God had for her. Her bondage to what might have been was broken. Peace had begun to mend the torn and shattered threads of her emotions and to weave them back into something that promised brighter days ahead.

She had learned that Peter was dead, and in thinking of him now she could begin to feel not bitterness but pity. The verse in Ezekiel came to her attention: *"I take no pleasure in the death of the wicked."*

"Nor must I. It is enough that God has let Trace live. Soon he will come to me. . . ."

Sir Douglas had also returned to Fort Vancouver, and though he remained as determined as ever to win Oregon for England, he was in a mellow mood—though still threatening to disown her if she married Trace. But no sooner did he say this than he began musing to himself how he might get Trace to work for the Company—this time in Hawaii.

Savana only smiled and continued to wait eagerly for news of the *Okanagan*. She knew Trace was recovering from a serious gunshot wound and that he could not come to her as he promised until he felt well and strong.

During the weeks that passed, Rebecca had become a close companion, and she laughed over Savana's concern about her younger sister, Callie, having any emotional claim on Trace's heart.

"You needn't worry about Trace," she said. "I always did think his interest was waning. There was a time two years ago when Callie would have married him, had he asked, but he didn't, and then he disappeared for a year somewhere up in Alaskan waters. Anyway," said Rebecca as they walked along together, "I received a letter from Callie recently from St. Louis. She confessed that her secret infatuation with Yancey isn't easily put to rest, and she doesn't think it's fair to Trace to enter a marriage. Not when Yancey would be her brother-in-law. They'd see too much of each other and it would lead to problems."

Savana felt relieved, and yet there were times when she struggled with feelings of uncertainty. She wanted Trace, but not on a rebound from an unrequited love triangle. He must want her alone, not Callie.

"Does Yancey know?" she asked Rebecca as they walked across the compound toward Mrs. Warrender's cabin for supper.

Rebecca sobered and tucked a wisp of dark hair under her bonnet. "I don't think so. They haven't seen each other in several years. And Callie would never tell him. She considers Yancey too wild to settle down. Callie's determined to come to Oregon—even if she has to marry a missionary to do it!"

Savana looked at her, shocked. "You mean actually marry a man she doesn't even love?"

Rebecca shrugged and didn't appear the slightest bit shocked by the idea. "Don't they do that in England—arranged marriages, I mean?"

"Well . . . yes, but—"

"Many of the Christian women are doing the same back east. The marriages are being arranged in the church so they can send out couples as missionaries. Single women aren't accepted by the mission board."

Savana didn't know how she felt about the idea. She paused in the clearing, smelling the sweet aromatic scent of pine trees. Rebecca looked up and, shading her eyes against the late afternoon sunshine, glanced across the compound toward Fort Vancouver.

"Looks like we have a visitor."

Savana followed her gaze. "Mrs. Warrender will need to set another plate—"

Savana stopped, her heart squeezing in her chest.

"What is it?" asked Rebecca. "Do you know him?" Then Rebecca stopped, too, and smiled.

As a familiar figure walked toward Savana, she clutched the ribbons at her throat that trailed from her hat and took several steps in his direction—then she ran to meet him, her heart singing. *Trace! Trace!*

Savana felt herself swept into his strong embrace. She lifted her face toward his, warmed to her soul by the flinty blue eyes that claimed her for his own. Her heart leaped, then began to race wildly as her lips met his and her arms wrapped about his neck.

"What will Bellomont have to say about a Boston agent in his immediate family?" asked Trace minutes later.

"He's painfully adjusting to the idea," she said with a smile that slowly faded. "But is it me you truly want, Trace, or a girl back in St. Louis?"

His eyes flickered and his hands tightened around her. "The woman who has made me completely forget a boyhood infatuation is all the woman I'll ever want."

"Are you sure it was only infatuation?" she asked.

"It's you I love, Savana. I am certain of that."

Her heart lifted with joy, and she couldn't resist a small taunt. "I'm glad to hear that, because she's already written her sister. Callie says she still has fire in her heart for Yancey. Looks like you lost."

He smiled. "It's no loss. I was wondering how to tell her about you when I arrive at Senator Baxter's house. I was worried how she would take it. The Lord has erased my dilemma." He sobered. "But there's another dilemma that is of more importance between us than the senator's daughter."

Dilemma? She felt troubled under his gaze.

"I must return to St. Louis for a time," he said. "I am still under orders from Washington City. I'll be reporting back to Senator Baxter on the mission at New Archangel, then to Andrew Jackson." His hands tightened about her back.

"Savana, in time, thousands of American pioneers and their families will be leaving Independence by wagon train to come to Oregon. And when I've finished my report to the President, I'll be talking with Yancey about taking on the responsibility as a scout. More missionaries will be coming as well as pioneers—a Dr. Marcus Whitman and his wife, Narcissa, and a couple named the Spaldings."

He looked at her. "I'm called to help make Oregon a territory of the United States. Can you accept that? Can Bellomont?"

Her eyes searched his as they held tightly to each other as though afraid their divided loyalties would tear them apart.

"Trace, I've already found where my loyalty belongs," she said softly. "It is to the Lord of all nations, and to you. With Ruth in the Old Testament, I can say with the sincerity of my heart—*Where you go, I will go; and where you lodge, I will lodge: your people will be my people, and your God, my God.*"

"I'll cherish those words, darling Savana." His head bent toward her and he kissed her softly.

"Are you ready to visit St. Louis and meet Yancey? And when I've finished the work that brings me there, we'll go to New Orleans for our honeymoon."

Her eyes melted into his. "Sounds exciting—are you going to abduct me aboard the *Okanagan* again?"

"Not a bad idea . . . but on one important condition."

"And what is that?" she murmured.

"That Jason Lee marry us before we leave."

"I was hoping you'd say that. . . ."

# AUTHOR'S HISTORICAL NOTES

Dear Reader:

As I enjoy researching history, I generally accumulate more information than can be smoothly incorporated into a novel of this scope.

From the rich history of this period, I have condensed into a manageable time frame the events that shaped the three-nation struggle to settle the Pacific Northwest. The history itself is accurate, and the mind-set of the three nations is represented through the fictional lead players in the story.

Listed below are some interesting historical facts about events used in the book:

1. Sutter actually bought Fort Ross in 1841—in time for the big gold rush of '49.

2. I used the name San Francisco for easy reader identification, but it was called *Yerba Buena* until renamed in

1847. It is the Spanish term for the abundance of rich mint plants—literally "Good Herb." In 1840 the Hudson's Bay Company had a trading fort on what is now Montgomery Street. William Glen Rae, son-in-law of Fort Vancouver's Chief Factor John McLoughlin, was in charge.

3. The town of New Archangel is presently called Sitka, Alaska.

4. Unfortunately, the Russian-American Fur Company's treatment of the Aleut Indians is historically accurate. A priest from the Russian Orthodox church at New Archangel did eventually journey to St. Petersburg to inform the czar of the Company's cruelties, and St. Petersburg sought to put an end to the practices.

5. The Hudson's Bay Company's interest in a new trading fort on the Stikine is historical, and so is Peter Skene Ogden's expedition. He was turned back by Russian patrol boats in 1834. England did get their treaty with the Russian Company in 1839, guaranteeing the delivery of food and making Fort Ross obsolete. The British built their fort on the Stikine, but by then America was well rooted in Oregon.

6. The Methodists established a mission to the Flathead Indians in 1833, and Jason Lee arrived at Fort Vancouver mid-September 1834. Much to the distress of the Hudson's Bay Company, Jason was treated favorably by British Chief Factor John McLoughlin, and eventually the Hudson's Bay Company sent out a Company man to report on his behavior toward the Americans.

7. New Caledonia is known today as British Columbia, so named by Queen Victoria when it became a Crown Colony in August 1858.

8. The details of the California cattle drive by Ewan Young and others are accurate. The drive took place in 1837.

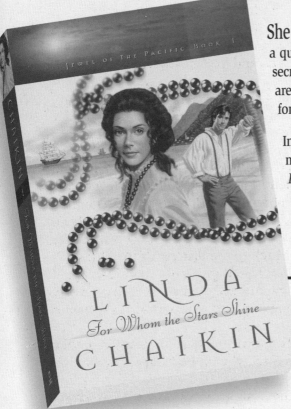